TAKiNG THE FiGHT OFF WORLD...

Operation Retribution Part 2

PALADiN SHADOWS SERiES, BOOK 8

A Novel by **Aidan Red**

▲

Edited by Tina Perdue

To my wife for her patience, tolerance and encouragement. Many thanks to my family and friends for their past and continued encouragement and assistance.

Taking the Fight Off World...

Their war against the slavers goes galactic. Suspect freighters are boarded enroute and their nefarious cargos commandeered. The shippers added defensive fighter escorts and Shara led her squadron on numerous intercept missions in response. They knew the number of fighters would increase with time, but Shara did not expect to come face to face with the Warlord Prince's heavy battlecruisers.

Chapters

Eighty-Seven
Sunday, December 25
Christmas Day

Hearing Cheral's scream of distress, Shara was out the back door, coat in hand and running for STSX parked just west of the main house before Greg could excuse themselves from their Christmas morning gathering and follow her.

She was up the ladder and had STSX powered up and ready by the time Greg closed the aft portal.

'I'll fly, love! Get into your Blue! Apache Two's been hit, bad!' Casi said as she lifted STSX up through the shield's dome and began the steep climb. *'Sorry, love. She's nearly straight up above us. Oh no! Cheral's physically hurt and Two's been torn open. She's losing suit pressure. We're going to have to go out and bring her in.'*

Stran saw the images Casi was seeing. *'I'll go out. I'm in Blues and I'll get the EVA suit on as soon as you're stabilized.'*

As they approached Apache Two, Casi was shocked when she saw the amount of damage inflicted on the small fighter. The right pylon and cannon were gone and the whole right side of the ship was torn and pealed open, Cheral was hanging in the skewed seat by her safety straps.

Casi slowed and slid STSX in beside the remains of Apache Patrol Two, matching its spin, then she turned STSX's aft portal toward the battered ship. *'Okay, love. We're about as close as I can get without actually seeing.'*

Stran stepped into the airlock between the inner and outer aft portal panels and secured the EVA suit's helmet seals. "Open the outer portal," he said and STSX complied.

'Your placement is perfect, Bren,' he said as he extended the ramp and reached out to the fighter. He quickly pulled the few remnants of cockpit debris out of the way and unclasped Cheral's seat harness. He pushed his helmet against hers so he could feel her move in response. "I've always wondered what it would be like to hold you in my arms,"

1

he said as he picked her up and turned back to STSX and the open portal. "Hold onto me."

Her eyes opened heavily and she half smiled at his teasing.

'I don't mind,' Shara said to both of them, and then she turned to the ship, "STSX, can you collect the fighter so we can bring it back down?"

"YES. IT IS SMALLER THAN KKLC14, BUT IT CAN BE RETRIEVED."

"Thanks, STSX."

'We're in. Come down and help me get her into Medical.'

Casi was halfway down the ladder before he finished his thought, and with him half in and half out of the EVA suit, they got her laid out on the right couch. Casi keyed the console on the bulkhead above Cheral's head to get the preliminaries started while Stran removed his EVA suit and returned it to the hangers.

When he returned, Casi already had Cheral's helmet off, the pressure suit unzipped, her left arm out of the sleeve and Medical's arm band in place. Casi was holding a blood stained cloth against Cheral's right side.

"Give me a hand. We need to get her out of the pressure suit," Casi said as they felt STSX move. "He's collecting the fighter while we get her stable." Shara pulled Cheral's boots off and unzipped the suits legs.

Stran nodded. "I heard you ask him to retrieve it, love," Stran said and lifted Cheral's head and shoulders.

"I think wearing her Blues with the suit helped stop some of the shrapnel," Casi continued as she tried to gently pull the suit off Cheral's right arm. "STSX, tell Major Kooich he needs to get someone up with Cadet Tigs on escort. Then take us to Obscure as soon as you have the fighter secured and alert Kiile that we need one of his Medics and a stretcher to meet us."

"And who's that other one?" Ted asked when Rusty and Carole had given him the details about a young woman he saw at the bakery on Main, "Tall and brunette?"

"That would be Millie," Carole said before Rusty remembered.

"She's early twenties, daughter of the owner's son. And she's not seeing anyone."

Rusty offered Thom a refill of her holiday cider. "Are you on the hunt like Ted here?" she asked with a wink as she set the carafe on the end table beside the couch.

"No, I'm not," Thom laughed, "but I'm keeping my eyes open in case I get lucky like Wally and Dan." Then he smiled at Carole with her brightly colored, two blossom corsage and turned to Wally. "I really am curious though. How do you get that lady at the flower shop to find you such pretty flowers this time of year? Honestly, when I go by her shop, I never see anything like those."

"I don't know, Thom," Wally said with a shrug. "I just tell Mary what I need and who they're for, and she does the rest. I think she's trying to make me look better than I am."

"Aah," Thom smiled, realizing Wally had given him an idea. "If anyone needs help—"

Thom was interrupted when Rusty pushed herself up off the couch and hurried to the foyer and the front door. Carole followed quickly as Rusty opened the door for a couple with a little girl.

"You must be Dan," Rusty said as they stepped in and Carole began hanging their coats on the wall pegs. "I'm Rusty and you know Carole. And you must be Blaire." Rusty bent to offer Blaire her hand. "I'm so glad you could come."

"And this is my wife, Mandy," Dan said when Rusty straightened and took her hand.

"Welcome, welcome." Rusty continued as she led them into the large living room. "In the two chairs are my other daughter Shelly and her husband Jim Woods," she said as Jim stood up and shook their hands. "And the one with the dolls is Carrie Anne."

Blaire instantly went and knelt down beside Carrie Anne, introduced herself and asked what the doll's names were.

"And this is my husband, Marty," Rusty continued as he got up from his overstuffed chair and greeted them.

"Welcome Dan, Mandy," he said and then pulled two more overstuffed chairs closer to the group.

"Please make yourselves comfortable," Rusty said. "Dinner's still about a half an hour away."

Mandy turned slowly, looking at the rustic beauty of the great room. "You have such a wonderful home here. Was this your family's home?"

"Yes, Mandy," Marty said with warm memories, "it is. My father built this place when I was young and we've been here ever since."

Rusty offered them something to drink, and Marty again praised her holiday cider. When they decided, Rusty hurried off to the kitchen.

As they took the chairs Marty offered, Mandy turned to Carole, sitting beside Wally on the long couch, holding his hand. "I took your advice and Friday Blaire and I took the walk up Main Street to check out the shops. That little clothing shop up on the north end looks very interesting."

"Sally's Casuals?" Carole asked, knowing it was the only one at the north end.

"Yes, that's the one," Mandy smiled. "I didn't think I would ever get Blaire out of there."

"Sally has a keen eye for what looks good," Carole admitted.

"Carole said you just got here?" Shelly asked. "Where were you before?"

"Eastern Arizona," Mandy said, "Safford." Her tone saddened as she mentioned it.

"I was away a lot," Dan interceded. "Mandy and Blaire had to, sort of, fend for themselves. It wasn't a lot of fun for them."

"Sorry," Shelly said in surprise. "I didn't mean to pry or anything."

"You didn't," Mandy said, brightening. "I knew how Dan's job could be when we got married, but even then, things didn't turn out like we had expected."

"Well, Wally told us he's here to stay and maybe you can be too," Shelly said happily. "I know I miss the valley sometimes, and the way we were when we got married." She caught Jim's hand as she spoke. "But things are better now, and I think they will continue to improve. Maybe they will for you too."

"So," Dan said, looking at Wally, "you've decided to stop jumping around and drive a stake into the ground?"

"Yes," he answered, "I have. We have people here that need us, Dan. And I want to be someone they can count on."

"And I think I see one of those people," Mandy said slowly as she looked at Carole and then at her hand. "You weren't wearing that when I last saw you." Mandy got up and reached out to Carole. "May I see?"

Carole smiled and slowly extended her hand. Ted and Thom leaned closer when they realized what Mandy was talking about.

"I guess you really have," Mandy said and Carole smiled at her reference to their private conversation. "Congratulations. When?"

"Yesterday," Carole said, feeling her face warm.

"Have you set a date?" she asked.

"No," Carole said and smiled at Wally, "but soon."

Their conversation took a more general heading and after a while, Wally found himself standing in front of the large picture window with the view of the valley, even though the fog kept things hidden after the first two or three miles. Watching him, Carole knew his mind was working on some detail of some problem, a trait she had come to understand and accept. She stopped beside him and slipped her arm in his.

"What is it Wally?" she asked, almost afraid of interrupting his thoughts.

"Tuesday, coming home," he said, slightly louder than a whisper, "I helped a couple having car trouble down by Grants. Did I tell you about them?" He looked down at her and she shook her head. Then he continued, "They had a flat tire and a flat spare, so I took them back to Grants to get them fixed. Nice couple, middle aged, coming up here to visit her sister for the holidays."

"That's not unusual, Wally," she said, wondering why this had him thinking.

"I know," he smiled, "but what is unusual is that they seemed afraid and in a hurry." He turned and put his arms around her. "And when I talked with the station attendant fixing the tires, he showed me the front tire they removed from the truck. It had a bullet hole in it."

"Oh, Wally," she said and tilted her head back to look at him. "They were running away from someone."

"Looks that way," he said softly. "And I have to find out who."

▲ ▲ ▲ ▲ ▲

"Thank you, Annie," Shara said as she toasted the meal, "for doing such a splendid job on dinner. And thank you Matti and you Cara for being such an important part of our family."

Annie blushed and glanced down at the table, feeling especially honored to be seated with everyone at the main table. "Thank you, Mrs. Shara. It's been our privilege and pleasure to be here for you."

Matti and Cara smiled brightly and raised their glasses in response to Shara's toast.

Greg scanned the group around the long table. "Anyone for seconds?" he asked and held up a dish of cobbler. "There's a lot still waiting for someone."

"If it's alright," Ani Tigs answered Greg's question. "I'll take some back for Captain Haak."

"Certainly," Shara said. "She'll be sorry she missed the gathering, but she can have anything we have left over—"

A loud argument in the back yard interrupted Shara and she and Greg got up to investigate when the back door opened suddenly.

"You aren't supposed to be out of Medical yet!" Kiile's loud and concerned voice followed a hobbling Cheral through the door. Supporting her right side with a crutch, Cheral stopped in the archway without uttering a response and let Kiile catch up.

Shara was instantly at her side. "What're you doing?" she asked in a pitched voice. "You shouldn't be moving around, much less standing here. Kiile? How could you—"

"Shar!" Cheral said, "Stop. Medical has me patched up and I'll go back quietly," she turned and glared at Kiile, "after I've visited a while." She slowly moved another step into the room as if reinforcing her resolve.

Before she could say anything more, Greg slipped around on her left side and scooped her up.

"Greg!" she shouted in surprise. "Put me down." She protested all the way into the living room and continued after he gently placed her on the loveseat with her legs stretched out, her back to the fire.

"Shara, some cushions please," he said, completely ignoring Cheral's continuing rant.

"Stay put!" Greg commanded when she swung her good leg down and started to push herself up. "Or I will carry you back to Medical myself."

When she stopped squirming, startled by his unyielding tone, he leaned her forward and stuffed a cushion between her and the sloping arm of the loveseat.

"Now that you've proven you have no common sense at all," he said in a calmer, gentler tone, "I will see what I can find for you to eat. You are hungry, aren't you?"

Sheepishly, she nodded and he turned to the table.

Matti quickly brought a couch tray and slipped its foot under the edge of the loveseat and positioned the tray top in front of her. Cara arranged a place setting on the tray top and Matti smiled at Cheral. "If you squirm any more you'll spill everything. Mrs. Shelly's little Carrie Anne caused less trouble."

When Greg returned with a large plate of food, a sampling of everything on the table, he saw Shara lay one of Medical's hand scanners on the side table. She nodded to him as he made a grand gesture of serving Cheral. "And what would you like to drink, water, tea or coffee?"

Cheral wrinkled her nose.

"Knowing what Medical has given you," he smiled, "I won't offer you anything stronger."

She chose tea and watched him as he walked back to the dining room where many faces stared back at her. Some smiling and others still astonished.

"Captain," Ani said as she stepped forward and knelt down beside the couch. "I was so scared while I was listening and then when I knew you had gone after that ship. I wanted to come and help so badly."

"I know, Ani," Cheral said and caught her hand. "But you did the right thing. Even if the station wasn't in peril, your job was to be there. I thank you for not forgetting your duty."

"You really shouldn't be here," Ani repeated the general feelings.

"Yes, I should, Ani," Cheral said softly, "for reasons you don't know about." Cheral smiled. "Also, my family needs to see that I am not going to let this little set back slow me down."

"Little set back?" Greg asked as he knelt beside Ani and placed the mug of tea on the tray.

"Yes," Cheral said firmly, staring back at Greg and knew he remembered how he hid his injuries after Corsecain. "I know that with a little time and Medical, I'll get a new ship and I'll be right back out there."

"I know you will," he said and smiled at Ani. "But give it more time than a few hours." He stood up and looked down at her. "Now eat and don't squirm so much. Shara won't like you bleeding all over her favorite loveseat." He turned and saw Kiile watching from the end of the table. "Kiile, take a chair and get something yourself. She's not going anywhere and STSX will tell us if she disobeys me again."

Ani giggled as he walked away, then softly she said, "It's nice to have a commander that cares about his people. You're very lucky, Captain, to know the colonel so well."

"We all are, Ani," Cheral said and forked a piece of turkey.

⚐

When Cheral had finished eating and the tray cleared away, Paul pulled a straight backed chair up beside the loveseat and sat down. Cheral smiled at his closeness and the comfortable feeling of the house as everyone settled in the living room and continued the conversations started at the table.

"Sorry Grandpa," she said softly. "It wasn't supposed to happen this way."

"No need to be, dear," he answered. "You did your job, and did it well. He didn't get away, and Shara and Greg got you home safe."

After a few minutes, Cheral's head began to nod and Greg smiled without straying from the discussion he was in. When her head slumped forward and to one side, Shara got up and hurried to her, glancing at Greg's smile.

Everyone watched quietly, especially Ani, as Greg leaned down and scooped Cheral up from the loveseat and followed Shara into the bedroom hallway. After a moment, the conversations suddenly resumed as Greg and Shara returned.

"You know she called me," Shara said softly as they entered the dining room. She touched her forehead, "In my mind."

Greg stared at her a moment. "No, I didn't know that." He half smiled. "That will make her so happy."

"Happy? Why?" Shara asked.

8

"She had just started hearing and sensing people when she was shot in Pitcarthy," he explained and stopped beside the table. "And it all went away. That's why she has a communications link implanted behind her right temple. The loss and the uncertainty of it ever coming back depressed her."

"I see," Shara said. "But why'd she call me?"

"You're her family, Bren," he said and smiled. "I think she needed to know you were there when everything came apart. If something could be done, she knew you could do it."

Shara sighed deeply and looked at the walls and their bedroom beyond, where Cheral was sleeping. "Did you put something in her tea?"

"Just a little," he admitted with a sly glance at the hallway. "STSX told me what Medical suggested and I knew that with a full stomach and the warm fire, it wouldn't take much. We'll let her rest a while and then I'll help Kiile get her back to Obscure and Medical."

Monday, December 26

It was early and Greg sat in his robe in the overstuffed chair in the dark living room, pondering the little changes he saw in Shara. The house girls were not up when he fixed a pot of coffee, filled a carafe and settled in their favorite chair to think. He knew something was bothering her, but she kept her mind closed and he could not get a reading on the concern.

This was the second time this week, after a slightly stressed day and wonderful love making that she had turned cold during the night and pushed him away, not wanting to snuggle like she always did. He was confused and concerned.

He'd see if she was feeling bad again, like she had been Thursday morning when she slept in until after eight. Eight was still early, but it was late for Shara. She was up and down many times around and after midnight, and finally settled down about four. It was the first time since they married that she had such a troubled night and when she finally fell asleep, he let her sleep until she felt like getting up. He did not think it was odd at the time when she declined breakfast and went straight out to the horses. After an hour or so with the horses, she seemed her normal self, appreciative of his company and back in their normal regimen.

Friday was more relaxed and Saturday seemed very pleasant, with Shara enjoying time with Coleen and time with the horses. But last night started as another fitful night and she finally settled down around one. He sipped his coffee and tried to remember the details of the previous day, the light breakfast, which she barely ate, and the stress of the morning when Cheral's fighter was destroyed and they barely got to her in time. That was enough, he admitted, to upset anyone. And she had concerns about Cheral all through the evening, especially after she defied Medical and Kiile and came to dinner.

The Christmas dinner was a wonderful spread, and the hands and the house girls were thrilled to be 'part of the family' again and to eat at the main table with everyone, including those invited from the 'mysterious place' in the woods. He thought about Shara's appetite at dinner and realized she had not eaten very much then either. He had not really paid any attention, and even now he thought Cheral's incident was a major cause of her lack of hunger.

'STSX,' he said quietly, '*have you detected anything wrong with Shara?*'

'*NO. SHE IS HEALTHY.*'

Greg took STSX's words at face value and then asked, '*Have I done something she does not like?*'

'*NO. YOU ARE HER MATE AND SHE IS VERY PROUD TO BE YOURS. SHE FEELS GREAT AFFECTION AND PRIDE FOR YOU. YOU CALL THE DEDICATION 'LOVE.' SHE DOES NOT WANT TO BE ANYWHERE YOU ARE NOT.*'

He rubbed his chin, and wondered why he was seeing a change when STSX told him she was fine and they were both still completely committed to each other. He emptied the carafe into his cup and had taken a sip when he felt Coleen get up and leave the guest bedroom. He watched her as she came into the dining room, turned to the living room and sat down on the loveseat facing him.

"She can feel your worry, Greg," Coleen said. "You have to let her work this out."

"What? What does she have to work out?" He looked at her, completely lost. "We've shared everything with each other, and now... There's something she's not telling me."

"Greg," she said softly. "I know she loves you more than anything. She lives her life every day for you, and would do more if she could. Just like you do for her."

"But something's different, wrong," he said and finished his cup, "and I don't know what to do to help."

"If you want to help, Greg," Coleen continued, "give her room and support her. Just be there for her and stop trying to take the blame for what's troubling her. Just be there for her, like you've always been. That will mean more to her than anything else you could possibly do.

"You've already consulted your ship, right?" she asked and when he nodded she continued, "and I take it he and that thing you call Medical says she's alright?"

"Yes, they do."

"Then listen to them," she smiled, "and just be there for her and whatever it is will work itself out."

Coleen got up, bent to him and hugged his shoulders. "Now stop your worrying and go back to bed."

When Coleen went back into the guest bedroom and closed the door, Greg got up, took the empty carafe and cup back to the kitchen and returned to their bedroom. He hung his robe up and as he crawled back into bed, Shara quietly rolled over and snuggled as close to him as she could, sighing softly as he curled his arm protectively around her and held her close.

⚔

Shara woke him with a long kiss as she stretched her body against him and stroked his back. He blinked awake and returned her kiss, realizing it was barely light outside and she was frisky and playful.

After many moments of togetherness, she led him into the shower where they lingered passionately for many more. Finally, they dressed for the day and Greg began to think he was letting his mind play tricks on him.

Coleen and Brendan were up and chatting in the living room when they came out and joined them. Shara took a cup of tea and they had just sat down at the table when Jill and Nick came in.

"Major Kooich and Leeana took an early escort shift this morning," Jill announced as she picked up two cups from the pile on the table, handed one to Nick and poured, "and said they'd eat after they got down."

"I just spoke with STSX," Shara said as she covered Greg's hand with hers, "and he says Cheral is doing very well considering last night's exertion. Kiile's Medic, a Captain Meara Wrth, got all of the shrapnel out after we got her down, so her carelessness last night did not significantly aggravate her condition. Obviously the pain killers were working."

"Well that's very good news, indeed," Coleen said. "Did she say why she felt so determined to come, instead of listening to Medical?"

"When we took her back," Shara said glancing at Greg, "she woke up enough to tell us she was afraid she wouldn't get the chance to say 'thank you' for us coming to get her. She knew she only had minutes left when she saw her suit was punctured, nearly deflated and that she was losing a lot of blood. She couldn't move to help herself."

"I know that scared her," Greg added. "She remembers the pain of Pitcarthy before she blacked out, but yesterday she thought she was going to have to watch herself die, alone with nothing but the emptiness of space to comfort her."

"Oh my," Jill said, her hand quickly covering her mouth. "But you said she's going to be fine, right?"

"Yes, I did," Shara said with a smile. "And today new things are starting."

"Kiile is up looking over the space station," Greg said, picking up the telling as Matti brought breakfast plates in and set them in front of Nick and Jill. "And if he's happy, they will plan to begin installing some defenses tomorrow."

"And their new lieutenant," Shara said as Cara set the next two plates in front of Coleen and Brendan, "Lieutenant Riviera, will have new scanning equipment to use and the admiral will have a new communications console so we can speak directly with him if a danger arises."

"Please begin. Don't wait on us," Greg said to everyone and then continued. "And the director has agreed to have four new patrol fighters here Wednesday, onboard the next, normally scheduled supply ship. And since we are in a real combat situation, Cheral will not be docked the cost of the fighter she lost yesterday."

"How did you manage that?" Shara asked as Matti set a plate before her and Greg. She suddenly hesitated and Greg felt a brief sensation of dizziness and nausea. "I mean…" She glanced up and looked at Jill and then at Coleen, quietly eating and she slowly got up. "Would you excuse me a minute?" she asked unnecessarily and turned toward the hallway, catching the edge of the table with the slightest hesitation before she hurried on.

Coleen got up and followed Shara, stopping at the closed bedroom door. She tapped gently and slowly opened it. "Shara? Can I do anything?"

She found Shara in the bathroom, curled over the toilet, clutching her stomach. A second heave caught her as Coleen stepped in and gently held her shoulders. Coleen waited, holding her until her trembling stopped and she sat back on her folded legs.

"Greg doesn't know, does he?" Coleen asked.

"No," Shara said, crying softly. "He can't know. He can't..."

Coleen was confused. "Why on earth not?"

"He can't know," she insisted. "Not yet. Please don't tell him." Her eyes pleaded as she looked at Coleen. "I'm his partner. He counts on me on every mission. I can't let him down. I've got to be there for him." She slowly surrendered to a fit of sobs.

"How long?" Coleen asked gently.

"I figured out Friday what's going on. It was six weeks ago last night," she slowly admitted. "The night we got married. After I recovered from being poisoned, STSX was thinking way ahead of me. He had Medical fix me a potion; one of its concoctions." She almost laughed, "I couldn't very well go to a store with everything that was going on at the time. Then when Greg and Cheral left, I couldn't see any point to keep taking it. I didn't know when he would be back, if ever." She sighed and shook her head slowly. "When he did come back, with the excitement of his return, our getting married and everything else that happened that day, I forgot to start taking any more until the next day." She looked up at Coleen. "Stupid of me, I know. It wasn't a 'Morning-After' type of thing, so even if I had of, it wouldn't have been soon enough. It takes two days for the doses to give protection"

"Shara," Coleen said softly. "You have to tell him."

"No! I can't," she snapped. "Promise me you won't tell him."

"Shara, I—"

"Promise me!" she demanded.

Coleen stared at her, seeing the hard steel of her temper in her eyes, the fierce determination and the forceful conviction in her face and voice. "You're not thinking of termin—"

"No! Of course not," she interrupted sharply, trying to keep her voice down. "I just can't tell him now! Promise me!"

"I won't tell him," she sighed. "I think you're wrong to keep this from him, but—"

"You mustn't tell him," she interrupted, her expression again vulnerable, her lips trembling. "He won't let me help if he knows. It will put him in more danger."

"Shara, please tell him. Soon!"

"No! And you promised!"

▲ ▲ ▲ ▲ ▲

Deputy Thom Baine took a seat at the counter in Jerry's café like he always did for breakfast before starting his first daylight rounds. The middle aged waitress slid a cup his way and filled it.

"You're usual?" Joan asked, hesitating as if she expected him to surprise her and order something new.

"Yeah," he smiled. "I'm in a rut."

She placed his order and came back to talk. "You haven't been here long enough to be in a rut. What's the trouble?"

"I think I've been in a rut for years," he explained. "That's kind of the way this business is. Can I get a glass of orange juice?"

"Sure," she said and went to the kitchen, "That's something new."

Thom laughed. "I guess it is." Then he decided to ask. "Do you know anything about that woman at the flower shop?"

"Mary? She's a great gal," Joan started.

"No, not Mary," he stopped her. "The tall, thin and pretty, auburn haired one that always wears the long, layered skirts. Eddie, I think her name is."

"Aah, Eddie," she smiled and shook her head. "She's not much on men. I don't know the real story, but I know she's ignored or sent away everyone that's gone after her."

"She sounds interesting," Thom said with a warm thought. "What's her background? I mean, from what you're saying, I take it she's not married, or not seeing anyone."

"Well, you're right there," Joan said as she brought his plate and set it in front of him, "she's not married and she's not seeing anyone.

She finished college a few years back with a degree in floral design or something like that. She's been working for Mary since her junior high school years and is really good at it."

"So why is it she doesn't like men?" he asked as ate.

"Like I said, I'm not sure," Joan said, thinking. "No, I don't know what happened. She dated one of the rancher's sons in high school for about a month maybe, but nothing since."

"Is her family from here?" Thom asked.

"Not originally. They moved when she was very young and her dad left when she was in grade school."

"Wow," he said with a start. "That had to be hard."

"I'm sure it was," Joan agreed.

⋏

After driving his route again, Thom stopped by the marshal's office to check on a few facts before he walked the Main Street beat.

"Good morning, Thom," Wally said when Thom entered and settled at his desk. "Everything all right?"

"Morning Wally," Thom greeted. "Congratulations again. Everything seems to be quiet this morning." He switched his monitor on and entered his access codes. "Do you know anything about a Collier family, Wally?"

"Name's familiar," he said without looking up. "What about them?"

"I'm not sure yet," Thom said as he opened a search. "Aah. The Colliers bought a small acreage down by the twin buttes, south of the Jordan place. Hmm, about twenty-one years ago. A couple with a young daughter."

"That would make the daughter at least in her twenties," Wally said and looked over at Thom's intense study of the monitor.

"Yeah," Thom said absently. "Twenty three to be exact."

"I see," Wally smiled and turned back to his own monitor. "And you're what, twenty-four, five?"

"Father left when she was in the ninth grade," Thom continued reading from his screen, "and the mother held onto the acreage for another two years until the daughter was in high school, but was finally forced to sell to make ends meet. She bought a place at 306 West Birch. Hmm, that's between Fox and Julia." Then a thought that had been nibbling at Thom slowly surfaced. "Wally, do you have those lists you made up on the missing people?"

Wally looked up with a start. "Yes, under Abnormal Situations. Missing and Lost Items."

"Aah, there you are," Thom said softly as the computer responded to his request. "Daniel Collier. I got to wondering if he was missing when there was no record of a divorce or anything. Just a vacancy."

"Did you take care of that tracking transmitter like I asked you to," Wally asked.

"Not yet, but I will in a few minutes," Thom admitted. "It'll be easier to do when I'm not driving."

"Who's the daughter?" Wally asked as Thom switched his monitor off and stood up.

"Eddie," he smiled, "in Mary's flower shop. "Gotta walk my beat. Call me if you need anything."

Thom tapped his earpiece and closed the office door quietly as he left Wally smiling.

Eighty-Eight

Thom took his time as he walked the six blocks down the west side of Main and checked each of the dark stores he passed. He stepped in and said "hello" at each that was open or just opening. At Maple, he crossed and started east, having already checked on Hap's and the convenience store on his driving route and headed to the college and the tracking beacon the remote led him to. When he had completed Wally's request, he went back west on Fir and checked the First Valley Bank, walking through the drive thru lanes as he went.

Sally was just opening her casual clothing shop and he waved when she looked up from sorting the display racks near the front of the store. Then he walked on.

Diagonally across the street from the marshal's office, he stopped in front of Mary's Flower Boutique and looked through the front window and the wonderful floral arrangements adorning the display space. His gaze settled on Eddie, bent over a potted arrangement on the working counter at the back of the front room, wearing a long, green apron to protect her pretty blouse and long terra cotta skirts. The colorful blouse reminded him of an autumn day with sunshine speckles dancing through the trees.

He took a deep breath, turned to the door as he checked his wrist watch and knocked.

Eddie looked up and came and opened the door.

"Hi," she said with her usual courteous smile and quiet voice.

"Hi, Deputy Baine," he said, hoping he wasn't being too formal, "I was wondering if I might talk to you a minute."

"Sure," she said and opened the door wider to let him in. She relocked the door once he was inside and turned back to her work on the counter.

"It's Eddie, isn't it?" Thom asked.

"Yes," she said. "And you said you wanted to talk to me about something?"

"Yes, ma'am," he said. "I have two things to ask about. First I understand you grew up here and I've been asked by the marshal to follow up on some people that went missing recently."

"Oh?" she said in surprise. "And who would you be asking about?"

He was watching her as she gently worked the soil in the pot and set the stems of the arrangement she was creating and almost didn't hear her question.

"Uh," he hoped he didn't seem too distracted. "A Mrs. Clark and her daughter, Della. I understand she had a son, but I haven't been able to find him."

"I knew Della."

"Do you have any idea what happened to them?" he asked.

"No," she said without looking up from her work.

"Can you tell me anything about them? Either of them?" He waited and she slowly put the pot aside and turned to face him. She leaned back against the counter and folded her arms in front of her.

"And what would you like me to tell you, Deputy Baine?" she finally asked.

"It's Thomas. Please call me Thom," he said. "I'm new here, as you know, and I don't know if they are missing because they just decided to skip out one night and not tell anyone or because they were forced to leave for some reason. It isn't natural for people to just leave and leave no trace, leave no forwarding information, or to leave and not tell their friends they were."

"So you've picked two people that have disappeared to go around and ask about?"

"No," he said defensively. "I have a list of over fifty people that I need to investigate and I needed to start somewhere. If any of them have left involuntarily, I have to find out why, who was behind them leaving and what we can do to find them."

He stopped, hoping his honesty wasn't becoming too much, and patiently held the penetrating, distrusting look in her eyes. "I have other people to ask as well, but I thought you might have known Della in some of your college classes. I understand she was also interested in botany and floral work."

"She was more interested in the science in forestry," Eddie finally admitted. "And I did know her fairly well." She hesitated and he thought she was thinking about what she should say. "I heard the marshal was checking on the missing people and I know that's making some folks nervous."

"No one should be nervous," Thom said trying to reinforce the marshal's sincere support of the town. "But if something wrong is happening, we have to stop it. The families here have to understand the marshal and those of us in his office are trying to protect them."

He stopped and suddenly felt embarrassed. "I'm sorry, I don't mean to get up on a soap box."

"No, no," she said, smiling for the first time, "You're doing a great job with that soap box."

He laughed. "Thanks, I think. I'll try to be less out spoken."

"Well..., Thom," Eddie said, stressing his name, "I'll think about Della Clark and let you know if I can think of anything that might help you find out what happened to her. I've been curious too."

"Thank you," he said.

She started to turn back to her flower pot when she remembered. "You said you had a second thing to talk about?"

"Aah, yes," he sighed and glanced away for a moment. "The second is more personal."

"Okay," she said and resumed her patient, guarded stance.

"The marshal said he's been getting flowers and corsages from you, ah, the store," he said.

"Yes," Eddie admitted, "he's placed a number of orders with us."

"And they are really great," he said enthusiastically. "The marshal said you were trying to make him look better than he really is."

She smiled at the thought.

"And I assume you know it worked," he said. "Making him look better."

She cocked her head, unsure of his meaning.

"The marshal and Carole are engaged," he explained. "Saturday. Christmas Eve. He attributes part of his appeal to the corsages and flowers."

"I'm glad," she said, again smiling sincerely, "but I'd never claim the flowers made her accept him."

"Well, he thinks they were a definite help," Thom continued. "And that brings me to my second topic."

19

"Oh?" she asked with a new sparkle in her eyes. "Someone thinks he needs help too?"

"Yup, I do," he started to explain. "I need something very pretty to break the ice with someone so she'll know I think she is a very special and talented person. I figure if the flowers helped the marshal, then maybe, just maybe, flowers might help me."

"So, you've been in town for two weeks," she eyed him suspiciously, "and now you think you're ready to hustle one of the local girls?"

"I know I've only been here two weeks," he said, a little offended, "but I am NOT a 'hustling' type. I've had a few girlfriends over the years, and—"

"Couldn't make any of them stick?" she asked pointedly, her smile almost a memory.

"No, I couldn't," he admitted. "Either I did something wrong, or my job would get in the way. Both of them were wonderful women, but my job kept me moving around. Neither of them could accept that."

"And now you think it's different?" she asked, the barbs still there.

"Well, the job is," he said, "and maybe I am too. I like the valley and I like what the marshal's offering, a permanent job in one place, an opportunity to settle and help a town and no longer jump from one problem to another all over the state. I want to stay here and be a part of what I see here."

He waited, watching her as she mulled over his words.

"Sorry," he said sheepishly. "I'm not looking for a quick relationship or a fast time. That will come, or not, whenever it's supposed to. You can tell all of your girl friends that, but I saw someone that I think is very pretty, has a lot of talent and I would like to tell her so."

Eddie watched him for a long moment and then glanced down at the floor. "I guess I was a little judgmental Thom. I'm sorry. If you'd like to say something nice to a girl with flowers, we can help."

"Thank you, Eddie," he said.

"Okay Thom?" she asked returning to her previous formal tone. "What are you looking for?"

"I'd like a small, durable table bouquet in a low vase that will look good on a dining room table for maybe a week," he said slowly, describing a vision he had. "I want vibrant colors that change with the light so they look good at dinner in room lighting and great at breakfast in the morning sunshine. I want her to see them first thing in the morning as a boost to face the day, an encouragement that today will be the best day of her life, and to be there to brighten the end of her day. Something that tells her she has a friend if she ever needs one. No expectations or strings attached."

Eddie stared at him, unblinking. "I... don't think flowers can do all of that."

"I sure hope they can," he said, confidently. "I've seen what you can do with flowers."

She smiled and looked at him for a long moment. "I have some varieties in the back that I use for special customers," she finally said and turned to the aisle beside the work counter.

He followed her into the cool room and watched as she picked samples from the numerous niches. He pointed to various ones and suffered her criticisms and accepted her suggestions, purposefully making choices that would make her pick the better selections. When they had exhausted his options, she led him back into the store.

"I think your choices will be wonderful," he said trying to not show the excitement he felt in her suggestions.

"I can have an arrangement ready this afternoon," Eddie said and stopped at the front counter.

"That will be great," he said. "Please call the office when it's ready and I'll come by."

It was midmorning and Ben was standing in Abe's small, cluttered den, watching the slowly moving dots on Abe's computer monitor. The red marshal's dot was in the parking lot behind he marshal's office building on Main, and the three deputy's dots were scattered about the town. One stopped near the mill, another at the college's south side parking lot and the last was moving north, up Donovan.

"They do not seem to be following any sort of a pattern, do they?" Ben asked absently as Abe handed him a cup of coffee.

"Not really," Abe agreed. "That's why Don wants to be able to know where they are at any given time. He can call and I can tell him."

Ben leaned forward and tapped the screen. "This one by the college just went out," Ben said and Abe leaned closer to see. "Oh, there it is," he said and pointed to the parking lot in front of the administration building." Ben stared at the monitor and rubbed his chin. "It was over here a minute ago."

"Must be jittery," Abe said. Sometimes the cold will make them intermittent or make them send out a slightly different position when they are not moving. Nothing to worry about, Ben. It's somewhat normal in this kind of weather."

"Okay," he smiled and took another sip from his cup. "If you are not worried, then I am not either."

▲ ▲ ▲ ▲ ▲

Taking lunch as usual at Hap's, Wally entered and crossed the sparsely occupied dining room and took his stool at the end of the long bar. Everyone there said "Hello" and wished him the 'Best.' He was upbeat and happy when Carole stopped behind the counter.

"What would you like?" she asked as she leaned close, over the counter.

"You. And a side of... you," he teased.

She gave him the two daily choices and he said, "Monday, chicken fried steak."

Before he could say anything more, she placed his order in the hand unit.

"Wally?" Carole asked as she returned and filled his mug with coffee, "We need to talk about a date."

"Sure," he said. "Tonight?

She blushed. "How about sometime this week?"

Surprised, he looked at her. "I have to wait so long?"

"Wally, I'm serious," she said.

"Carole," he said confused. "I..."

She took a deep breath and faced him. "Wally. I know this is sudden, but I have no family besides mom and dad and Shelly and I would like Shelly to be here for the wedding."

"Certainly. She should be here," he said.

"Could we get married before she goes back to Virginia?" Carole said, her voice pleading.

"Sure," he said and nodded in agreement.

She stood up quickly and then went to collect his plate from the window.

"Do you have anyone that you want to be here?"

"Just you, the deputies and Dan's family," he said. "Oh, Greg and Shar and their clan."

"Do you want a formal, church wedding?" she asked, but he sensed a concern.

"Carole, I want to marry you, and yesterday wouldn't be too soon," he said, "but your folks might think this week is a little fast. They may want it more formal, more organized. They may want to invite their friends, other ranchers, whoever." He hesitated and smiled. "For me, I'm a guy that is extremely happy his girl has said she'd marry him. Tell me what you want and I'll do my part to help make it happen and I'll be there."

She stared at him a moment and then squeezed his hand. "Wally Lima, I love you so much. Thank you for being so understanding. I'll talk with Mom and Dad and then we can pick a date."

⋀ ⋀ ⋀ ⋀ ⋀

Thom stared at the incredible arrangement of flowers. He knew they would be great, but Eddie had created something more, a lot more! His knees felt unsteady as he turned the vase and nodded.

"This 'is' unbelievably beautiful," he said to Mary as she watched him checking the arrangement from every side. "I've never seen anything like this." He looked up, grinning uncontrollably.

"We do try very hard to make the customer happy" she said with a broad smile. "I'm glad you like them."

He suggested that he should pay for them and she took his banking card, and as she started processing the transaction, he slipped a sentiment card into the arrangement.

Mary returned his banking card and handed him his receipt as he slowly turned the vase, studying the bouquet again. He absently pocketed the card and receipt as he straightened up. "My god, this arrangement is 'beautiful,'" he whispered, shaking his head and turned to the door.

Surprised by his sudden departure, Mary stared after him as the door closed. Then she looked down and realized he had not taken the flowers. "Hey, Thom!" she shouted as she grabbed the vase and hurried to the door. She looked up the street in both directions, but when she didn't see him she closed the door and started to the cool room.

She was almost there when she noticed the card, and stopped abruptly when she realized it had Eddie's name on it.

▲ ▲ ▲ ▲ ▲

"I'm so sorry," Lieutenant Debira Glean said as she leaned closer to Cheral's Medical couch. "We were already down and inside and never heard any of your calls."

"I know," Cheral said. "It's okay. I'm told Cadet Tigs managed fine."

"I'm not talking about Cadet Tigs," Lieutenant Debira said, "and you know it. Major Mooren got MKCC5 up, moved the schedule around and reassigned times for the escorts. Tigs was fine, but we should have been up to help you."

Cheral smiled at her. "Thanks. I'm not sure it would've actually helped, though."

"Might've given those mines another target," Lieutenant Debira smiled, "and spread the damage out a little."

"Maybe," Cheral agreed, not really wanting to debate the possibilities.

"We never heard your 'May-Day,'" Debira continued. "And, Neel and I were both surprised the colonel himself and his lieutenant were the ones that found you."

"Well," Cheral smiled, knowing she had called and Shara heard her! Then she continued, "They're like that. Always ready to help."

"You're very lucky," Major Glean said as he entered the compartment. It was obvious he had been listening at the door. "Apache Base says the colonel reached you in less than six minutes after you were hit. Lieutenant Casi was flying and the colonel pulled

24

you out of what was left of your ship."

"I remember the right side was torn open," Cheral admitted.

"Torn open?" Debira chuckled. "More like MIA."

"They brought the remains of your ship back when they brought you down," Major Glean said. "They're going to start salvaging it tomorrow."

"Salvage?" Cheral said, startled and pushed herself up. "They're not going to repair it?"

Debira looked at Neel and then looked back at her, "Captain, it's not repairable. They haven't found the right engine or very many of the separated parts—"

"I need to see it," Cheral said, swinging her legs off the couch and sitting on the edge.

Surprised, Neel said, "Captain, I don't think—"

"Don't! Please," Cheral said, softening her voice and reached for the crutches at the head of the couch. "I need to see it."

Major Glean took her outstretched arm and Lieutenant Debira took her other arm and they lifted her upright. "Just like a fighter pilot, Debira," he said, smiling as he handed Cheral the crutches. "Stubborn to the core. Can't do anything without checking on their ship first."

"I know," Debira said, looking at him sideways. "I'm mated to one."

▲ ▲ ▲ ▲ ▲

"It looks like the turrets will be a pretty easy installation," Kiile was saying when Matti brought him a beer and a new carafe for Greg and Shara. "About ten hours on each one, or both if Thirty-Four can spare the Marines to do them at the same time."

"I'm certain the admiral would be appreciative if they were both done together," Greg said. "The sooner the better. How about the Shields?"

"I'm planning the shield generator installation first," Kiile confirmed, "Starting first thing tomorrow or as soon as the pieces are gathered and checked out."

"That's good," Greg said and looked at Shara. "We heard today from the director, that they intercepted a flight of two Traders' Union freighters out of the Colbr System. Two hundred captives on each one."

"Very good," Major Kooich admitted. "Is he still giving your Campaign the credit?"

Greg squirmed slightly. "Yes. He says all of his interceptors are red banded in Able Squadron colors."

"You need to correct him," Leeana quipped. "He should remember that Able is Apache."

"Speaking of 'remembering,' how's the cross-training coming?" Greg asked and nodded.

"Very well," Major Kooich admitted. "Leeana's been flying most of our missions in the last week and Lieutenant Kaal has been sharing their missions for over a week now."

"As a matter of fact," Leeana added, "All of the nav-coms have been flying escort and patrol missions for over ten days. The major's also been using the Advanced Cadet Training Syllabus to train us in the more complex spatial combat maneuvers and strategies."

Greg smiled and nodded appreciatively. "You will need that training in the very near future, I'm afraid," he admitted softly.

Tuesday, December 27

Brendan and Greg were visiting with Jill and Nick at the dining room table when Major Kooich and Leeana opened the back door and led the group of four in. Greg rose and greeted them, absently glancing around for Shara, but quickly remembered that she and Coleen had gone out to the horses right after breakfast was finished and the plates cleared.

"Good morning, Major," Greg said and gestured to the living room.

"Colonel," Major Kooich said formally when they stopped in the center of the large room. "Major Bradg and his mate, Lieutenant Mri Bradg of Q-LLRT12, and Major Pti Fila and nav-com, Lieutenant Lori Tam of Q-KCMM9."

Greg extended his forearm and greeted each of them. "I am very pleased to meet you and to have your assistance in this campaign."

"Thank you, sir," they replied, almost in unison. "The pleasure is ours, sir."

"When did you arrive?" Greg asked.

"Early this morning, your time, sir," Major Bradg said.

"We were about two pars behind Q-LLRT12," Major Fila added. "It is a great pleasure to meet you, sir." Standing close behind the major, Lieutenant Tam nudged her sharply.

"Then I presume Major Kooich has arranged your billeting," Greg said without acknowledging he noticed the exchange.

When the four of them nodded, Major Kooich explained he had provided the standard spiel for new arrivals.

"Lieutenants?" Greg asked when Major Kooich had finished. "Do either of you have any pilot training experience?" He continued when they shook their heads. "That is about to change. Major Kooich will explain my training program and I will apologize now for having to start you behind the others. But that is the way it works."

"Yes, sir," Lieutenant Tam said. "We have heard that you are implementing some accelerated pilot training and that you taught your lieutenant. Both of your abilities and accomplishments are widely known among the Shadows, especially Lieutenant Casi's."

Greg smiled. "We are in a combat situation," he continued, "with a local duty to perform at the same time. Major Kooich will give you the full picture and my expectations. As soon as the Squadron is ready, we will be engaging in a number of off world sorties."

"Sir?" Major Fila asked. "Will we have the opportunity to meet Lieutenant Casi?"

Greg reached out and felt Shara in the tack room, but she wasn't listening. He was puzzled, but did not let it show.

"Yes, you will," he said, "At the moment she is unavailable. We will be down at Obscure later today and I will be certain you get the opportunity."

"Sir?" Lieutenant Tam asked again. "You're headquarters is in such an unusual setting for a command center. May I ask why you chose such a beautiful and unusual location?"

"Lieutenant," Greg smiled, "this is Casi's and my home and I agree the location is very beautiful and unique and not what one expects for someplace called 'headquarters.' Casi raises horses and teaches competition riding." He continued when she looked at him, puzzled. "It is a terran equestrian sport and something she has done it since she was a small child." He gestured to the pictures hung on the long living room wall.

"Thank you, sir," she said.

"Thank you, Colonel," Major Kooich said. "I shall take our new crews back to Obscure and introduce them to the rest of our squadron."

▲

Coleen followed Shara out to the horse barn and into the tack room where Shara grabbed an oil cloth and began fondly oiling a competition saddle. Coleen grabbed a second cloth and asked what she should start with.

"Sorry to leave so quickly after breakfast," Shara said as she pointed to a set of straps and belts. "I felt like I needed to get outside in case breakfast didn't set right."

"Are you feeling better this morning?" Coleen asked as she started on the straps. "Hope I'm doing this right."

"Just wet the cloth and then rub the leather," Shara said. "Yes, so far I'm feeling fine. The nausea hasn't started coming everyday yet."

Shara turned to the work and tried to not think, hoping she wouldn't broadcast too much of her uneasiness.

"You know he's concerned?" Coleen finally asked.

"Yes," Shara sighed. "I know he feels my moods and feelings very keenly. He always has. It's one of his better traits. And his patience for me comes in an extremely close second."

"Have you gotten to ride much?" Coleen asked, feeling she needed to change the subject.

"Maybe once since you were here last," Shara said after thinking about it for a moment. "The heavy snows slow things down a bit and our mission is getting more involved, more intense at times." She glanced toward the house, "And today we have two new ships joining the squadron, and tomorrow new supplies and replacements will be arriving. Each day, Greg and I seem to have more and more on our plates."

"I know you do," Coleen said encouragingly and realized Shara was turned toward town, eyes unfocused.

Shara held her hand up, forestalling Coleen's questions, knowing she would hear.

'STSX,' Shara said silently, *'Did you hear WL-One's request of*

Five?'

'*YES.'*

'*Do you have the list of people Greg compiled before the attack on Point Obscure?'*

'*YES.'*

'*Please access the database recovered from Ahaar's complex concerning each of the names WL-One has requested. Archive a copy of all family connection and lineage data discovered and transmit a copy to WL-One.'*

'*ACCESSING.'*

'*Thanks, STSX.'* Then she refocused her thoughts and turned back to Coleen, "Sorry. It seems our new marshal is researching a few of the local missing people. I'm hoping the database we found at Ahaar's complex will be able to help him."

Coleen smiled. "Has the data been as helpful as you had hoped it would be?"

"Yes and no," she admitted. "Part of our problem is learning how the data is filed and sorted. Captain Woods, Jim, has had a number of his cryptologists and coder/decoders working on the file structure, but it is slow work. It's not a database structure we're used to."

Then Shara listened and faced the house. "Looks like Major Kooich is taking the new crews back to Obscure. We'll have to go down and see Cheral shortly." Then she stopped and looked at Coleen. "I'm sorry we seem to always be running off somewhere and leaving you and Brendan."

"That is quite all right, Shara," Coleen said and caught her hand. "We understand and are extremely glad to be able to spend whatever time you can spare, either or both of you, the son I thought I had lost and the daughter I never expected to have. I owe you a lot of thanks for many, many reasons. So, please don't be concerned when you have to spend time doing your jobs. That is more important."

Shara stepped forward and hugged Coleen tightly. "I have an idea for tonight. Let me talk to Greg and see what he thinks."

Wally studied his computer system monitor and the 'Missing and Lost Items' files. He had called up the list he had compiled from his investigations after Shar had allowed him to see the data she and Greg had collected.

Scrolling down the list, he first checked the more recently missing people and was surprised when Della Clark and her mother were not on the list. He confirmed her name with a number of college students and when he checked residency records, he also found their names missing. There was a brother Steve, but no one at the address on file had seen him, in ages.

He made himself a note, knowing Della was supposed to have gone missing around the fourth of October, and her mother around the twenty-third of October, the same time the sheriff and his deputies disappeared. He knew who he would ask.

Wally settled down with the list and started trying to connect the names of the missing with the names of families that still lived in the valley. He had started this cataloguing effort to see if he could see a link between any of the families that lost someone and those that had been stirring up trouble, like Russ Tooke, the fellas behind the bank and others. Anger over missing relatives was somewhat understandable, but aggressive, vigilante action was not. He felt it was imperative that he make a list, sort it and determine the most likely candidates so he could talk to them and reassure them he was working the cases and trying to apprehend the responsible parties. They were either reacting out of fear of not knowing or they were acting out planned, determined, subversive aggression.

Part way down the list, he saw the name Collier and remembered Thom's comment the day before. Daniel Collier was Eddie's father and all indications were that he was 'taken.' Like the others, when they disappeared, most of their belongings were reported missing, giving the appearance that they packed up and left for some reason of their own. But Wally had noted a few that had left with too much of their stuff, like Bob Jordan's nephew, or some that left with little or nothing of their own. After Shar and Greg explained the slave trading organization they were fighting, and how Shar and Jill had been specifically targeted and kidnapped, he felt the term 'taken' had become a more appropriate first choice for the missing people.

Wally studied the paltry information he had on Daniel Collier and realized that the only information he had was that Daniel had worked as a services coordinator for the college. He specifically managed the receipt of supplies for the various departments on campus, and that he left on the sixth of May, nearly nine years earlier, when Eddie was fifteen, in the ninth grade. He decided he should ask about Daniel and about Della.

He tapped his earpiece and asked, "WL-One? Can you contact Remote Five?"

"YES," the answer came back immediately.

"Please send this list of missing people and specifically the names of Della Clark and Daniel Collier to Remote Five for the colonel, Greg. Ask him if they have any family connection details or other significant information concerning these people and especially the two names I have identified."

A moment passed and then WL-One replied, "REQUEST SENT."

If anyone has more information, he told himself, *it has to be Greg and his team.*

Eighty-Nine
C.3482.380

Intelligence Director Kraast reread the message that scrolled across his communications monitor for a third time. He felt uneasy, almost ill as his eyes followed the string of words, and whatever memory had been pleasant in his day, vanished.

He reached for the communications console toggle and selected the chairman's code.

"Sir, Director Kraast here," he said when the connection was made and the gruff, tired voice answered.

"What is it, Kraast?" Chairman Sorgat asked tersely.

"More bad news, I'm afraid," he answered.

The chairman waited.

"More lost shipments," he added.

"Put Director Korveel in the conversation."

"Yes, sir," he said and toggled the appropriate console keys. When Merchandise Director Korveel's link connected, he continued.

"The two freighters from the Colbr launch facility," Director Kraast said into the continued silence. "I am just informed that all six of the fighter escorts were neutralized and the freighters boarded. The information is much the same as with the freighter out of Betolle."

Still the chairman waited silently.

Director Kraast began to sweat and sat uncomfortably in front of the console. "The transmission from one of the freighters states they were hailed by two Peace Force patrol cruisers and blocked by two red-banded heavy fighters. The bridge was stormed by—"

"Red banded?" the chairman's gravel voice asked.

"Yes. Yes, sir," Director Kraast said. "Just like the last boarding, the heavy fighter had a red band around its forward central body."

"I don't remember that detail," the Chairman replied. "Is it of some significance?"

"I... do not know, sir," Director Kraast replied meekly. "We think it must be, and are checking. I do not yet have an answer at this time."

"Hmm," the Chairman muttered softly. "Have you ever heard of heavy fighters having any such markings?"

"Never," Director Kraast admitted. "They have always been subtle, nearly invisible against the background. Therefore, I have inquired of our agents secreted within the Rings," Director Kraast explained, torn by the conflict that he created when he had called the chairman first, before he thought about all of the things he should have set into motion first.

"Director Kraast?" Director Korveel asked, "Have you a plan to stop future boardings? It is obvious that we cannot allow them to continue."

"Yes, that is obvious," Director Kraast agreed. "Our agents at each of our launch facilities will seek out the informants and will purge them, to ensure our launches remain secret. Betolle and Colbr are now known, but the hope is that we can keep the others secreted."

"Good," Director Korveel said absently.

"Second," Director Kraast continued, "I will increase the fighter escorts to six per freighter and I will instruct the freighters to travel only while fully cloaked."

"I would have thought that was obvious," Director Korveel said.

"I agree, but it appears it was not," Director Kraast disagreed. "They were detected and stopped. If they were properly cloaked, they would not have been detected."

The connection remained silent for another long moment.

"Thank you, directors," the chairman said dryly. "I want to know more about this red band."

The connection dissolved and Director Kraast keyed the appropriate consoles to put his delayed plans into motion.

⋏ ⋏ ⋏ ⋏ ⋏

"Good morning," Wally greeted from behind his desk when Thom came in and switched his monitor on.

"So far," Thom agreed as he continued to the coffee urn and filled a mug, "I'd have to agree with you. Other than being a bit chilly, that is."

"Yeah," Wally admitted and leaned back in his chair. "It seemed a bit colder this morning, but I think the weather is supposed to hold until late in the weekend. Rounds go okay?"

"Sure," Thom said as he settled on his chair and turned to face his monitor. "Anything happening here?"

"A little," Wally admitted. "You were looking at that list of missing people the other day and I decided to ask a favor or two." He had Thom's undivided attention. "I now have proof that eight of those on that list were 'taken' and shipped off world."

Thom's mouth dropped open.

"Without actually going and investigating, undercover," Wally explained, "my friend can't tell if they are still alive or whether they have been shipped elsewhere. I have information on the original destinations for those eight."

"How on earth," Thom asked softly, "did you come to get that information?"

"Open the list and click on one of the icons attached to a name," Wally said. "There are only eight at this time, but more will be coming."

"Anything on 'Collier?'" he asked as he scanned the list.

"Not yet," Wally said, "but I asked specifically about Della Clark and Daniel Collier."

"Yeah," Thom said as he checked the attachments, "Eddie said she'd let me know if she thought of anything about Della that I should know. That's a strange one."

"Do you realize she's not on the list?" Wally asked. "And neither is her mother."

Thom quickly sorted the list and scrolled through the appropriate section. "Well, I'll be..."

"Thom," Wally said, turning serious. "I want you to go down to Clay on Friday and then to Hawthorne on Saturday and talk with the city police offices to see what their take is on these missing people. Knowing what we do about why they are missing, you might find them to be a little reluctant to talk."

"You think they might be in cahoots with the slavers?" Thom asked as he pondered the possibility.

"From what I've been told," Wally continued, "Sheriff Black

and his deputies here in Riggin were. I find it hard to believe they were acting alone and the other valley offices ignored what was happening."

"So, it's more than just possible." Thom stared at him.

"Yeah, so be polite and don't push. Keep your questions official based on public records," Wally instructed. "Oh, and you will take WL-One for backup. Leave Thursday night and stay in one of the tourist motels in Clay and again in Hawthorne. Let me know what you find out when you get back."

"Okay," Thom agreed and started making notes. "I'll make arrangements."

"And be sure your cruiser isn't bugged or tracked." Wally smiled at Thom's nod. "By the way, my friends are coming into town tonight and are going to stop by to discuss some information concerning all of this. Can you come back into the office around six-thirty?"

"Sure."

⚔ ⚔ ⚔ ⚔ ⚔

The Marine pilot eased the transport alongside the space-side end of S.S. QuickSilver, stopping just below the center solar panel array.

He turned to his nav-com, "Have you contacted Admiral Baker?"

"Yes, sir," the nav-com replied. "He has removed his personnel from the upper sections of the core. Any minor noises we make should not be of significance to their crew."

The pilot unstrapped and drifted up, out of his seat and pulled himself along the ceiling hand holds toward the central passageway. Once out of the cockpit, he righted himself and found the EVA suited loadmaster waiting.

"We are in position," the pilot said.

The loadmaster nodded and turned to the two teams of six marines each wearing similar EVA suits, waiting beside the two uncrated, man height turret modules and the two smaller core power modules. "Seal your suits!" the loadmaster shouted and the Marines donned their helmets and began the process.

The pilot pulled himself back inside the central passage and closed the pressure door. With a swing of the latch handle, the seals inflated. He listened to the Marines in his earpiece as they prepared for depressurization of the cargo bay and waited beside the hatch watching the bay camera video screen as the cargo bay indicator turned from green to amber and then to red.

⋏

Lieutenant Wardly opened the admiral's office door and said, "They're top side, John. Lieutenant Riviera says she has their IFF, but they are still not visible or showing on her scanners."

"Thank you, Anne," Admiral Baker said with a smile. "Their Chief Warrant Officer Kyle said they would be cloaked while they work. Does Townsley know?"

"Yes. I alerted him when Riviera confirmed their IFF."

"Very good, Anne," he said. "They said it would take six to eight of our hours to install both top and bottom turrets, so I guess we will wait and see if they need anything from us."

⋏ ⋏ ⋏ ⋏ ⋏

Wally and Thom were quietly discussing the afternoon rounds and conversations they had with the various store owners. Some complained about the snow piled on the sidewalks or in the curbside parking spaces by the plows, while others embraced their day with anticipation; no two felt the same and kept rounds interesting.

At a few minutes after six-thirty, the front door opened and Shara led Greg in, followed by a man and a woman neither of them recognized. Jill and Nick came in last and closed the door behind them.

Wally stood up and extended his hand to Shara and then to Greg. "I was really surprised when you called and said you wanted to come into town. Thom, this is Greg and Shara Malone. Shara's better known around here as Smallwood."

"Oh, yes. Glad to meet you," Thom said. "I guess I know more 'of' you from the ranch and talk around town. Good to see the rumors are true."

"Two folks you should meet," Greg said as he turned to Coleen. "My mother, Coleen Cassel and her husband Brendan Cassel."

"Your mother?" Wally quickly stood and shook her hand. Then he shook Brendan's.

"Yes," Greg said, smiling. "Shara found her about the beginning of the month. It's a long story. I'll share it with you sometime, but all those years I thought she was gone, she wasn't. Just misplaced."

"Well," Wally said. "I'm so very glad that you found each other and I'm glad to meet you." He turned and gestured to Thom. "This is Thom Baine, one of my three permanent deputies."

"You remember Jill Thomas and Nick Jordan?" Greg continued as they all shook hands.

"Yes," Wally said, and Thom said he was glad to meet them as well.

"Nick?" Greg asked, "Would you take Coleen and Brendan to look at a few of the decorations and tell them about some of the town's highlights while Jill, Shara and I talk with Wally and Thom?"

"Sure," he said and turned to open the door. "We'll stay close in case you need anything."

"Take Three with you," Shara said as they stepped out. "We won't be too long."

When Nick closed the door behind them, Wally offered them each a chair. Greg remained standing and watched both doors.

"Like I said," Wally started, "I was very surprised you would come into town. With so many folks on one side scared that you're alive and the rest hoping that you are. You know there will—"

"We know Wally," Shara interrupted. "But there are two things we need to do. The first is talk to you about Della Clark and her mother, and the second is stopping the gossip. I am alive and I am married and heaven help anyone that tries to change either of those two facts."

"Okay, okay," Wally said with a broad smile, accepting the reality and emotions in her words. "And what did you want to tell us about Della Clark?'

"Four college students," Greg explained, "were the judge's first choice in collecting locals to fill in when the slaver's quotas ran short by one or two. They were nick-named 'Shoppers.' Bradley Jenkins was the judge's primary go-to-guy and when he tried to collect Della on the fourth of October, I stopped him and while he was unconscious, I hid Della where he couldn't find her. My mission partner, Cheral, kept her informed on what happened daily and supplied her with everything she needed, food, toiletries, clothes, you name it."

"When we overthrew the slavers," Shara added, "Greg had our undercover military help move Della and her mother to a new location and Jim says they would normally give them new names. We were afraid that either the judge or Harry Woods might find them again."

"That's why," Greg continued, "you don't have any reports or data to support them being missing. They aren't. They're just safer now."

Thom looked at Greg, Shara and then at Wally. "Are they telling the truth?"

"Thom," Wally said and held up his hand. "I forgot to mention that everyone you have met tonight has a Peace Force POI tag. Most of them are similar to yours, Dan's, Ted's and mine." He turned to Greg, "May I tell him?"

"Thom," Greg shook his head slightly and said instead, "Shara and I work for the Peace Force. We are Shadows, undercover investigators. Jill and Nick are trainees, cadets, learning to do the same things."

Thom consciously closed his gaping mouth, again.

"When you go to Clay and then down to Hawthorne," Greg continued, "we expect there might be some resistance to your being there, especially after you ask a few questions. Therefore, Jill and Rose Mitchell will escort you on our remotes Three and Four. You will have Wally's remote and our Remote Five will continue to support Wally, Dan and Ted here in town."

Thom did not say anything and just continued to stare at him.

"You will not see Jill or Rose, just like you don't see Remote WL-One," Shara said, "but they will be close and if you need them, all you will need to do is ask them." She tapped the side of her head, a gesture to his earpiece. "WL-One will monitor and record everything you encounter or say and hear."

"Any questions?" Wally asked when Thom shook his head to clear his thoughts.

"Do I really need an escort?" Thom finally asked.

"Thom," Wally answered. "Before you arrived, Carole and I were shot at in the woods southeast of here while I was following a hunch of mine, Carole was attacked after work behind Hap's for talking to me, I was attacked by six at the bank at Main and Fir for asking too many questions, and I was shot twice, just north of the River on Mill. So, I am very glad to have Greg's offer."

"Sorry, Wally," Thom said. "Greg must be the friend you said you met when you were kids in foster care."

"Yes, he is," Wally said with a smile. "I didn't realize he was here until just before you three arrived."

"Do you have any questions, Jill?" Shara asked as she turned to Jill, quietly sitting in a chair behind one of the desks, listening.

"When?" she asked in return.

"Thursday night and back Saturday late, if all goes well," Wally said.

"We'll fly you and Rose down," Shara added, "So you will be there when Thom gets there. We'll pick you up in the evening and back the next day."

"Unfortunately," Wally looked at Thom and chuckled, "you'll have to drive."

"Okay," Jill said and got up. "We'd better catch up with the others if you're going to dispel all of the rumors."

"Thanks Greg," Wally said and shook his hand again.

Thom followed Wally's example and then watched them, still caught up in his surprise as they left and the door slowly closed behind them.

Wednesday, December 28

Kiile watched from the south lip of Obscure's launch bay as the Class XI freighter, extending a couple hundred feet past the limits of the portal on both ends, settled into a low hover over Obscure's open bay. A few moments after the freighter was secured under the shield's dome and cloaking verified from the outside, he noted the loading dolly lift his shipment receiving sergeant to the man sized hatch that opened just forward of the main cargo holds. It took more than an hour to complete all of the arrival necessities before the main hatches finally opened and the unloading dollies floated up from the launch bay and disappeared inside.

He was not surprised when Cheral, walking with the barest of a limp, and the other two cadets stopped beside him to watch the unloading of the replacement patrol fighters. The first two were standard Class 1 fighters, identical to the ones the cadets had brought with them when they arrived two weeks ago, but the second two, Class 2 patrol fighters, drew surprised questions, including the obvious 'who gets those?'

Twice the size of the standard Class 1 and capable of carrying two persons, one being the pilot, the Class 2 fighter was a significant upgrade to the training machines. By design, and with the looks to go with it, the Class 2 fighter was a formidable fighting machine. Not as sophisticated as the Q-Ship, but with its improved fire power and enhanced electronic systems, the Class 2 was still the rarely fulfilled dream of every cadet.

▲

Cheral watched with quiet envy as the graceful Class 2 fighter's departed the freighter and gently parked in the same spot where she and the cadets had parked when they arrived. Though her private goal was to eventually earn a Q-Ship, especially after living and breathing Q-STSX1 for the previous three years, she could not help but wish for an assignment.

Looking around, knowing the colonel or Major Kooich had already made their assignment choices, she was unable to settle on an appropriate 'who' in her own mind. Since there were only three cadets here, she wondered if they were to receive more cadets instead, maybe cadets with advanced training that would claim the Class 2s. That made more sense as she thought about it and after seeing what she did to her fighter, seeing how much of it was destroyed and missing, she was certain she would get Moss' beat up and unreliable Ship Four as her deserved replacement.

With a reluctant sigh, Cheral reentered the portal hatchway and descended the curving corridor of steps to the launch bay and eventually arrived in the Mess for a late breakfast. She knew she was restless, a pilot without a ship. Even if she was just a cadet pilot without a ship, she felt the separation from flying and training very keenly. She had spent so much of her recent life aloft, on board a fast fighting ship, and now, after weeks of hands on training and the one-on-one contact with aerial combat, she felt adrift. Even with her ground time, working undercover, she had STSX and his comfort and security to retreat to at any hour of any day.

She slid her tray in front of the choices and selected a light assortment of foods and a mug of coffee. At the end of the nearest table, she sat down and started eating slowly.

She looked up when Seventeen stopped and asked if he could join her. She nodded, thinking company might distract her from her dreary thoughts. He sat and sipped his coffee with her.

"How're you feeling, Captain?" he asked, quietly making small talk.

She knew he was concerned, everyone had been concerned when the colonel brought her in and STSX deposited the barely recognizable remains of her ship on the launch bay floor.

"Okay," she said and smiled at him.

"That's good," he remarked, "especially with new fighters on deck."

"Yeah, well," she sighed, "after the way I treated my last one, I'll be lucky to get—"

"Stop, Captain," Seventeen said sharply. "I wouldn't say you mistreated that ship, though I will admit you used it up." She stared at him when he chuckled. "You made the kill and stopped that fighter from telling the rest of the universe what he found or thought he found. And, albeit with help, you made it home to fight another day."

She looked at him, surprised. "So you think it's all right to trash a fighter if the end justifies it?"

He held his smile, his voice soft. "Captain, in combat we have missions, and missions have objectives, and the outcomes can be satisfactory or unsatisfactory. It is normal to incur damage in reaching the objective, and whether it is justified is determined by the acceptability of that outcome and the effort that went into trying."

"The major that I flew with, even as a cadet, treated his equipment better than I did," she said adamantly. "He always explained his care of his equipment meant he and his crew had a way to get home."

"So," Seventeen asked, "Your major never lost a ship? Every mission was done from a safe offensive distance?"

Seventeen eyed her as she hesitated and remembered the major's attack in Corsecain when his ship did not survive and the story that he carried pieces of it inside him for days while he rescued and delivered two dignitaries to safety. She remembered the number of times he had charged in after planning his path carefully to reduce his risks as much as he possibly could, but in reality, he could have lost everything, including his life; the many times he confronted his enemies alone, keeping her and Kiile as a supporting, perimeter defense; when he was shot by the sheriff's deputy; when he escaped from Shara's sports coupe near Clay; when he scouted the launch facility alone and when he went after Shara after she had been captured.

"No," she finally admitted. "He never fought from a safe distance. He prepared, but he did lose a ship once. He accomplished his objective even after being wounded." She looked up at him. "I guess you're right. He always focused on the objective and how to reduce the risks. He really never did play it safe."

"I didn't think so," Seventeen said. "He may have explained that keeping a ship in good order was the goal, but I have never heard of the colonel playing it safe to protect the equipment."

She smiled, reminded that everyone knew she had flown with the colonel.

"I think you have learned his tactics," Seventeen said, "better than you think. Wounded, yes, but you achieved an acceptable outcome in meeting the objective at hand. Not bad for a cadet, Captain."

"Thanks," she said and sipped her cool coffee. "I guess I did."

"And now," he said, "for a cadet with nine kills on the board, you're second only to Lieutenant Casi."

She laughed. "I've a long ways to go to best her, in many more ways than the number of kills."

Thursday, December 29

"Colonel," Lieutenant Riviera said as she studied the horizontal scanner screen. "I don't know what they did when they installed the cannons, but ever since, I've been automatically tracking their IFF positions."

"They're letting us track them?" Colonel Townsley asked with a little surprise in his voice.

"Yes, sir," Lieutenant Riviera said. "I can filter them out, but my default now has them." She looked at his perplexed expression and knew he wasn't sure of this new development. "Personally, sir, I like it that they are telling us where they are. It is so much better than guessing like I had to do before, not knowing who was on which side, who was shooting who. This is much better."

"I'm certain it is, Lieutenant," he admitted. "I guess I'm just overly cautious, especially when it comes to allying ourselves with strangers."

"Well, sir," she said and tapped the screen, "we are, and they are

43

back to install the shield generators. At least I think that is what the admiral said they would be doing."

"Did you see them on Monday?" he asked. "I mean their IFF signature?"

"Not until they powered the turrets and set the controls up with Weapons," she said. "They also said that the installation of the shield would not affect our ability to scan."

"Have you picked up any other targets?" Colonel Townsley asked as he remembered.

"No. We still haven't seen any of the intruders," she replied. "Their colonel said we would only see them if they saw them first and lit them up."

"Let's hope they see them first," he said and turned to the central hatch, "like they have been. I'll be in the admiral's office, following their progress, if you need anything."

⋀ ⋀ ⋀ ⋀ ⋀

Captain Haak, Cadet Tigs and Cadet Moss stood 'At Rest' in front of Captain Iims' dais as he started his morning briefing.

"Cadet Moss," Captain Iims began. "Patrol Fighter Four is being temporarily confined to maintenance and re-identified until they can figure out what its problem is. You are assigned one of the new Class 1 patrol fighters as Patrol Four."

"Yes, sir," Cadet Moss said happily. "Thank you, sir."

"Cadet Tigs," Captain Iims continued. "Your existing Patrol Three is being re-identified and returned to the cadet pool. You are assigned one of the Class 2 fighters as Patrol Three. Congratulations and good luck. Familiarization and cockpit orientation will begin in half an hour."

"Yes, sir," Cadet Tigs said brightly. "Thank you, sir."

"Captain Haak," Captain Iims said and looked at her a moment before continuing. "I am glad to see you are recovered."

"Thank you," she said. "I am."

"You are assigned the other Class 2 fighter as a replacement for your damaged Patrol Two. Between it and Cadet Moss' old fighter, Maintenance may be able to come up with one suitable for use."

"Thank you, sir," Cheral said, hardly believing her ears.

"Familiarization and cockpit orientation is in half an hour," Captain Iims said, "along with Cadet Tigs. Cadet Moss," he turned to Moss, "Flight drills are in one hour. You've missed a few."

"Yes, sir," Cadet Moss said happily.

"Any Questions?" Captain Iims asked.

"Sir?" Cadet Tigs asked. "Are we expecting more cadets?"

"Yes, cadet," Captain Iims replied. "If you are wondering about the two unassigned Patrol Fighters, maybe three, they are for our use as spares or replacements. The colonel is certain we will sustain more combat damage and he wanted to have back up equipment on hand. A spare Class 2 fighter will come in two weeks with the next group of cadets. Those cadets will bring their own patrol fighters and additional replacements. Anything more?"

"No, sir," Cadet Tigs said. "Thank you, sir."

Captain Iims glanced at the cadets and then shouted, "Dismissed!"

ᴀ ᴀ ᴀ ᴀ ᴀ

Ben and Abe had just returned to Abe's house, after stopping at Jerry's Café on Main for a quick lunch. The weather seemed unduly cold for a clear day and Abe quickly went to the kitchen and made a fresh pot of coffee. Ben dumped his coat on an overstuffed chair in the living room and followed Abe as far as the dining room.

"Any idea what Don is planning?" Ben asked as Abe hung his coat on the back of a chair.

"About what?" Abe asked in answer.

"About what he is going to do about that marshal and his questions," Ben said. "He has been too quiet."

"I know," Abe agreed, "and he has not told me anything."

"Abe, it has been over two weeks since we told him about the women with the red headbands," Ben continued, half to himself. "Almost three since Pat shot the marshal and those women showed up."

"He did say he wanted to know what the marshal has found out," Abe said and poured them each a mug of coffee. "And we were told to follow him and listen to find out."

"But, so far we have nothing to show for it," Ben said, sounding dejected.

"Yeah, and he is not going to put up with it much longer," Abe admitted as they walked into the den and switched the tracking monitor on.

Abe sat down in the folding chair in front of the computer and Ben stopped at the end of the desk absently watching the street in front of the house with the college stadium across the empty block beyond. Abe was jotting down the time and locations of the five dots on the screen when Ben absently said, "There goes one of the deputies."

Abe looked up from the screen. "Where?"

"Just went by," Ben said, glancing at Abe. "Came around the corner from the north and went toward town." Ben gestured past the window.

Abe looked back at the monitor. "There is no dot on Birch." He looked up at Ben. "Damn!"

"No dot?"

"No dot," Abe restated, "Come on. There are three that are not moving and we're going to see what they are."

Abe grabbed his coat from the dining room chair and hurried out the front door. Ben scrambled to keep up.

Ninety

Friday, December 30

Eddie sat in an antique straight-backed chair in her dining room staring at the beautiful bouquet centered on the round, intricately carved pedestal table. Monday she had spent most of her day creating the arrangement for the new deputy, Thomas Baine, trying to figure out ways to match the flowers and greenery with the vision he explained when he ordered it. She had taken an early dinner break so she could check on her mom, so instead of her, Mary had called to tell him the arrangement was done and was there when he came to pick it up.

Still confused, she remembered her initial surprise and then her anger when Mary showed her the bouquet and the card with her name on it. She was surprised that he was giving it to her, and then her temper flared, arguing that he made her spend hours to make her own present! If he wanted to give her something, she told herself that he should not have made her make it!

Driving home, she almost threw it out of the car's window, twice, but she had admitted it was too nice to just throw away. She even considered giving it to her mom, but she knew her mom wouldn't appreciate it. So she finally took it home with her and set it in the center of her dining room table where she sat and stared at it in continued confusion and irritation until the night was almost morning.

Tuesday morning, she barely noticed them in her hurry to get to work. Angry that her irritation and late night had caused her to over sleep, she was still in a foul mood when Mary came and opened the shop. She tried to explain to Mary how she felt, but that just made the way she felt sound worse. The afternoon passed slowly and she kept looking at the door, expecting him to come in and say something he might think was cute and encouraging. She was ready for him, ready to argue with anything he had to say or any excuse he might present. But, he did not come and after work, still upset with Thom, she went by to see her mom. The continued, unhappy status from the nurse just made her day sink lower. At home, she tried to eat, but she did not have an appetite for food and she opened a brew and sat, staring at the flowers.

Wednesday morning was better, a little. She studied what she had done when she made the arrangement and thought about why she did the things she did as she ate a cold cereal breakfast with a cup of coffee. At work, she found herself absently creating a 'new' bouquet, trying some of the different things she had thought about while she studied the arrangement at home. And when Mary came in and opened the shop, Eddie felt like she was a little more sociable, maybe a little less angry. At lunch she went and checked on her mom, but the nurse was still not encouraging and Eddie went back to work feeling empty inside. That evening, with her chin in her hands, she stared at the bouquet and slowly began to cry for her mom and the life that was take away from her, from them.

Thursday was somber, her mom did not recognize her again and the loneliness made her day almost unbearable. Mary understood and tried to help, but nothing seemed to. That afternoon when she got home, unmoved by the clearing weather, she popped the top on a brew and sat down at the dining room table. As she stared at the center piece, a shaft of late afternoon sunlight slipped in through the window and the bouquet suddenly blossomed with its vibrant colors, illuminating the room in its cheer and she remembered Thom's words, that he wanted her to see the flowers first thing 'to be encouragement' and 'to be there to brighten the end of her day.'

But after her dad left, leaving them in the lurch and the insensitive, uncaring way men had treated her and her mom in the years after, she found it hard to be encouraged and see her days brightened. When her mom got sick, her mom sold her the house for a minimal amount, but the cost of her medical care had nearly bankrupted them. She remembered how angry she was at her dad when she found the forgotten insurance policy in the few things he had left behind. It was the only good thing she could remember happening after he left them.

She still wondered what had changed, why he had just simply packed up and left while she and her mom were at the school's spring musical. He had always been so supportive of her and the things she did, but that day he said he had to work late. And that was the last she saw of him. Her mom collapsed, distraught and blamed herself. Neither of them really recovered from that night.

She had trusted her dad completely. That's what a kid did, and then he let her down in the worst way. And now, after eight years, this Thom Baine gave her his fine speech and tried to make her believe he could be trusted. She wondered if people, especially men, could really be trusted. Was there such a thing as 'no strings attached?' The few people she talked to about the new deputies had indicated Thom seemed a reliable sort, not chasing skirts or talking down to anyone. She wondered what he was really like.

She pondered the conflicting feelings she harbored as she absently toyed with the card Thom had placed in the bouquet. She watched it without thinking about it, flipping it back and forth between her fingers, seeing her name carefully and clearly hand written on one side of the envelope.

Suddenly she stopped and looked at it closely and realized it was an 'envelope.' She slowly opened it and took the folded card out. Nervous, she laid it on the table and took a long sip of her brew.

Printed simply on the front of the card, he had written 'Friends…'

She unfolded the card and saw Thom's neat, clear handwriting inside,

'…lend an ear when you need someone to listen,

…lend aide when you need someone to help,

…lend comfort when you need someone to care,

…lend a smile when you need someone to cheer you,

…lend you a shoulder when you need someone to share your burden.'

Then at the bottom, he had added,

'No strings, no expectations. You have a wonderful gift, and I think you are wonderful yourself. Thomas.'

⅄

Eddie had finished her breakfast and had put her bowl and coffee cup in the kitchen sink. She sat and stared at the beautiful bouquet in the center of her dining room table, admiring the cheerful, bright colors, knowing they would still be vibrant for another two, maybe three days. She got up and drove the short distance to the flower shop and had the first two of the days orders finished and in the cool room before Mary came in and opened the store.

Mary was surprised at her progress and was even more surprised when she saw the vibrant, colorful arrangements in the cooler.

"Mind if I take the afternoon off?" Eddie asked as Mary checked off items on the order sheet. "I'll have those ready before lunch."

Mary looked at Eddie still intent on her next order and finally said, "Sure. Anything going on?"

"No," she answered in her normal tone, but she smiled as she looked over at Mary. "I haven't taken an afternoon off in months, and I'd like to."

Mary nodded and turned back to her lists, "Okay."

▲

By noon Eddie had closed the cool room on her last arrangement and told Mary she would see her in the morning. Then she drove down to Hap's and parked in back. She remembered it was Friday before she pushed the door open and faced the already loud, pulsing music. She stepped inside and took stock of the dining area and then saw the marshal on a stool at the end of the long bar, and Carole behind the bar filling his mug from a coffee carafe.

She walked around the bar and stopped beside them.

"Hey, Carole, Marshal," she said happily. "I heard congratulations are in order."

"Thanks Eddie," Carole said. "I haven't seen you around in a long time. I'm glad you came by."

Wally said "thanks" as well. "Eddie, would you care to join us?" he asked and offered the stool beside him.

"Sure," she said and sat down. "Have you guys set a date yet?"

"Well," Wally started, "Carole was trying for this weekend, but apparently there is too much that has to happen and it can't be done that quickly. I think I'm just along for the ride from here on out."

Eddie chuckled.

"It'll probably be the end of the month, January that is," Carole said, correcting herself. "Will you come?"

Surprised, Eddie blinked. "Sure. I don't get out much and that will be a great reason."

"No gifts," Carole said. "We don't need stuff, just our friends."

Thom's card and his words suddenly flowed through her mind and she smiled.

"What can I get you?" Carole asked as she set a glass of water in front of her.

"You know, I'm off for the rest of the day," Eddie said, "so how about one of those spiced beers and a grilled cheese." Then, when Carole took her order to the window, Eddie turned to Wally, "How are you and your new deputies settling in. Someone told me you're going to stay and be our long term marshal."

"That's right," Wally admitted, "forever or longer if I can manage it. I think the deputies are happy to get the chance to settle down as well. At least I know Dan is. His wife is here now and he's looking forward to enrolling Blaire, his daughter, in school next week and she's about as happy as I've ever seen a seven year old kid be."

Carole returned and set Wally's burger without fries in front of him and an auto-chill stein in front of Eddie.

"How about the single guys?" Eddie asked and sipped the beer. "I hear they've been checking out some of the girls I know."

"I guess that's to be expected," Wally admitted and took a bite of his burger. "Hopefully they're polite and courteous. Ted's the social one. He started looking for dances and gatherings the week he got here. So I guess 'checking out the girls' might be a suitable way to put it."

"He asked Wally if he could have tomorrow night off," Carole said with a chuckle, "so he could party a little." Eddie watched the comfortable, almost playful interaction between the two of them as Carole continued, "So Wally gave him the night off, but also the morning rounds on Sunday."

Eddie laughed at Wally's ploy as Carole turned and retrieved the grilled cheese. Eddie started eating while it was hot, partially to keep herself from asking about Thom.

"Are you going to join the 'rowdies' tomorrow night?" Carole asked as she quickly glanced around the room.

"Probably not," Eddie admitted. "I usually don't go out, especially on crowded, holiday nights."

Carole glanced at Wally, her eyes questioning.

"You could join Carole and me," Wally offered. "I'm off duty until about nine, and then Dan and I have to monitor the public conduct for the rest of the evening."

"No," Eddie said quickly. "You'll want to be alone—"

"Eddie," Carole interrupted. "We're going to have a quiet dinner at my place until Wally has to go on duty. I'd like some female company if you're not doing anything."

Eddie stared at her, uncertain of what to say.

"Besides," Carole continued. "We haven't visited in a long time."

Finally, when Eddie could not think of any excuses, she accepted. "What time? Can I bring something?"

"Around dark," Carole said, "and not really. Do you like wine?"

Eddie nodded and said, "I'll bring some snacks and a couple of bottles of a great, dry red." Then, when she finished her sandwich, she asked Wally, "So you've got one deputy out partying tomorrow night, and you and another, you said Dan, are on duty, where's the other one? I thought there are four of you."

"He might be back," Wally said, "but maybe not."

"He's away?" she asked, wondering if that was why he had not come by the shop to bother her like she expected him to. Every time she cracked the door open with a guy, they always pestered her until she went out with them or she sent them on their way, and usually she just sent them on their way to save time.

"Yeah," Wally said as he finished his coffee. "I had an assignment for him and he left last night."

"Oh," she said, not expecting that answer and realized Thom had been here all week and had not pestered her, not once. He had given her space, no pressure.

"So what're you going to do with your afternoon off?" Carole asked as she cleared her plate.

"I think I'll look for a new blouse and some nice looking boots," she said happily, "The shops are never open when I get off work and I usually don't have much time at lunch."

Carole asked softly, "Sorry, but how is your mom doing?"

Eddie inhaled deeply. "About the same. Her memory's all but gone and the nurses are not very optimistic. They think it's only a matter of a few weeks."

"I'm so sorry to hear that, Eddie," Carole said. "You let me know if there is anything you need or that you want us to do."

"Thanks, Carole," Eddie said and forced a smile. "At least mom's not in pain." Then she turned to Wally, "Thanks for coming to our little town and I'm glad you're going to be a part of it."

She paid Carole for the lunch, got up and went shopping for

herself for the first time in many months.

▲ ▲ ▲ ▲ ▲

Thom pulled his patrol car into one of the 'official' parking slots in front of the Clay Police Station and shut it down. He checked his notes and took a deep breath before he stepped out and locked the car. With a slow glance up and down Main Street, stretching his back as if the ride tired him some, he tried to get a feeling for the town. Then he straightened and stepped up onto the sidewalk and entered the offices.

He stopped at the chest high counter and smiled at the woman behind it. "Can you tell me if Chief Russell is in?"

The woman looked up and smiled in return. "He sure is," she said. "Who may I say wants him?"

"I'm State Deputy Thom Baine from Riggin," Thom replied and the woman got up and stuck her head into an office along the wall behind the counter.

When she returned, a stocky man in a brown uniform followed her out.

"Good morning," he greeted. "Chief Russell. How may I help you?"

"Do you have a place where we can talk privately?" Thom asked without sounding too dramatic. "I have a few things I'd like to discuss if you have some time."

"Sure, sure," Chief Russell said and gestured toward the office he came from. "Can Marie get you some coffee or anything?"

"Coffee would be nice," he admitted and smiled to Marie as they stepped into the Chief's small, but tidy office.

The Chief pointed to a chair and then sat down in the worn leather chair behind his desk. "Did you drive down this morning?" he asked, gauging the time of day against how long he knew it took to drive from Riggin.

"No," Thom said casually. "I drove down late last night and stayed at that nice motel on the south side of town, Bob's Cabins."

"Oh," the Chief said, obviously surprised by his answer.

"I figured I'd get a good breakfast, on the marshal, you know," he said with a wink, "and then see a little bit of your town since I've never been here before."

"Well, I will admit it is small," Chief Russell said, "but we sure like it."

"I can see why," Thom agreed as Marie brought a tray in with two mugs, a carafe and a small basket of sweet breads.

"Thanks, Marie," Chief Russell said and gestured for Thom to help himself. As Thom filled a mug for himself and passed the carafe to the chief, the chief asked, "So, what is on your mind?"

"It's sort of hard to know where to start," Thom said, dissembling to show a little less confidence. "The marshal and us deputies were assigned to Riggin after Sheriff Black and his six deputies disappeared sometime around the twenty-second of October. No one we've talked to seems to know anything or has seen anything we can use to close the books on their disappearance. You know; was there foul play involved? Did they just skip out and if so, why?"

"Yeah," Chief Russell said softly. "We heard about them being missing."

"Obviously," Thom continued, "the marshal wants me to check with anyone that might have known them to see if there's anything we should know."

"Wish I could help you there, Deputy," the chief said, "but things were quiet around here and we did not see the sheriff or any of his deputies much."

"Nothing unusual happened around that date?" Thom asked absently. "No kids or hunters playing with bright lights or ground shakes?"

"Aah, we did have a couple of high school kids that claimed to see a light fly over and felt the ground shake," the Chief admitted as he thought about it, "but we never figured out what they might have seen or felt."

"Us either," Thom admitted as he flipped through the pages on his digital notepad. He started to say something but stopped and said, "Excuse me," and tapped his earpiece. "Yes?" he asked, listening to someone on the other end of the connection. Then he said, "Okay, I'll meet you when I'm done and we can talk about it," then he turned back to the Chief. "Sorry for the interruption. Where was I? Oh, yes," and he focused on the notepad.

Chief Russell watched him intently, seeing the earpiece for the first time when Thom spoke. "Something important?"

"What? Oh," Thom said seeing the chief's look. "No, no. My partner went looking at shops while we talked. Just wanted to show me something. What I was going to ask you about next are the other people that have gone missing since that time."

"Others?" Chief Russell asked, sounding surprised.

"Yes," Thom continued, acting as if he had been more interested in his notepad than to the chief. "About the same time the sheriff disappeared, we have a Brian Woods. He headed up the mill in Riggin, but we thought he might have come this way when he left."

The Chief shook his head. "No, none of us have seen Brian since maybe, early September."

"Hmm," Thom muttered and looked back at the notepad. "I also have a Harold Danley who was an official at the mortgage and loan here in Clay. He and Harry Woods disappeared about mid-November." Thom looked up. "I suppose someone has inquired about Harold."

"Yes," the Chief said. "We checked out his house and his office, talked to his coworkers and neighbors but have not found anything that would say where he went or why?"

"Don't you think that's odd?" Thom asked with a puzzled expression.

"Odd?" Chief Russell asked and then said, "Yes, I suppose it is. When we could not find anything that indicated foul play, I just supposed he was away on a trip. But now that you bring it up, I have not seen him for over a month."

"Okay," Thom said and went on. "The circuit judge? The marshal tried to get in touch with her after he arrived. He had a detainee and needed the circuit judge's advice, but he never made contact with her. A Judge Bernice Reeds, I believe." He stopped and looked up at the chief. "She has a home here, I understand."

"Yes, yes she does," the chief said, suddenly perspiring and seeming a little nervous. "Come to think of it, I have not seen her lately either."

"That is odd," Thom said, rubbing his chin as if he were pondering some unspoken thought. "Well, if you find out anything about them," he handed the chief one of his cards, "please call me at our office in Riggin."

"I will," the chief said, "I certainly will."

Thom folded the cover on his notepad closed and started to get up. "Oh, and when you check on the judge and Harold, please look into a Malcolm, Charley and Seth Clotter. They live around here as well and have been missing since around mid-November also."

Then Thom stood up and extended his hand to the chief and noted his hands were sweaty when he returned the gesture. "Anything you can give us will be greatly appreciated. The marshal has a report to make and needs to address as many names as he can."

"I will see what I can do," the Chief said. "That is a lot of names to address."

"Yes," Thom agreed absently as he stepped out of the office and into the area behind Marie and the counter. "In the last ten years we have over fifty to investigate and thirty-five of them lived between here and Grants."

The Chief nodded. "Who is the marshal making the report for?"

Thom looked sideways at the chief and smiled wryly, "He's a state marshal, Chief Russell."

Then Thom smiled at Marie and thanked her for the coffee and said to the chief, "Thanks for the help. If I don't hear from you in the next couple of weeks, I'm sure the marshal will have me come back to visit. Thanks again." He walked through the door and looked at the clear sky. "I was going to say 'enjoy the great weather,' but I think it's getting worse again. Good bye." And Thom closed the door.

When he slid into the patrol car, he noticed the blinds on the office's front window move, as if someone was watching his next move and released the blinds when he turned around. He smiled. The chief was very uncomfortable and he knew Wally was right, he had better watch his back.

"WL-One," he said into his earpiece, as he started the car and backed out of the parking slot, "monitor the conversations in and around the police station for the next half an hour, then give me a status."

He drove slowly up the street, watching to see if anyone was following him. He told Jill he'd meet them and he did not want anyone to see.

⋏

Thom stopped at a small city park just south of the city hall building and stretched out on a long bench beside a picnic table next to a large pine tree. He was glad the wind had relaxed as he leaned against the tree.

"You were followed here," Jill said, standing near the table, completely invisible.

"It's the one that was listening from the office next to Chief Russell's," Rose added.

"Yeah. I have our remote recording whatever happened after I left," Thom said. "Ought to be interesting. The Chief was getting very nervous."

"I know," Jill said. "The one that followed you wanted to just make you go away and I know what that means, but the Chief reminded him who you are and that you had a partner waiting for you."

"I'm glad you called, Jill," he said with a smile as he casually gazed around the park. "It was a good opportunity to add to the ruse, and I'm glad you let me know the man next door and Marie were listening in. Kept me from going too far off script."

"Is Wally really writing a report for the state?" Rose asked.

"Not in the way the chief thinks, Rose," Thom laughed softly. "But we do need to get some answers."

"Wally already has the facts on the judge, Harold, Brian, Harry and the three Clotter brothers," Jill admitted. "But he can't put those facts in a report, even if their stories are known."

"What?" Thom said and turned toward Jill's voice. "He already knows what happened to them?"

"I think you're asking about the wrong list. Wally knows that Shar and I were there when the judge went 'missing' and that we were there when Harry shot Shar and he was killed," Jill added, "and that Shar, Greg and Kiile were there when Malcolm and Charley Clotter went missing. Wally shot Seth after Seth tried to kill him and Carole. He also knows that Shar and I were there when Pat went missing, after he shot Wally twice in the back and that Kiile's men were there when the six that jumped Wally at the bank went 'missing.'"

Thom thought to himself for a long moment. "What else do you and Wally know or were 'there' for when it happened?"

"A lot," Jill said. "But I may have already said too much. Wally, and probably you, will need to sit down with Greg again and let him give you as much of the story as he is allowed to give. The unknown stories are about the people that have gone missing four months or more ago, not the recent ones."

"So, when you talk about the slavers—?" Thom started to ask, redirecting his thoughts.

"Wally gave you a basic overall description of what's happening, planetside and off world, but Greg will have to explain anything you need beyond that." She paused a moment and then continued, "WL-One is coming and the one following you is waiting by the city hall building to see if you're meeting your 'partner.'"

"Could I pick one of you up along Main Street to make the 'partner' legit?" Thom asked.

"I'm in street clothes," Rose said before Jill could answer.

"We both are," Jill added. "But, yes, Rose can find a suitable place and unveil and you can pick her up and head out of town. Are you finished here in Clay?"

"Not quite yet, but I need to satisfy the tail and lose him before I check out some addresses."

"How many do you have, Thom," Rose asked.

"Five," he said. "Drive-bys and a couple of digital images."

"Take Rose with you and I'll follow with WL-One and Four," Jill said. "When you've got your info, head south on your way to Hawthorne and Rose can rejoin me."

"Sounds like a plan," Thom said and stretched as he slowly got up, held his hand over his ear as if he were talking to his 'partner' and then ambled back to his patrol car.

Saturday, December 31

While Greg and Kiile were reviewing supply requirements and equipment allocations for Obscure, Casi hovered near Hawthorne and waited for Deputy Baine to finish his business there. When he signaled he was ready to head back north, Casi dropped down and picked up Jill, Rose and the remotes. Casi bid Thom a "Good Trip" and took STSX aloft.

Enroute, STSX received a request to join up with Cheral and Cadet Tigs on their first patrol duty since Cheral's sortie on Christmas day and Casi altered course to make the interception. Jill took the right side jumpseat and Rose the left, as they eagerly inhaled the views from the cockpit, mesmerized by the cloudscapes and the view of the rugged country around the valley and across the state as they climbed through the thinning air. Casi took note of the extensive cloud bank building to the northwest of the valley.

Casi stayed focused on both the sensations she had and the scanner's IFF trace of Cheral and Cadet Tigs' patrol fighters as they flanked the space station in the southern swing of its orbit over South Africa.

"I think we should check out the second launch facility," Casi said as she leveled STSX just above the atmosphere and followed the displayed intercept course.

"Sure," Jill said as she looked at the 3-D globe beside the pilot's cushioned chair. "Is that Cheral?"

"Yeah. Cheral, Ani and the station," she replied and swung a little farther south and east of the station's track.

"I know Major Kooich has a remote watching the activity," Casi continued, "but I just want to see for myself."

STSX made a slow pass round the cloaked 'island' and recorded visual and thermal data. On the second pass the scanner picked up slightly warmer thermal streaks in the water extending radially from the island's coordinates in two directions.

"UNDERWATER TRANSPORTATION DETECTED," STSX said.

"Really?" Casi said softly and magnified the scanner image. "That would make sense. There are no obvious docking structures," she continued as STSX rolled into a tighter turn.

Casi suddenly felt like the ship was spinning and jerked the controls. Jill and Rose both looked at her, startled by the twitch and watched as Casi leaned forward, her head unsteady.

"Shar? Are you all right?" Jill asked and reached out to touch her arm.

'RELEASE THE CONTROLS,' STSX said softly in Casi's mind. 'WE ARE STABLE.'

Casi relaxed her grip and caught the armrest as she turned the chair to aft facing. "Excuse me," she said and hurried down through the floor portal.

"Shar?" Jill called after Casi, her eyes wide at them being alone in the cockpit.

"WE ARE IN NO DANGER. THE LIEUTENANT IS FINE."

After many long moments, Casi slowly drifted back up and returned to the pilot's chair. Guarding her thoughts, she turned and smiled at both of them. "I think that last turn got to me."

"Has this happened often?" Jill asked, watching her closely.

"No," Casi lied. "And I'm fine." She glanced around at the indications as she strapped herself back into the seat, gripping the armrest as her head threatened to spin again. "STSX told you so. Now, let's catch up with Cheral."

▲

'*Good morning, cousin,*' Casi greeted silently as she brought STSX alongside Apache Two's presence.

'*Shar?*' Cheral asked in surprised reply. '*Where are you? We don't have you painted.*'

'*Right beside you,*' Casi chuckled. '*I haven't broadcast our IFF.*'

'*Who's with you?*"

'*Just Jill, Rose and me this morning,*' Casi answered. '*How's the patrol duty coming?*'

'*A little boring,*' Cheral admitted.

'*And the new ship?*'

'*The ship is a real treat,*' Cheral said, her voice brighter. '*Doesn't take voice commands, but all of the systems are a nice step-up from the Class 1s. I still can't believe they assigned them to Ani and me.*'

'*Why shouldn't the Campaign's two cadets with the best engagement performance records and the highest number of kills get the good ships?*' she teased. '*You've earned them.*'

'*Did Greg have something to do with this?*' Cheral asked, suddenly suspicious.

'*Not that I know of,*' Casi said. '*I think this one came from the director.*'

Ninety-One

Carole already had the round dining room table set for three when Eddie arrived, allowing them to relax and visit before dinner. Wally took the stuffed chair near the front door and left the couch for Carole and Eddie. He sat quietly listening as the two women caught up on the general happenings around town, what their mutual friends had done since school or were doing now.

"So?" Eddie asked, changing the subject slightly. "Where were you Wally, before you came here to help us out?"

He sipped his coffee and thought about his answer. "I spent three months in the wilds trying to catch poachers up near the reservation," he explained without going into too much detail.

"Poachers?" Eddie questioned with a raised eyebrow. "Isn't that something the game and wildlife people usually do?"

"Usually," he nodded and sipped his coffee again.

She waited and watched him, her expression asking for more and he knew it would be impolite to challenge her insistence.

"Seems there's a jurisdiction issue when it comes to the Indians," Wally slowly explained, "and a bit of an interpretation issue when it comes to what is poaching and what is not, and some differences in those interpretations depending on who's accused of doing the poaching. The Indians have some special allowances that many folks don't know about."

"Sounds like it could get complicated," Eddie admitted.

"It was," he continued after another sip. "But when I finally saw the man and his wife committing the 'crime' I realized the warrants forgot to mention they were Indians, making things very complicated. To spare you all of the boring details, I'll just say that they were exonerated, under those 'special' allowances concerning protected game under state law. So, I enjoyed the late summer in the high desert, mostly alone, with all expenses paid by the state. But I was glad for the change when I was asked to come here and fill the vacancy."

Eddie smiled and sipped her wine. "And how long were you here before you realized you liked city life and not being alone in the wilds?"

"Actually, I've always liked both," he said. "I like being away from towns some, but I'm not a hermit."

"I guess what I'm wondering," Eddie said, changing her direction, "is how long after you got here did you look up and noticed Carole?"

"Oh, direct question," he smiled and glanced at Carole. "I was here, what, two weeks and three days before we actually spoke to each other? We'd seen each other at Hap's, and I had gotten her name from one of the other waitresses, but we hadn't talked to each other. She's too pretty to not notice."

Carole looked at Eddie and laughed. "Wally was usually deep in his work and didn't talk much until the day when we first spoke. And that day, he came into Hap's for lunch as usual and was more interested in asking about Shara's car wreck. He had been out to her ranch and Hank had shooed him away, so he started asking around town."

"I guess," he said a little abashed, "you could say it still took me a little longer to really 'see' Carole."

Eddie chuckled and shook her head. "And why were you asking about Shara and the car wreck? That happened before you got here."

Wally explained how skeptical Carole was of his motives and how he tried to convince her that he was just cleaning up open files from the sheriff's office, but also how her questions made him dig deeper into other things he discovered, finally forcing him to ask her to just sit down with him and tell him what had been going on in the valley. "When I went out to her folk's ranch and she gave me the history, that's when I 'saw' her and realized how much she wanted to help and how much I like having her help. That's when I knew I wanted to be with her."

"By the way, Eddie," Carole said, smiling at Wally. "The rumors that Shara and Jill are alive are true. We knew Shara was alive and well when we met with her about a month ago. But apparently the car wreck wasn't an accident and when some of the people from the Family realized she hadn't died in the wreck, they tried to kidnap her and Jill. They escaped and she and Jill hid out at her ranch. They didn't say anything until those responsible were caught or dealt with."

Wally nodded and got up when the oven timer buzzed for his

attention. "Looks like dinner's about ready."

"She's alive?" Eddie asked as if Carole was joking. "And Jill's not missing?"

Carole smiled, "And Tuesday night, about seven thirty, Jill and Nick walked into Hap's, as casual as anyone, followed by Shara and her husband Greg,"

"'Husband?'" Eddie couldn't believe her ears. "Shar's married? I... I..."

"She is," Carole said. "Yes, our local, wonderful, reliable, defiant tomboy. The same one that slugged Richard Bowling for tellin' folks they were engaged without asking her first six or seven years ago, and the same one that's put all the other fellas in this town in their places, swearing off relationships of any and all kinds. Well, she's happily, no, radiantly and happily married to Greg Malone."

"Malone? Malone? Wasn't that the fella Sheriff Black was after?" Eddie asked, trying to remember the details.

"The charges weren't true," Wally said from the dining room as he finished setting the food on the table. "All of the sheriff's warrants have been recalled and voided."

"That's a relief," Eddie said as she followed Carole to the table.

Conversation changed to the subject of foods and preparations once dinner started in earnest and Carole mentioned that Wally prepared most of it, the casseroles and the seasoned vegetables, gravies and sauces. Carole admitted that she only got to cook when Wally's work filled his time and he couldn't spend the time in the kitchen. Eddie commented that she seldom cooked a full meal and being invited was a real pleasure.

When dinner was finished, Wally cleared the table and set out clean napkins, stem-less wine glasses and a chiller with a bottle of chablis and the bottles of red that Eddie brought. Carole set a plate of thinly sliced cheeses, bread thins and fruit slices on the table for a light desert and their congenial evening continued.

Wally had rinsed the dishes and resigned them to the dishwasher when a knock at the door interrupted them. He answered it and let Thom in.

"Sorry to interrupt, Wally," Thom said and glanced around the room.

"Hello, Thom," Carole greeted. "Please come in. Do you know

Eddie Collier?" she asked as he stepped into the dining room.

"Thank you, Carole," he smiled and looked at Eddie. "Yes, we've met. Nice to see you again, Eddie." Then he turned back to Wally. "I'd like to speak to you before you go out on rounds, if you have a minute."

"Certainly," Wally said and ushered Thom to the far side of the living room where they would not disturb Carole and Eddie.

Carole resumed their conversation, but noticed the number of times Eddie glanced at Thom and Wally, deep in their own conversation and oblivious of their existence.

"When they talk business," Carole said, "they forget everything else."

"It seems important," Eddie admitted and glanced once more. "Do you ever get involved with Wally's work or are you left on the outside?"

"As a matter of fact," Carole said with a smile, "we discuss almost all of his work at one time or another. I've gone out with him on investigations. I've been shot at. I've been attacked. I'm sort of in the middle of it all. He's very quick and very protective, but I like learning what he does."

Stunned, Eddie just stared at her.

"Excuse me," Wally said as he stopped beside the table. "Eddie, could Thom speak with you a minute. I think he has some information that you'll like hearing."

When Eddie nodded and said "yes," Wally gestured for Carole to join him in the living room and for Thom to take a seat at the table with Eddie.

"Thanks," Thom said as he sat down in Wally's chair across from Eddie and leaned forward with his forearms on the table. "I don't want you to think I'm prying or anything, Eddie. What I have to say will not be repeated to anyone else by me. Publicly, only you will know about this unless you tell someone else."

Eddie waited, her expression cooling into the same one he had seen in the flower shop.

"We did some investigating," Thom began, "trying to see what we could find out about your father's disappearance."

"You what?" her voice pitched in surprise. "Why do you bring him up, especially on a happy night like this? When I'm—"

"Eddie, please." Thom looked down at the table, and then continued softly when she paused, "I think you should know that your father did not willingly leave you and your mother."

"What?" She stared at him, uncertain that she heard his words. "How can you say that?"

"Your father did not run off and leave you and your mother." Thom looked at her and held her eyes, seeing the turmoil and conflict she was feeling. "Your father had to work late on the night he disappeared. He had to go to Clay that afternoon to untangle a problem with the shipping office there. The college would not let him wait a day to resolve it, so he went and missed your night at school, but when he got there he was 'taken,' kidnapped if you will."

He hesitated and saw the disbelief in her eyes.

"Eddie, your father was stolen from you by a slave trading organization and shipped to a labor market." Thom saw her inhale sharply. "I have a copy of a manifest that confirms he and fifteen others were taken that night."

"How?" she asked, barely a whisper.

"I can't explain to you how I know or where I got the information," he said softly and slid the folded sheet of paper to her. "But this lists your father and the others by name. We've confirmed they are all on the list of fifty-three Wally has been investigating. The names and dates all agree. I was away checking on some of the others and just got back."

Eddie slowly unfolded the sheet and noted the highlighted name. "Where's Dangcee? I've never heard of it."

"No, you wouldn't have. It's a mining colony, where people are enslaved to provide manpower in the mines," he admitted softly. "I got another report today that confirms your father did not go quietly. He fought them the best he could, but was subdued and shipped away. He did not voluntarily turn his back on you. He was stolen from you."

Eddie looked at him, her eyes filling with tears as she listened to his words and felt the paper in her fingers. "You're sure?"

"Very sure, Eddie," he said. "I will never lie to you." He took a deep breath and continued, "When they took the people on that list, they sent others to remove their personal belongings to make it look like the person left on their own. We're seeing where they did this over and over in the past ten years, maybe even longer."

"Is he...?"

"We don't know yet," he said, wanting to hold her, to comfort her, but he honored his word and remained in his chair. "I am told an undercover agent near Dangcee will see if he can find out if he's there, if he's been taken somewhere else and if he's still alive. I don't know how long it will take, but we have friends that will keep looking."

She looked at him again, and he held her eyes softly.

"When we find out more, I will tell you," he said and slowly straightened.

She wiped her eyes with the napkin and watched him, then slowly she said, "Thank you, Thom."

"You're welcome, Eddie," he said softly as he got up. "I wanted you to know as soon as we knew." He nodded and forced a smile, hoping the news would help ease her feelings of abandonment and longing.

Thom said his goodbyes and turned to the door as Carole sat back down at the table.

"Ted's on at four," Wally told him as he stepped out onto the porch. "Dan and I will cover nine to four. You can pick up tomorrow evening's shift. Go home and rest now."

"Okay," Thom said, "Call me if anything comes up."

Wally closed the door and turned to the dining room.

"I hope that was all right, Eddie," he said as he paused beside Carole's chair.

She nodded and wiped her eyes again with the napkin. "A little overwhelming."

"I'm sure," he said and gently squeezed Carole's shoulder. "I've got to change and get ready for work. Just remember that if you have any questions or need to talk about anything, we're here if you want."

Then Wally turned and retreated to the hall bath and closed the door.

⚔

After Wally had gone and Eddie had soothed her turmoil with another glass of red, she asked, "You and Wally? You've only known each other, for what, six weeks?"

"Yeah, about that," Carole admitted. "But they've been the best ones in my life."

"I don't mean to be snooping," Eddie said, "but it doesn't look like he's moved in."

Carole blushed. "No. No, he hasn't. We both have our own places and have only, just started talking about where we want to live after we get married."

"Hmm," Eddie muttered with a smile.

"Don't think we don't get tangled up together on occasion," Carole said defensively, "'cause we do. But there're too many gossips in town and I don't want them saying things they shouldn't, especially about the new marshal and his deputies."

"You're concerned about that, aren't you?" Eddie said as she realized the feeling in Carole's words.

"Yes, Eddie. I don't want the town to think badly of them. Wally really has the town's interests at heart and they need to trust him. And I don't want the town to think badly of how I was raised or about mom or dad." She smiled and refilled her glass. "Besides, Wally and I will have plenty of time to share a household in another month, four weeks from today."

Eddie sipped her wine and wrestled with her questions, then finally asked, "What do you think about Thom?"

"Thom?" Carole asked and then put her thoughts together. "Well, I don't know either of the single guys very well, but out of the two, I'd say Thom is definitely more settled, more sure of himself, in his desires, his manners, considerations and in his abilities. Ted still acts too young for his age, in my opinion."

"You won't believe what he did," Eddie started. Slowly, she explained Thom ordering the bouquet and then described her roller coaster week that followed. When she took Thom's card from her shoulder bag and showed it to Carole, she recalled his actions this evening, when he sat down and told her about her dad, the actions she mentally noted but did not think about at the time. How he stayed reserved, neutral, factual and caring in the way he delivered his message, and how he stayed just out of reach and made no gestures she could misconstrue.

"Sounds sincere to me," Carole admitted. "Wally was my friend before we became anything else. He showed me how he felt by protecting me, being there for me, not letting me be alone after I was attacked, and by sharing his gift of cooking, possibly the 'thing' he's most passionate about."

"Yeah, but you started interacting almost immediately," Eddie observed.

"After seeing him at Hap's regularly for lunches," Carole said, smiling at herself, "and after one dinner date where I pretty much interrogated him, I decided I wanted him to know I was interested if he was." She sighed, "He didn't take long to show me he was."

"Does he know about you grandfather's conditions?" Eddie blurted out, immediately wishing she hadn't. "Sorry Carole, that's really none of my business."

"It's okay, Eddie," she said. "Everyone in town that's been here more than six months probably knows about them. But Wally didn't. When I explained what they were and that I wouldn't break the conditions and what that might mean to us, he was okay with it. He understood and said the land is mine and not his. He's okay with it even if I want to make the separation of ownership legal."

"Wow," Eddie said softly and took another sip of her wine. "That's not like any of the guys around here and I know you've had your share of problems with them."

"Refreshing, isn't it? But Eddie, it doesn't hurt to have a beer with a guy," Carole added, turning back to the subject of Thom, "and you can just leave it there if you don't click."

"I've been angry at men for such a big part of my life," Eddie said. "Having a casual beer or a date doesn't sit very well with me."

"Well, it doesn't look like Thom's pressing you for a relationship," Carole surmised. "His card sounds to me like he might be amenable to one, but more than that I think he's trying to help you to be happy again."

🜲 🜲 🜲 🜲 🜲

"Thanks for stopping by, Rose," Greg said as he led her through the dining room and into the living room. "Would you like anything to eat, or a drink maybe?"

"I could use a little to eat," she said, "If that's not too much trouble?"

"No trouble," he said, gesturing for her to take a seat by the fire and turned to the kitchen.

When he returned and sat down in his overstuffed chair, Jill and Shara came through the dining room and joined them.

"Matti's fixing some sandwiches and a couple of brews," Greg said as Jill settled on the loveseat beside Rose. He looked at Shara as she warmed her hands in front of the fire. "Would you like anything?"

"Yes," Shara said with a sideways smile at him. "But I'll just nibble on a sandwich also. They were a little late at the pick up so we're all a little hungry." Then, feeling sufficiently warmed, she settled on Greg's lap.

Matti came in and handed Rose and Jill an auto-chill stein, then turned to Shara.

"A carafe of tea and a couple of mugs, please," Shara said softly and Matti hurried back to the kitchen, almost running into Cara as she came out with a tray and a platter.

When the sandwiches had been suitably attacked and the immediate urgencies of hunger and thirst quelled, Greg asked if they had anything to report.

"Well," Jill said, quickly washing her last bite of food down, "Deputy Baine has certainly had practice dealing with these types of situations."

"Sort of," Rose added, "rolled the grenade under Chief Russell's table and let him stew, wondering when it would go off."

"Really?" Greg asked, surprised.

Jill went on to explain the conversation Thom had with Chief Russell and how the clerk, Marie, and another police officer had listened in from outside and Rose added other details as she remembered them. She added that both Four and WL-One recorded all of the conversations in and outside of the chief's office.

"Because Chief Russell thought Deputy Baine had a partner with him," Jill continued, "we had him pick up Rose a little ways west of the police station so their tail could see them join up."

"That must have satisfied the officer that was tailing him," Rose said, "because he stopped following Deputy Baine after that."

"The remotes didn't see anyone else," Jill said, "so Deputy Baine went on and got pictures of the five addresses on his list."

"One of the places he stopped at," Rose added, "was Judge Bernice's mansion."

"Oh," Jill said, "when they stopped there, I wondered if Kiile had ever opened up the collapsed tunnel."

"I believe he has," Greg said and waited for Jill's thought.

"That could be good," she said softly. "Since Deputy Baine stirred the pot so well, the tunnel would be a great way for the marshal and the deputies to keep track of what happens now. I mean," Jill said, watching Greg's controlled expression, "the chief's going to 'do' something, and the tunnel would let them get into Clay without being seen."

"Jill Thomas," Greg said, a smile slowly growing on his face, "that's a great idea. Have Five mention it to WL-One and to Kiile."

Jill sat back in the loveseat, realizing how far she had leaned forward while she was explaining the day and her thoughts, then smiled at Greg and Shara and then at Rose.

"We rejoined Deputy Baine a little after daylight this morning in Hawthorne," Rose said. "Shar dropped us behind the cheap motel he stayed at on the south side of town. Deputy Baine had finished an early breakfast at the diner next door and he was waiting for us.

"He went straight to the police station there, but their chief had not shown up yet," Rose continued. "That was about eight fifteen."

"I sent Four on a search around town to see if their police chief was around anywhere," Jill added. "It found him on a ranch south of town and back east a few miles. Four had also recorded a call his office made after Deputy Baine left, letting the chief know he was in town and asking to see him."

"Deputy Baine spent a big part of the morning in his car in front of the police station," Rose continued. "Then he broke for lunch and spent some time in the media section of their town library,"

"When that didn't bring the police chief out into the open," Jill said with a smile, "Deputy Baine went to the town hall and the city clerk's office and began asking questions and searching the deeds and land transactions records."

"By the time the offices were closing, he had collected a thick pile of stuff," Rose said. "And when he left, the chief and two deputies were outside waiting for him."

"We'd let Deputy Baine know they were assembling," Jill added quickly, "so he wasn't caught off guard."

Rose excused herself and made a trip down the hallway to the necessary and Greg apologized for not giving them enough time after they got there. Shara got up and slipped into the kitchen and returned with a second pair of auto-chill steins.

"You've been talking yourselves dry," Shara said and gestured toward the steins when Rose had resettled on the loveseat. "Please continue."

"Well," Rose started again, "the chief was not very sociable, rude actually, and demanded to know what Deputy Baine was doing there, why he was asking all of the questions he was asking, and why was he upsetting everyone in his town, stirring up old hurts and bad feelings."

"Deputy Baine simply reminded the chief," Jill said, "that if he'd met with him when his office told him he was there, he would have asked the chief the questions and no one in his town would have known he was there. Deputy Baine also mentioned that the only information he asked about was in the public records."

"The chief didn't like Deputy Baine's answers," Rose admitted, "but he really couldn't do much about a state deputy visiting."

"For a few minutes I thought the chief might actually try to do something," Jill said, "but he thought better of it and tried to back away from the tension he had created. When he realized that Deputy Baine knew his office had called him, the chief asked where Deputy Baine's partner was."

"Deputy Baine just said his partner was checking on some other things for him," Rose said. "And the chief's face got red. He started telling the deputy that he had no business coming to his town and snooping around. His voice got louder and his face got redder."

"We moved ourselves and the three remotes into a semicircle behind the chief and his deputies," Jill said, "and told Deputy Baine where we were positioned. I thought it was going to get ugly."

"But Deputy Baine walked straight up to the chief," Rose said, "and stopped and stared him right in the face. He said that if the state felt it needed to ask a question, it would. And if the chief didn't have anything to hide, he'd better get real cooperative. On the other hand, he'd said, if the chief had anything he didn't want the state to know about, that he'd better get it good and hidden, and quick."

"The chief was stunned," Jill said, again smiling. "And Deputy Baine turned and pushed past the chief and got into his patrol car. We followed him north out of town to be sure no one was following, and when we were sure, we called Shar for a pick up."

"We waited over Clay," Rose said, "to be sure he didn't have any trouble from Chief Russell, and he didn't. Then Shar brought us back." Rose glanced at her watch, "Deputy Baine should be getting into town any time now."

Sunday, January 1

The morning went quickly with Shara more eager and spry than she had been all week. She and Coleen rode for an hour before the weather began to thicken, forcing them back in. Greg and Brendan had gotten to know each other a little better with Brendan expounding on the benefits of the warmer climes of Florida and the ocean and gulf fishing that he'd come to love. Greg admitted a warmer climate was a temptation when the winter howled across the valley.

"What's a temptation?" Shara asked from the coat room as they hung their coats up and shed their boots.

"Warmer weather," Brendan said when they joined them in the living room.

Shara hugged Greg as he stood in front of the fire, her arms tightly around his waist and her head firmly against his warm chest. "Would be nice for a visit, but I like the cold. Makes snuggling so much more fun."

When Shara released Greg and turned to look for coffee, she caught Coleen's concerned stare. '*Hush!*' she said privately and did not let Coleen dampen her spirits. "Do we have any coffee?"

"I was just going to ask Matti for a new carafe," Greg said and started to the kitchen.

Moments later, Greg returned with Matti close behind. "She wouldn't let me bring the tray," Greg shrugged as Mattie set the carafe and four mugs on an end table.

"It's not a bother, Mr. Greg," Matti remarked casually. "I'm supposed to do this and you're supposed to be with your mother and Mr. Brendan." She nodded and quickly went back to the kitchen.

Greg smiled, "I guess I've been told."

Shara chuckled and began to pour for everyone. Coleen and Brendan settled on the loveseat and Greg took their usual chair.

When Shara settled on his lap, she asked, "Are Major Kooich and Leeana on patrol this morning?"

"They were earlier," Greg confirmed, "but they are presently working with Kiile on the final details of the piggy-back slings for the patrol fighters."

"Does he have something ready?" Shara asked.

"He says 'yes,'" Greg admitted. "After lunch sometime, we'll go out to Obscure and see how it works."

"Are you really going to carry the fighters," Coleen asked, concerned by having only heard Greg talk about the idea there at the house.

"Yes we are, mother," he said. "It's the only way I can get the fighters to the scene of the battle. They just don't have the range. We'll have four ships capable of carrying the fighters and only two fighters going. That way if a Q-Ship is damaged, we can still get the fighters home."

"It just seems so risky," Coleen sighed.

"It is a little," Greg admitted. "But I need the extra support and they need the experience."

"When will you have to go?" Brendan asked, gently sipping his hot coffee.

"There's a suspicious launch expected Tuesday or Wednesday, our time," Greg said and glanced down at Shara, curled on his lap, holding her mug with both hands. "It'll take about six of our hours to get there, so we will have to be ready to leave at a moment's notice."

"How will you know when?" Coleen asked, "if that isn't an improper question to ask."

"There are two Q-Ships, like KKLC14," Greg explained, "waiting at two suspected course change points. If they've guessed right, and they've been pretty good at guessing with the last three intercepts, the first will alert STSX and we'll leave. If our calculations are correct, we'll reach the second before the freighter and its escorts start their third leg."

"Sounds like a lot of 'ifs' to me," Coleen said.

"It is," Shara admitted, "especially when you consider how far we have to go to make the intercept. If they've changed their routes along the way, we could miss them entirely."

"But we have to try," Greg said with more firmness than he meant. "Every ship that gets through is another couple hundred innocent people torn from their lives, stolen for the profits of the black markets."

Shara felt his chest heave in anxious breathing and she gently patted his shoulder, hoping he would calm quickly.

"Sorry," he said after a minute. "At least now, we know how many they have taken and where most of them were sent when they left here."

Shara tilted her head and looked up at him and then glanced at Coleen and Brendan.

"The database we captured the day we found you," Greg continued, forcing himself to slower, calmer words, "has given us a great deal of insight into the Trader's operations. They had four launch facilities here on earth and the Peace Force's Marines shut down three of them before we came to the valley looking for the last one."

"We gave Wally," Shara said when Greg paused, "data on one of his missing people on Friday and yesterday we were able to confirm that Greg's entire list of missing people are in that database."

"It proves they were stolen," Greg smiled, "and sent off planet. Now we know where to look and we have names of who we're looking for. And, we have proof of who's behind the shipments. The director was very pleased."

Coleen watched Greg, surprised as he talked. "How many have been taken?"

"One hundred eleven thousand, six hundred and seventy-three," Greg said and looked at her and then at Brendan, "from this planet. You were also listed mother, but for some reason your shipment was delayed and then you were listed as lost. That would've been a very upsetting notation if I didn't know that you were 'lost' because you were rescued."

◢

They had shifted to the pleasant subject of Coleen and Brendan's visit and how soon they might want to come back out when Jill led Nick in and stopped in the coat room.

"Did you know it's snowing again?" Jill asked as she hurried through the group and stopped in front of the fire.

"We'd noticed a few flakes," Coleen said, pointing to the tall, narrow windows on both sides of the fireplace. "How is it away from the house?" she asked, referring to the influence of the shield dome.

"Not too bad yet," Nick said as he stopped beside Jill. "Forecast is for another two to three feet by midday tomorrow."

"Sure you don't want to stay?" Shara asked Coleen in jest.

"Don't get me wrong, Shara," Coleen said, "I really do like your place here, but I think spring and summer will be a lot more enjoyable."

"Certainly less cabin-bound," Nick said as he led Jill to the longer couch.

"How was your Dad?" Shara asked when they sat down.

"He's doing all right," Nick said. "It was a quiet week for him and the hands and this morning they were bracing for the next few days. Mostly, he's going through the motions, trying to keep the ranch going and looking forward to the spring and a few new horses."

"It must be hard," Shara said. "How long has it been?"

"It's our second Christmas without mom," Nick said with a deep breath, "but it's getting better, or so we keep telling ourselves." Nick glanced at Jill, then added, "I think I'm going to help him run the place, after we get married. We've looked at a spot on a low cliff overlooking the river, and I want to build us a place there. Dad's happy to sell me the acreage."

"Very good," Greg said as Jill squeezed Nick's arm.

Nick was just refilling his coffee mug when Major Kooich and Leeana came in and added their coats to the wall rack in the coat room. Matti stuck her head out of the kitchen door and asked if they wanted anything to drink and disappeared again when they answered her.

"Major, Leeana," Shara said waving them in from the living room. "Come get warm." She kissed Greg on the cheek and then got up to greet them.

"It's going be another bad one," Leeana said. "KKLC gave us a forecast and it doesn't look good."

"It won't be too bad under the shields," Major Kooich said, "but we'll need to try things out before it gets too serious."

"We'll plan on later this afternoon," Greg said.

"We're going to take Greg's mom and Brendan back where it's warm," Shara said with a chuckle, "then we can come out."

Matti brought the major and Leeana's drink requests and turned to Shara, "Lunch can be served whenever you are ready."

"Kiile and Cheral should be here soon," Shara said. "Let's eat when they get here."

Matti nodded and turned back to the kitchen.

"I'll see if I can hurry them along," Shara said and Matti waved as she slipped through the door.

Shara settled back on Greg's lap and focused her thoughts. *'STSX, please ask if Kiile and Cheral will be here soon. Tell them Matti is asking.'*

A few moments passed and then STSX replied, *'CHERAL SAYS THEY ARE ALMOST THERE.'*

"Colonel," Major Kooich said as he sat down in an overstuffed chair and Leeana sat on the arm. "I have the crews selected for the mission."

Greg smiled and nodded, "That's good. Four Q-Ships and two fighters?"

"No," the major said. "I decided on five Q-Ships and three fighters. STSX1 of course, KKLC14 and TTYF8 will be the command group. I had the rest of the crews draw straws for two more to go and KCMM9 and MKCC5 were the long straws. The remaining three Q-Ships will manage the home front."

"Does KCMM9 have any combat experience?" Greg asked.

"Some," Major Kooich replied. "They have been in three engagements, either as second wave or backups. This will be their first under rules like yours."

"Rules like his?" Coleen asked. "What's that mean?"

"That means," Major Kooich smiled and turned to Coleen, "that everyone fights, even the cadets."

She did not know what to say, and just looked at the two of them.

"It also means," Shara added, "that it's not practice. The old hands watch out for the cadets, but we don't step in unless it's really necessary."

Matti interrupted the banter and led Cheral and Kiile in. "We'll have lunch on in about five minutes, Mrs. Shara."

Ninety-Two

Greg, Shara, Major Kooich and Kiile stood in the center of Obscure's launch bay and watched Cheral settle into the Class 2 fighter and close the canopy. Arrayed around them, Leeana waited in KKLC14, Franni waited in TTYF8 with Major Mooren in the jumpseat, Cheral in Apache Patrol Two and Wilm in Apache Patrol Four.

"STSX," Greg said softly, "Please ask TTYF8 and Apache Four to hover in the middle of the bay."

Major Kooich and Kiile stepped to one side and Shara followed Greg as he made a space between them to allow Apache Four to maneuver. Slowly, cautiously, Cadet Moss drifted Apache Four into position, steadied at two feet above the floor and then retracted the landing struts.

"Hold that position," Greg said casually, and then he turned to Kiile, "You're sure this will work?"

"Yes, Colonel," Kiile smiled back, watching him through the space under the patrol fighter.

"Okay, STSX, have Franni move above Apache Four and set up for connection." Greg turned to Shara, "You take Six and I'll take Seven."

The two remotes settled quickly and they each mounted and drifted up to keep a close look on the two ships and their movements. Greg noted that Major Kooich and Kiile were also mounting remotes.

They watched, barely daring to breathe as Franni maneuvered the much larger Q-Ship up and over the patrol fighter. Concerned, Wilm stared up through his canopy as the Q-ship loomed closer and closer.

"Tell Cadet Moss to relax," Greg said. "His turn will come in a minute."

Slowly Franni let TTYF8 drift over the fighter, approaching from the right rear quarter, and gently settled closer to Apache Four.

"We're using the optical communications bulb on the belly to align the ships," Kiile said in the near silence of the bay. "There," he said when the fighter twitched, "they have an alignment."

Slowly TTYF8 lowered until they were a couple of feet apart and Apache Four seemed to bounce slightly.

"Engaging magnetic stays," Franni announced and suddenly the two ships seemed to lock together, separated by the two feet of seemingly rigid air.

"Very nice, Lieutenant," Greg said softly. "Apache Four, please power down."

They watched as Cadet Moss went through his cockpit routine and ended with both hands in the air.

"Apache Four is Power Off, sir," Wilm replied and looked at the colonel.

"Thank you," Greg said and looked up at Franni.

"TTYF8, please lift another ten feet or so and turn around one hundred and eighty degrees."

Greg smiled as Franni put TTYF8 through the requested maneuver and stabilized their position.

"Apache Four, power up and regain hover."

After a moment, Wilm announced, "Powered and ready, sir."

"Okay, Lieutenant," Greg said with a shrug. "Drop him."

Apache Four suddenly dropped a couple of feet and Wilm quickly caught it.

"Apache Four," Greg continued without any comment on the separation. "Move out from under TTYF8 and hold. TTYF8 rotate one hundred and eighty degrees and hold."

When they both had repositioned, Greg turned to face Apache Four.

"Apache Four, join up with TTYF8."

Shara moved closer to Apache Four and followed him as he turned and repositioned for the approach. Wilm brought Four under TTYF8 from the rear and slowly rose up until they had about five or six feet of separation. Apache Four drifted slowly until the optical links aligned, and both ships twitched. Then Apache Four rose up slowly until it bumped into the 'rigid' cushion of air and TTYF8 bounced slightly.

"Engaging magnetic stays," Wilm said and the two ships rotated into alignment and again locked together.

"Very nice," Greg said. "TTYF8, please rotate one hundred and eighty degrees again."

When the two ships had moved to their new position, Greg asked, "Apache Four, can you open your canopy and egress your ship?"

Without answer, Wilm released the pressure seals and pushed the canopy aside. It just cleared TTYF8's belly.

"Yes, sir," Wilm answered. "It looks like I can."

"Thank you," Greg said. "Close up and separate again."

He patiently watched as they went through the steps and slowly drifted apart.

"Very well done," Greg said to both as they hovered near their original starting points. "You may land and deplane. KKLC14 and Apache Two, you're up next. Apache Two, please take up a low hover in the center of the bay."

Greg had KKLC14 and Apache Two repeat the exercises they had watched TTYF8 and Apache Four complete. He was very pleased that the Class 2 Fighter handled and joined up smoothly and that its larger size did not seem to cause any unexpected maneuvering issues. But when he asked Cheral to open the canopy after the second joining, they discovered that there was not enough clearance for the forward and rear canopy sections to swing up and allow a normal egress.

"Kiile," Greg asked and the four of them drifted in closer and hovered around the partially open canopy, "how much more clearance can we get?"

"Only about another foot or so," Kiile said rubbing his chin. "That won't be enough and if we go more than that, I think the ships will be too far apart and unstable on a long journey." Kiile drifted back and looked at the first repulsion pads, mounted just behind the canopy of the fighter and on KKLC14's belly. He shook his head as he puzzled the situation.

"Colonel," Cheral said from inside. "It's not as nice, but I could use the belly hatch behind the second seat, in the equipment bay."

Greg looked back through the canopy at the tight quarters, "Show me."

Cheral reclosed the canopy and unbuckled. She turned out of her seat and worked her way back past it and then past the second seat and as Greg lowered himself to look under the fighter, Cheral swung the hatch inward and dangled her legs through the opening.

"Less than two minutes," he said with a smile. "Do you think it will be easier without gravity?"

"No," Cheral laughed. "I think it's a small challenge either way. We can always go up and check it out."

"Okay," Greg said. "Back in the cockpit. When you're ready, separate and land in your original space. Debrief huddle in the center of the bay when you get down and have deplaned."

▲

When the pilots and Major Mooren joined Greg and the others in the middle of the launch bay, forming a small circle, Greg smiled at them and again gave them a 'well done.'

"Major Kooich," Greg said, "Your comments please."

"Thank you, Colonel," he said and then glanced at the four pilots. "I have to admit, for doing something that has not been done before you four make it look very easy. I want to thank Kiile and his Marines for figuring out a way to tether the ships together. Using the repulsion pads and the magnetic docking stays was a very brilliant idea. My thanks to whoever though that one up—"

"Sir? You don't think I thought that up?" Kiile feigned surprise.

"USL15," Major Kooich said formally with a stern look, "you may pass my 'thanks' to 'whoever' thought it up."

Cheral chuckled and the rest followed her cue.

"Yes, sir. Thank you, sir," Kiile said with a nod.

"Now," Major Kooich continued, "It is my intention that the fighter pilots will travel enroute in their associated Q-Ship and they will transfer back into their fighters before we enter the battle arena. But, as Lieutenant Haak suggested, we will go up and practice without gravity to be sure we can join up and transfer under any conditions. We might not get the luxury of a nice peaceful refuge before the fight. I will call a pre-mission briefing at 0600 tomorrow morning."

Then he turned to Franni, "Lieutenant, your comments on the practice session, please."

In turn, Major Kooich went around the group asking the pilots first as participants and then as spectators, for their comments, followed by Major Mooren and then finishing with Shara.

Satisfied that all of the questions had been asked and answered,

Major Kooich dismissed the group with another 'well done.'

⟁

"Major," Greg asked as the group dispersed and only the four of them remained. "Have all of the Q-Ships incorporated the engine upgrades that you put into KKLC14?"

"I'll have to check, Colonel," he said, thinking. "I know three of them have, but I'm not sure about the others."

"Make sure they all are upgraded," Greg said firmly. "As for the credits for the upgrade, the Campaign will foot the cost—" Major Kooich's expression interrupted his thought. "I know Major. The Campaign will also reimburse the credits for the upgrade to those that recently had it installed at my request."

Major Kooich smiled, but did not say anything.

"Second, I want our little recoding incorporated as soon as the upgrades are finished," Greg smiled slyly at the major and glanced at Shara, her eyes dancing. "I want to be able to get there fast and I want the speed available if we get into trouble during a fight."

Then he had a question flash through his mind. *'STSX, is there an engine upgrade for the Patrol Fighters?'*

Shara smiled hugely as STSX answered.

'YES. SIXTY PERCENT INCREASE OVER BASE THRUST IS AVAILABLE FOR THE CLASS 1 FIGHTERS AND SEVENTY PERCENT FOR THE CLASS 2 FIGHTERS.'

'Can we install the upgrades here?'

'YES. WE CAN DOWNLOAD TO STSX OR KKLC AND DISTRIBUTE TO THE PATROL FIGHTERS ACCORDING TO TYPE.'

'Do any of the fighters have the upgrade already?'

'NO.'

'Then do it.'

'DOING.'

He looked back to the major and smiled, "STSX says there are two upgrades available for the patrol fighters. He's downloading the two versions and with KKLC's help, will install them as quickly as he can." Greg went on to explain the differences in the two upgrades. "We'll see if we can rewrite them once we have them downloaded."

⚔ ⚔ ⚔ ⚔ ⚔

Dave Barns arrived early, picked a tall table in a quiet corner of Patty's Pub and ordered a dark lager for his wait. The peanuts were half gone and his lager seriously depleted when Don Nikle finally arrived and slid onto the stool beside him. Don waved at the waitress and ordered a double bourbon with a splash when she stopped at the table. Dave gestured for a refill.

"Must have been a tough day," Dave said and slid the peanuts to Don.

"Yes," he admitted. "I am still trying to figure out how to keep track of that marshal and his deputies."

"I am sure," Dave said and finished his stein. "How did he know Abe and Ben were bugging their cars and the office?"

"I do not know, but it seems he knew where the transmitters were," Don said, "no matter where we put them. Even the ones they put on his house and on his girlfriend's house."

"You said he put them on other cars?" Dave asked, remembering part of their earlier conversation.

"Yes, he did," Don half smiled. "Ran Abe around a bit before he realized he was being toyed with. But none of the voice transmitters have sent anything."

"Well, now what?" Dave asked as the waitress brought his refill and Don's drink. She exchanged the empty peanut bowl with a full one and then went to another table.

"The only thing I can think of is to hire some of the college kids and have them wander around town, reporting to Abe or keeping a log." Dave took a long sip of his drink. "I just do not have any good ideas right now."

"Did you know," Dave changed the subject, "the Smallwood and Thomas women have reappeared in public?"

Disbelief colored Don's expression. "So they are alive and have come out of hiding?"

"They certainly have. Tuesday night they showed up at that college hang out, Hap's Place. They were part of a group of six, I was told. The Smallwood woman was with a man our contact did not know, and the Thomas woman was with Nickolas Jordan and there was an older couple with them."

"What did they say about their absence?" Don asked, concerned.

"Not much, I guess," Dave said. "The Smallwood woman told some of her friends that she was lucky she did not die in the car wreck and nothing more of any substance."

"And the Thomas woman, how did she explain being gone?"

"All our contact said was that she said she had been away."

"Well," Don said. "You did say Harold saw them at the ranch when the judge tried to take ownership. So, I suppose it stands to reason they would not talk about what they have been doing in the almost three months of their absence. I think we need to find out what they have been up to."

"How?"

"I do not know yet," Don said and took a long sip of his bourbon.

"You will think of something," Dave said and raised his stein in mock toast. "In the meantime, I am sure you know one of his deputies was down here on Friday."

"Yes. I got an ear full Friday night," Don admitted, "and then again last night from the chief down in Hawthorne."

"Hawthorne? Chief Parks?"

"Yes," Don said soberly. "Chief Russell was concerned and nervous, but Chief Parks was in full attack mode. He claimed the deputy threatened him."

"Threatened him?" Dave stared at Don.

"When Chief Parks, in his usual belligerent manner, I am sure," Don continued, "demanded to know why the deputy was snooping around his town, the deputy said he had some questions and the chief was not available to talk with him."

"I bet that did not go down well," Dave said and took another sip.

"No, it did not. Chief Parks said the deputy tried to hide behind the fact that he was a state deputy and told him that if the state asked a question, he had better answer it. Chief Parks also said the deputy told him that if he had something to hide, he had better hide if really good and quick."

"Are you sure that is what the deputy said?" Dave asked, startled by the recital.

"Of course not," Don admitted. "I know Chief Parks as well as anyone and I know he only tells the parts that work to his benefit. From what I have heard about the marshal and his deputies from our contacts in Riggin, the last thing they are is rude or pushy. We also know the marshal takes his job seriously if pushed."

Don paused and snagged a handful of the shelled peanuts and washed them down with another long sip from his drink.

"No," he continued, "they are not dumb enough to openly antagonize anyone, especially if they want cooperation. I think Chief Parks may be developing a conscience or the disappearance of the bulk of the Council has put a fear into him."

"Do you think we need to pay him a friendly visit?" Dave asked over the rim of his stein.

"Soon maybe," Don said. "I want to see what he does this next week. If he is really rattled, he will do something he should not do. Have a visit with his deputies first, get their opinions of the meeting with the state deputy and let me know."

"First thing tomorrow," Dave said, "weather permitting."

"Make a call if it does not permit," Don said and waved for the waitress again.

Monday, January 2

Eddie was crossing Ash on her way back to the flower shop after picking up the sweet rolls Mary had ordered from Connie's Deli when she saw Thom leave the shop and turn north. She figured he was continuing his walking beat, but she was suspicious of why he might have stopped in the shop. She was not in the best of moods as the day had started out badly with a call concerning her mother and then continued to get worse in her mind. The stiff north wind and the continued, heavy snowfall did not help.

She had pondered Thom's news that her dad had been kidnapped and had not run out on her and her mother, but her suspicions warred with that possibility. She argued with herself that they could not know for certain what happened eight years ago even if they did conjure up a list of names for her to look at and by the time she pushed the shop door open and slipped in, she had decided that Thom Baine was just another insensitive man trying to lead her on for his own purposes.

She hurried to the back of the store, set the sack with the rolls on the corner of the work table and hung her coat on the rack by the cool room. "Coffee made?" she asked as Mary came out of the storage room.

"New pot," Mary said and set a short, wide mouthed white glass vase on the work table. She turned and filled two mugs as Eddie placed the rolls on two napkins and stared at the familiar white vase.

"I saw Deputy Baine leaving as I crossed the street," Eddie said tersely as she took the mug Mary proffered, still looking at the vase. "Did he order another bouquet?"

"Yes," Mary said and picked up one of the rolls. "My, my, these do look good."

"Damn," she said, half under her breath. "I suppose he had a detailed description of what he wants me to make?"

Mary looked up at her, confused as she tried to swallow the bite she had taken. "Not really. What's gotten into you, Eddie? What's the matter?"

"Nothing," she said and picked up the other roll and muttered, "Does he expect me to make all of my own bouquets?"

"I don't know what you're talking about, Eddie," Mary said and sipped her coffee. "He said he wanted something suitable for a night stand for the elderly Widow Banks down on Maple. She just found out her brother has terminal cancer and he wanted something to help cheer her up."

Eddie stopped mid bite and stared at Mary. "Oh," she mumbled through her full mouth and sheepishly turned to the work table and the vase Mary had set there.

"He asked if we could deliver it sometime this afternoon," Mary said and resumed eating her roll.

🔺🔺🔺🔺🔺

Lieutenant Riviera drifted quickly into the scanning room, coming as quickly as she could when her assisting tech called.

"What do you have?" she asked as she grabbed the hand hold that encircled the monitor.

"Ten new IFF targets showing," he said and pointed to a section of the screen. "We have one escort and I called you when the others showed up."

She looked at the screen and pulled herself closer to its surface as she studied the ten dots. "Three dots seem to be merging with three others."

"That's what it looks like," the Tech agreed. "Or at least they are close enough together our scanner thinks they are one."

"Well," she admitted. "It sure is hard to tell what they're doing, but it's good to see them and know they're there."

"It isn't an engagement," the tech said. "Movements are too slow and the escort has not taken up a protective stance."

"Some kind of maneuvers," Lieutenant Riviera said, studying the movements, "or a rehearsal for something coming up. They said things were heating up for them."

⚔ ⚔ ⚔ ⚔ ⚔

Major Kooich watched intently from KKLC14's jump seat as Cheral and Casi brought STSX1 and Apache Two together in a second, flawless join up.

"Very nice," Major Kooich said and KKLC14 transmitted to the seven Q-Ships and the three Apache Patrol Fighters. "Cadet Tigs, join up with KKLC14. Colonel, please watch the maneuvers."

"Will do," Stran said and gestured for Casi to release Apache Two and turn so they could watch Apache Three.

"Apache Two is clear," Cheral said softly as she added power and slipped back into the group encircling the joining exercises.

The cluster of ten ships drifted a couple hundred miles above the space station's orbit and about a hundred miles ahead as they fell around the planet. Stran had allowed the initial efforts to be visually uncloaked, but they were still sensor blocked. They were at risk of detection from the ground, but he wanted a smooth practice. As soon as each Q-Ship had joined with the smaller patrol fighter he would have them repeat the exercise fully cloaked.

He picked a position close to the space station so he could switch Q-Ships into and out of the escort position, allowing each the opportunity to engage in the exercise. He hoped there would come a time when the number of patrol fighters and Q-Ships were equal.

Stran and Casi watched with smiles as Apache Three easily

snuggled up to KKLC14 and locked in place. Cadet Tigs repeated the maneuver a second time without the barest bounce at lock up.

"Very good, Apache Three," Stran said when Ani separated and drifted away from KKLC14. "Now, park someplace and let KKLC14 join up with you."

They watched as Leeana guided KKLC14 in a turn to acquire Apache Three and then settled into the approach. Again, the join up was flawless and Stran was very pleased. When they had finished their second join up, Stran turned the exercise over to Major Kooich and settled back to watch as Major Kooich directed Apache Four to execute the paired maneuvers with each of the other Q-Ships. KCMM9 was the last as Major Kooich had KVWC33 switch places and they took a turn in the dance.

When Major Kooich announced a "well done," to the crews and all the ships settled in the circle around KKLC14, he gave the order for everyone to cloak and start the practice over again.

"Wing Leader," Stran hailed, "Let's do this one with shields up as well. In a Hot Zone, in preparation for combat, we will be operating with shields active."

"You heard the colonel," Major Kooich announced, "Shields Up."

"Remember," Stran added, "Patrol fighters must select top shields off before join up and the Q-Ships must select bottom shields off before join up. Feel your way in and lower your interfering shields before you get too close. There is no cushion if your shields hit each other."

The cloaked exercises took considerably longer with each pair moving more cautiously, partially out of concern of causing a collision and partially due to the lack of a visible target for closure. Stan noticed that only Cheral and Casi seemed to actually know where each other were during the exercises, sensing each other's ship. He watched Casi and smiled when he confirmed she was flying, eyes closed, concentrating completely on her feel of Cheral's presence.

During the last joining of each pair of ships, Stran had the cadets exit their fighters and transfer into their transporting Q-ship and then back again, ensuring that every crew had the routine firmly in mind. When each ship had completed their pair of veiled joinings and settled back into the loose formation, Major Kooich read the reassigned escort schedule and commanded that all three cadets and all lieutenants were to immediately return to Shadow Base and start a twelve hour mandatory rest cycle, reminding them the lieutenants had been engaged and flying for seven hours at this point. He dismissed the flight with another "well done."

⋀ ⋀ ⋀ ⋀ ⋀

Dave waited for Don in Patty's Pub again, but it was late enough he had asked for dinner menus when he ordered his dark lager. Don settled onto a stool next to Dave and ordered his preferred double bourbon with a splash when the waitress served Dave's lager.

When she left, Don asked, "Did you talk with Parks' deputies today?"

"Yes, I did," Dave said and sipped his brew. "Seems the chief's upset is his own doing. Both deputies admitted the Riggin deputy had not made any fuss when he got there. He went to the chief's office and asked to see him. He was told the chief had not come in yet and the clerk called him to see when he was coming in."

"Seems reasonable enough," Don said and hesitated while the waitress served his drink.

"The deputies figured Chief Parks had talked to Chief Russell and had made up his mind to hassle the deputy the day before. When they finally confronted the Riggin deputy in front of the city clerk's office, they said he was cordial and was fine until Chief Parks started in on him. That is when the Riggin deputy sort of laid the law down, if you will. He told the chief that being as he was a state deputy and was sent to ask him some questions 'in private,' Parks was expected to answer them."

"Parks sure would not have liked that," Don said.

"I guess he did not," Dave said. "That is when the deputy from Riggin told the chief that unless he had something to hide, he was expected to cooperate."

Dave and Don both sipped their drinks and looked at each other.

"Like I said," Don added, "those state guys will get real serious if you push them. And it sounds like Parks tried to push a little."

"Yes," Dave admitted, "And that will not be forgotten, I am sure."

"We will have to keep an eye on Parks," Don said, "to be certain he does not get that marshal stirred up any more than he probably has. I almost had him calmed down and just finishing open paperwork without asking a lot of questions, until Pat shot him and got him angry."

"He sure did that," Dave agreed, shaking his head with a scowl.

"Have you heard anything about Pat?" Don digressed. "Where he might have gone? Or anything?"

"Nothing," Dave confirmed.

"Too bad. Anyway, we had answers that would have made the marshal happy," Don said, thinking out loud, "but now, I think he has been digging a little deeper and has new questions. I do not think he is just finishing paperwork anymore."

"I will keep a close watch on Parks," Dave said. "We certainly do not want more state people nosing around down here."

Don nodded and opened the menu. "I think I am ready for a nice, thick steak."

"My thoughts exactly," Dave admitted and waved for the waitress.

⌂ ⌂ ⌂ ⌂ ⌂

Greg laid a soft, light blanket over Shara where she had withered on the long couch when they got back to the ranch. Assured by STSX that she was feeling okay, Greg turned back to the dining room table and took a seat across from Jill and Nick. Major Kooich and Leeana had retired shortly after a light dinner and he knew Leeana had probably crashed as well and that the major was either reading, planning for the upcoming mission or taking advantage of the mandatory rest time himself.

"Is she doing all right?" Jill asked when Greg sat down.

"Yeah," he smiled, "just tired. I worked them pretty hard today. The cadets and all of the lieutenants did all of the work."

Jill looked surprised. "So you discriminated against the 'weaker' sex today?"

"Yes," Greg said and smiled. "But if anyone tries to tell me women are weaker, I think I'll have to disagree with them."

"Any word on when you'll have to leave?" Nick asked.

"Not yet," Greg admitted, "but I do know where we will rendezvous with the Watchers when we leave. Major Kooich will have the engines in all of the ships upgraded and the code revisions uploaded tomorrow morning."

"Do you have tasks for us?" Jill asked, knowing he would have.

"Certainly," he said and poured himself a cup of tea. "You four, both of you and Rose and Doug will watch out for Wally and his deputies. I think Thom's trip to Clay and Hawthorne is going to start something."

"You think the Elders will try something?" Nick asked, suddenly more concerned.

"The Elders or that Chief Parks," Greg said softly. "Chief Parks feels like we are getting too close for comfort, his comfort, and he's like a powder keg with a sputtering fuse, liable to go off when we least expect it."

"Any ideas what he might do?" Jill asked.

Greg shook his head. "No way to really tell. So far, they've only tried to remove whatever has been in their way or that has been inconvenient for them. So they could try anything from causing an unfortunate accident, a car wreck," he raised his eyebrows, "a fatal tumble in the snow, to something much bigger. But by what you said and from listening to Four's recordings, there's a lot of fear and turmoil just under the surface. Chief Parks bothers me the most because he's unpredictable, and afraid."

"How should we watch out for them?" Jill pressed further.

"Remote One and Two are still watching the ranch and a periodic run around town," Greg said, starting to itemize their assets. "Three and Four are your transportation and immediate protection, and Five is linked to WL-One. Five knows all of our players and can find any of them by asking. WL-One will listen to you through Five and it knows all of Wally's guys and maybe a few others. So you have Wally and his deputies, and you have the four of you and you have six remotes at your command," he tapped his forehead to remind her that he and Shara *hear* her, "and you can *speak* directly to either of us and STSX through us."

"But STSX and Shara will be with you?" Jill asked, confused.

"We can direct traffic if you need," Greg said with a gentle smile, "even if we're half a galaxy away. Major Kooich will have KVWC33 tuned to you if you need to move your group any distance. Use them and don't try to save a few minutes and travel any long distances out in the elements. You're going to be the senior member, Jill, so think logically, plan any moves you have to make and plan how to use your assets, your group. Talk to Wally through WL-One and work together."

"Wow," Nick whispered loudly. "You sound like you think something is really going to happen."

"Nick, plan on it," Greg said, "and if it doesn't, be thankful. Tomorrow, we'll get extra Greymns out of the secreted stores in the feed barn. Don't go anywhere unprepared. Just like usual. If you need to go any distance, take your Brekshiirs, Jill, even if you have to hang them in your equipment bag under Three or Four."

He stopped and emptied his cup, then refilled it with warmer tea.

"Thanks Greg," Jill said softly and reached over and took his hand. "I'll try to be vigilant and do it right."

"Use everyone around you," he said with a smile. "Nick, Rose and Doug have experienced a lot of what you have. Use them, listen to them. Make any move you make count, think them through and then act. You know."

He looked at Nick. "And your job is to protect her. Just like you helped me, you watch her back and her blind side. She can't see everything at once, so be her second set of eyes."

Nick nodded, suddenly wondering if Matti might have some scotch stashed in the kitchen.

Ninety-Three

Tuesday, January 3

Wally was waiting for Carole when the three stepped out of Hap's back door just after midnight and locked up. Carole stopped at his open window and he watched as the other girls got into their cars.

"Follow me home?" she asked when the other two drove away and she turned back to Wally.

"Thought you'd never ask," he said as she got into her jeep.

He followed her up Baxter as usual, but he paid more attention to the two crossing streets before they turned onto Hickory. He parked in her drive behind her jeep, got out and followed her inside through the garage as usual. He wondered if he was too predictable.

Inside, after Carole closed the garage and the inside door, he hung their jackets on the customary pegs behind the front door.

"Glad to see you are wearing one of the jackets I got you," he said with a smile as she headed down the hallway to her bedroom.

"Thank you again," she said over her shoulder. "They're so comfortable and warm"

He hung his utility belt on the peg beside his coat, but unclipped the pistol from the holster and slipped it in the back of the waistband of his pants. Then he went into the kitchen and started a pot of coffee.

He touched his earpiece and asked, "WL-One, are there any voice taps around the house?"

"NONE," WL-One replied.

"Are there any persons loitering or watching the house?" he asked.

"NONE," WL-One said, but the response was a little longer in coming. "THERMAL AND ENHANCED VISUALS DO NOT INDICATE ANY ABNORMAL ACTIVITY."

"Thanks, WL-One. Let me know if you see anything unusual," he said as the coffee pot indication changed to Ready.

"Who are you talking to?" Carole asked as she came around the corner into the kitchen, wearing her low waisted sweat pants and matching top.

"Just checking in with the remote," he said and poured a cup. "Would you like one?"

"No," she said and turned to the living room, "It's too late for me to drink coffee. Now, a beer would sound good."

He pulled one from the refrigerator and followed her, switching off the kitchen light as he went. He handed her the beer and set his coffee on the end table beside the couch. As he turned to set down, he took his pistol from his waist band and put it beside his cup.

"Is something wrong?" she asked as he sat down and she snuggled close.

"Maybe not," he said and put his arm around her shoulder and pulled her close beside him. "But I feel like I need to pay a little more attention to what's going on around me, around us. I've been reviewing the recordings of Thom's trip last Friday and Saturday, and I've been getting a bad feeling about those guys in Clay and Hawthorne."

"You think they might come up here and start something?" Carole asked, skeptical.

"Yes, I think they might," he said and turned to look at her. "That's another reason I'm glad you're wearing the jacket when you're out. But right now, I think everything is fine. The remote says everything around here is normal and there are no new bugs planted."

"That is very good," she said and turned to lie across his lap, facing him. He reached up and dimmed the lamp as she caught his neck and pulled herself up and kissed him, long and tenderly. He held her tight to his chest and let the pleasure of the moments push his worries a suitable distance away.

⅄ ⅄ ⅄ ⅄ ⅄

The winds had finally settled into a gentle breeze and the clouds had begun to break up allowing patches of blue and shafts of bright sunlight to peak through when Thom parked his patrol car in front of the marshal's office after his rounds. He got out of the car and crossed Main to Connie's Deli for a quick bite of lunch. He stepped inside and stopped to remove his gloves and fur-lined cap as he absently scanned the room. He spotted a couple of unoccupied tables near the cashier's station and proceeded through the large dining area to the nearest one.

As he placed his cap and gloves on the table and turned to sit down, he noticed Eddie at a table in the back corner of the room against the opposite wall. When she glanced up and noticed him, he nodded with a pleasant smile and then took his seat and began to review the menu. He decided on a chicken Panini that he had once before, then went to the counter and ordered. He chatted briefly with the young woman behind the counter, then returned to his table, sat down, opened his jacket front and took out his notepad.

He began making notes from his last rounds and absently sipped his mug of coffee while he waited for his order. Slowly, he realized someone had stopped and was standing beside his table. He looked up.

"May I sit down?" Eddie asked.

Confused, but pleasantly surprised, he gestured to the chair across from him and smiled, "Certainly."

"I haven't seen you on your morning beat," she said as she sat down without looking directly at him. She laid her coat across her lap and absently smoothed it with the palm of her hand.

"I saw that you've been very busy when I've gone by," he admitted. "I didn't want to interrupt you when you come in so early to work."

"Oh," she said and looked at him.

Thom waited seeing that she was thinking very hard about something.

"I thought... I mean," she started and then hesitated. "Did your bouquet...?"

"Yes and no," he said, thinking of the one he had given her, surprised she had brought it up. "I ordered the most beautiful bouquet I have ever seen to let someone know I wanted to be a friend and to help her through some tough times, to know she wasn't alone. But I have it on good authority that instead, I caused a great deal of pain and anger. For that, I am extremely sorry. That was never my intention."

He waited again as she studied his face, his expression, as if she were trying to divine some added understanding from it. Before she said anything more, the young woman from behind the order counter brought him his sandwich and refilled his mug. He thanked her with a warm smile.

"I delivered the bouquet you ordered for the widow Banks," she said, redirecting the subject.

"Thank you," he said. "I hoped she would like them. The news of her brother was pretty hard on her."

"I think it was," Eddie said. "I talked with her a while and I think the flowers may help her." Again, Eddie withdrew into her thoughts before she continued. "I visited my mother this morning on my break," she said. "She had a beautiful furry stuffed bear and told the nurse that a policeman brought it to her. Did you—?"

"No. That would have been Dan Lupis," he said with a knowing smile. "I mentioned your mother's condition to Dan one day in the office over a cup of coffee. He apparently said something to his wife at dinner or sometime, and his daughter, Blaire, brought him one of her bears and said he should take it to your mother to keep her safe, so she wouldn't be afraid."

"But Dan doesn't know my mother," she said softly. "You don't know my mother. Why...?"

"We do now, Eddie," Thom said as he put his mug down. "We try to get to know the people in the town we serve, to know what makes them happy, sad, or if they are hurting. We can't do much except to be there, if and when they want us." He watched her a moment and then continued. "We can't fix what is wrong with most folks, certainly not medically, and we can't make people happy that don't want to be, but we try to do the things that we can do."

She slowly smiled, "You and your soap box."

He suddenly realized he was doing it again and looked away with a sheepish smile. "Sorry. I guess I do carry it around with me too much."

Eddie inhaled deeply and then glanced at the front door. "Please thank Dan for me. My mother doesn't remember who I am, but she remembers the kindness of the policeman with the stuffed bear."

"I'll tell him, Eddie," Thom said softly as she stood up and swung her coat over her shoulders. He stood up when she did.

"I really stopped and sat down to say thanks for telling me what you found out about my dad," she added. "I was so stunned, I don't remember if I thanked you or not. I'm actually still a little stunned." She looked at him with a faint smile. "And thank you for the flowers..., I think."

He watched her weave between the tables, crossing the dining room. She disappeared out Connie's front door before he sat back down. He smiled and started eating his now cool sandwich, wondering if he dared to hope, but quickly reminded himself, no strings, no expectations.

Wednesday, January 4

It was just after six when STSX woke Greg and Shara, telling them he had received a message from their Watcher; two freighters had departed a secreted base on one of Copus Two's moons in the Colbr System.

Greg and Shara showered and dressed for the mission and Matti met them as they entered the dining room.

"I know it's silly to ask you to stay safe," Matti said as she handed Shara two small plastic sacks. Greg went to the coat room and collected their coats and clothing carrysacks as Matti finished talking with Shara. "This one's for the major and Leeana and this one's for you, Mr. Greg and your cousin, Cheral. I've included some juices that are high in iron and calcium and some of Annie's high fiber and protein sweet breads. Now you better get going before Mr. Greg gets impatient."

Matti gently shoved her toward the door when she did not move, staring at her.

"Go now," Matti said firmly. "See you when you get back."

⚔

The area around Obscure's launch portal was stirred up into a full frenzy when STSX arrived and landed beside Apache Two. KKLC14 and Apache Three were in the process of joining up and TTYF8 hovered quietly to one side with Apache Four secured beneath it. A number of Kiile's troopers were scurrying about carrying small parcels from a floating pallet to nearby Q-Ships, disconnecting ground servicing umbilicals and ensuring all open external access panels were closed and flight ready.

Casi quickly lifted STSX and joined with Apache Two when Cheral settled into a low hover beneath them.

'I've sent Eight to bring you aboard,' Casi said to Cheral once she

engaged the magnetic stays.

Cheral opened the belly hatch and dropped the short distance to the ground. When Eight arrived, she took the handhold, stepped into the extended stirrup and lifted to the belly hatch, closed and secured it before drifting up to STSX's aft portal. Once inside, she removed her helmet, hung it in the equipment bay and heard Stran talking with Obscure's Launch Control and with KKLC14.

She hurried up the ladder and sat down in the left hand jumpseat, "All aboard. Is everyone else ready?"

"Just about," Casi said as she turned STSX to face the other assembled ships.

"Get a status, Casi," Stran said over his shoulder from the nav-com chair, "please."

"Apache Wing, launch status?" Casi asked and STSX broadcast the request to the other ships and Obscure Control. She heard the ships call in.

"MKCC5 is launch ready," Lieutenant Colbee Donnr's voice said.

"KCMM9 is launch ready," Lieutenant Lori Tam's voice said.

"TTYF8 and Apache Four are launch ready," Franni's voice said.

"Colonel, Apache Fighter Wing, KKLC14 and Apache Three are launch ready," Leeana's voice said.

"Apache Wing Leader," Casi said to the Wing. "Apache Leader and Apache Two are ready." Then to Stran, "The Wing is ready."

"Take us up to the outbound fix," Stran said, "and once grouped at the coordinates, go to the first Watcher's coordinates."

"STSX, do all of the ships have the outbound fix and the Watcher's coordinates?" she asked as she lifted STSX toward the shield barrier.

"AFFIRMATIVE."

"Thanks STSX," she said and turned to the wing, "Apache Wing, proceed to the outbound fix. Cloaking on, sensor blocked, and shields full. Form up on Apache Leader."

Casi added thrust and pointed STSX's nose high into the soft morning sky. KKLC14 followed seconds behind, followed quickly by TTYF8, KCMM9 and MKCC5.

"Impressive," Cheral said as they cleared the atmosphere and Casi told the flight to visually unveil. Cheral looked out the left and then the right side of the canopy. KKLC14 with Apache Three beneath formed up just to their left and slightly behind, and TTYF8 with Apache Three formed up off their right with the other two Q-Ships trailing in a right echelon off TTYF8.

"Yes it is," Casi said, following Cheral's gaze as she took in the view. "I had to take a look. I've never seen a formation of Q-Ships before."

"Neither have I," Cheral said as KKLC called in.

"Outbound fix achieved," Leeana said. "Wing is ready for the jump. Coordinates loaded."

"It's all yours, Bren," Stran said from the nav-com compartment.

"Apache Leader to Apache Wing, cloaking on. Jump," she said and shoved the thrust levers three quarters forward. "STSX, adjust thrust as necessary for the slowest Q-Ship's fastest speed." Then to KKLC14 she added, "Apache Wing Leader, match speed with Apache Leader. We want a formation arrival."

"Will do," Leeana answered.

Casi relaxed the best she could and leaned back into the cushioned pilot's chair. The importance of the moment began to weigh on her and she smiled, hoping they could actually pin-point and intercept the two freighters in the star-filled vastness ahead of them. She glanced back and took heart in the presence of the four other Q-Ships and three patrol fighters.

"Cheral," she said and turned to look at her. "I left some of Annie's sweet breads in a plastic sack in the galley. Would you bring them up? First drawer on the right."

"Sure," she said and unbuckled. "Would you and the colonel like a tea?"

Casi nodded, Stran said he would, and Cheral drifted down through the floor portal.

"Do you know how many escorts there are?" Casi asked Stran casually, going over tactics in her mind.

"Intelligence says the Traders have been increasing the number of fighters since the interceptions began," Stran said. "The last interception had six fighters for each freighter."

"So this one should have a higher ratio, more fighters," she admitted as Cheral came back onto the upper deck.

Cheral handed Stran the first container of ration tea, and then drifted back to the cockpit. She handed Casi a container and Casi secured it in her left armrest. Casi took the sack and checked the content, pulling a wrapped roll out and checked which it was.

She gave it to Cheral. "Do you mind passing this one to Greg?"

Cheral nodded and took the roll, then checking its wrapping, she turned and called, "Colonel, turn around."

When he did, she deftly tossed the roll in his direction.

"Thanks," he said and smiled as he caught it, then turned back to the monitors.

Casi found the high fiber roll Matti told her about and handed Cheral the remaining roll.

"Mmm," Cheral said after taking a bite. "Sure beats rations. Annie is really a keeper."

"Yes she is," Casi agreed and sipped her tea.

"Tell me, Cousin," Cheral said softly, "what it was like growing up in a place as pretty as your valley. This is the longest we have ever been in one room together so tell me about you and your upbringing."

Casi thought about it a moment, and then turned her chair to aft facing. "Greg, can you take this leg and let Cheral and me go down and visit?"

"Sure, Bren," he said and unbuckled. "I can watch for traces from up front as well as from back here."

"Thanks. I'll come back up for the next leg or when you want a break," she said and pushed herself up, tea container in one hand and the sack with her roll and Matti's juices in the other. Greg met her in the central compartment and she quickly threw her arm around him and kissed him firmly. "I love you, love," she said softly in his ear, "more than anything in my life. Thank you for coming to me, for everything you've done for me."

She released him and quickly drifted down through the floor portal. Cheral followed her before he moved into the cockpit. As he waited for STSX to readjust the pilot's chair he heard Cheral softly ask Casi, "Why did he call you Bren?"

▲ ▲ ▲ ▲ ▲

Dave was standing outside Patty's Pub when Don Nikle parked along the curb. He was thinking he might have been called for an early lunch and more discussion on how to track the marshal. Don got out of his car and stepped up onto the sidewalk.

"What is up, Don?" he asked. "Your message sounded a little strange."

Don stopped, facing Dave. "I want you to go up to Riggin this morning and gather twenty of our contacts from the college. Pick up weapons from my place on your way and distribute them among those you can gather."

"What are we attacking?" Dave asked in jest.

"I want that Smallwood woman and I want that Thomas woman! They are hiding at the Smallwood Ranch," Don said and glared at Dave. "They obviously have some significant part in the disappearance of Harry and Howard. They were there when the judge was captured and went missing. Now, I want no more interference from them. I want them stopped! Removed!"

Dave straightened, startled by Don's manner and tone. "Are you sure? I have never taken part in anything like this. What if I screw it up?"

"You will have to deal with me if you screw it up," Don said. "They are confident enough to go into town and tell everyone they are alive, so they are not expecting anyone to still be looking for them."

"What if they were baiting a trap?" Dave asked, a little tremble in his voice.

"Just do it!" Don shouted, louder than he meant. "Just do it," he repeated softly. "After dark, preferably around dinner time when they are least expecting anything to happen."

"But, Don—"

"No BUTS," Don snarled. "I want them or their bodies at my place by midnight!"

Dave stared at Don's back as he walked away and got back his car.

Carole giggled as Wally loaded two coolers in the back of his jeep along with bedrolls and a couple of rolled quilts.

"Where are you taking me?" she asked and squeezed him as he closed the tailgate.

"Aah, but you're going to take me," he said and gently guided her to the passenger door and helped her in.

"What are you talking about?" she asked as he got in and closed his door.

He keyed the garage door open and drove out onto his drive, closed the garage door behind them and turned onto the street.

"I have a day's supplies to use on your impromptu day off and I want you to show me where you want us to live our lives," he chuckled and turned back west toward North Forest Hill Road. "Which way, my love?"

She giggled and pointed and he turned north. In a matter of minutes, he stopped at the county road that led west to her folk's place and the Rockin' H.

"Go west toward mom and dad's for two miles then slow down," she said. "The turn's on the right."

As he neared the mileage, she started watching for the unobvious trail to the north. When she saw it, he turned and followed the winding path in the snow up through the narrow stand of trees. They had driven a few miles when the thinning trees gave way to a wide, slowly rising, snow covered plain. He was thankful the winds had blown most of the snow away, thinning it to a depth they could manage in his jeep.

"Stop by that stand of trees," she said, pointing a little west of their location. "Up against that rock outcropping."

When he stopped next to the outcropping, they got out and she quickly climbed up on the first tier of rocks. She hollered for him to follow her, and when he reached her, she turned him slowly around to face the valley as it spread below them, miles into the distance and miles to either side, east and west.

She sighed. "This is where I want to build a house," she said softly, reverently. "I can see west past the Rockin' H to the crags climbing up to the Spires and east to the ramparts of the rim mountains and as far south as the good Lord allows on any given day. We're four hundred feet above and ten miles north of town by road, a nice vantage point to greet the day. Or to say good night."

Wally nodded and smiled at the view. "This is certainly nice. But I thought you might inherit your dad's place."

"Someday," she said. "Mom and Dad will be around a long time and when they go, yes, I'll get title to their land." She hesitated a moment. "I don't want this to sound wrong or disrespectful, but I will get their land, though I don't really want to live in their house. I really hope that before it becomes an issue, Jim will retire and he and Shelly can move back and live there."

Wally studied the view and then turned to see the lay of the land to the east, the north and the west.

"Do you really want to live two and a half or three miles up from the road?" he asked as he scanned the surroundings. "I mean, it's a great view, but do you think it's practical?"

She caught his arm and snuggled close. "Wally, this is what I've dreamed of since I was a little girl. If I can raise and train horses like Shar did, then I'll be very content. And if you're here with me, I'll be ecstatic."

Wally climbed down to the jeep, grabbed a cooler and a quilt and quickly scrambled back to the snow-free rock ledge. He spread a blanket on the rock and sat the cooler on one side.

"I think this is a great place for a house," he said as he opened the cooler. "And now, we are going to toast the choice and partake of a lunch warmed over an open fire."

⅄

"You know," Wally said as they watched the last rays of the setting sun disappear between the Spires, the two side-by-side, steep sided peaks perched on the western rim nearly fifty miles away. He tightened his arms around Carole as she leaned back against him, sitting on the blanket on the rock outcropping, "this is the best place I know of to watch a sunset."

"Yeah," Carole said softly, "I've always thought so."

"I think we might have to build around this rock," Wally said, "so it can be part of our living room and we can sit on it and watch the sunsets every night."

"Good idea," she said and turned her head aside in an attempt to see him.

He leaned forward and kissed her cheek.

They watched the mountains until the light had all but faded into darkness and then they slowly gathered up the blanket and Wally dropped down beside the jeep. He helped her down with the help of his large hand lamp, and then threw the cooler in the back and closed the tailgate. When they had everything packed, he turned toward the valley and the lights of town. He pulled her close beside him.

"It is beautiful," he casually remarked, then turned her to face him. "But not as beautiful as you." Then he kissed her again and once again, he lost track of time and the moments slipped by.

They were nearly to the county road when WL-One's alert filled his ear, "INTRUDERS ARE ATTACKING THE SMALLWOOD RANCH."

"Shit!" Wally said and told Carole what the remote had told him.

"Go west!" she shouted and pointed as they reached the road. "Take the cutoff on the left just past dad's drive."

Wally stomped on the accelerator and swung the jeep onto the pavement.

᠕ ᠕ ᠕ ᠕ ᠕

"I wonder how they're doing," Nick said as he led Jill into the living room.

Jill cocked her head and *listened*. "I think they've met with the first one they called a 'Watcher.' At least they are in cruise and have not yet engaged."

Nick smiled and sat down on the loveseat near the fire. "It's creepy how you can do that."

"I know," Jill agreed. "I felt the same way when I first watched Shar do it."

Nick patted the seat next to him and she sat down and curled her legs under herself. She leaned against him and watched the fire. Nick looked around the room and at the tall, narrow, drape covered windows beside the fireplace, thinking how strange it was to be here, almost alone in Shara and Greg's house with them away. They had eaten early just as the sun set and the house girls had retired to their rooms and the hands to the bunkhouse soon afterwards.

It had been a quiet day of practice and drills at Obscure, followed by a light dinner and now the quiet fire. He smiled and thought of Jill nestled against him, his arm around her shoulder— He stiffened, seeing the quick glint of light in the darkness beyond the tall, thin window to the right of the fireplace.

"Can you really sense people when they're around?" he asked absently as he watched for the glint. It did not repeat.

"A little," Jill said. "Nothing like Shar, though. She can feel things on the other side of the planet, maybe farther. STSX says Cheral and I need to come and have another session in Medical to see if they can improve that further."

Nick got up slowly and turned the end table lamp off. "How about now? Do you feel any strangers?"

"No. Why?" Jill asked when she realized he wasn't trying to be romantic, but was watching the window instead. "What's the matter?"

"A glint of light," he said without turning. "Get the dining room light."

Jill was over the back of the loveseat before he had finished speaking. She switched the light off and froze as One called her, *'JILL THOMAS. INTRUDERS ARRANGING THEMSELVES AROUND THE MAIN BUILDINGS THEY ARE JUST OUTSIDE OF THE SHIELDS.'*

▲ ▲ ▲ ▲ ▲

After Stran made the formal rendezvous with the first Watcher, Q-JCCV4 joined their ranks and followed STSX on the second leg of their journey to intercept the two freighters. Casi and Cheral came back into the cockpit as STSX heeled into his course change and Casi quickly glanced back, sensing the formation. She was pleased that everyone made the change without any obvious issues.

"Is that JCCV4?" she asked, "in echelon off KKLC14 on their left?"

"Yup," Stran said softly and smiled as he absently glanced over his shoulder at the spot where the unseen ship was. "I wonder if they have the red stripes."

Casi felt her cheeks warm and Cheral smiled at her.

"Are they going to join the squadron? Can they keep up?" Casi asked, "Or have we slowed down for them?"

"Yes and sort of both," Stran said cryptically. "The director is processing their reassignment and they do have the standard thrust upgrade issued by the Force, but they don't have our code revision. So you're right in that we can't run the Wing as fast as we were."

"So they really *can't* keep up with Apache Squadron?" Casi asked with a sly grin.

"No, not yet. We'll fix that after they're reassigned," Stran answered and glanced back at her with a conspiratorial grin of his own. Then he sobered his expression and continued, "JCCV4 says we should reach the second Watcher with a couple of hours to spare before they expect the freighters to show up." Stran glanced at his scanner. "Do you want this leg, Casi?"

"Sure," she said eagerly. "I can handle the transfer as well."

"Okay," Stran said and swiveled the chair to aft facing.

When he unbuckled and pushed himself up, he caught Casi and turned her to face him. He kissed her tenderly and then slowly released her. "You're very welcome, Bren," he said softly to her. "Thank you too, for waiting for me to come."

Then he turned and pushed himself toward the nav-com compartment.

"Man," Cheral said with a chuckle as she settled in the right hand jumpseat. "You two need to get your heads back on the mission."

Smiling, Casi settled into the chair as it readjusted, secured the straps and turned it to forward facing. "Which 'mission' is that, Cheral?"

Time passed slower than it had before the leg change, and Casi attributed it to the rising tension of actually getting closer to the intercept. Her past exposure to combat had usually come quickly, suddenly dropped in her lap and her response had been nearly spontaneous, a reaction. This time, though, she thought, the time between knowing and preparing and getting there worked against them, allowing tensions and nerves to influence their moods. This was like, but more stressful than, their attack on Ahaar's Complex. In a way, she preferred to not think about it ahead of time, but she knew the planning lessened the risks.

Casi turned and glanced at where the Wing was on each side of STSX, and smiled at knowing what they were attempting. She double checked the scanner display and then the course STSX had plotted and displayed along the right side of the cockpit's forward panel.

"Q-JCCV4," she said through the optical link. "This is Apache Leader. I'm showing one-point-one terran hours to rendezvous with our other Watcher. Do we have the Watcher's IFF ID?"

"ID coming over," the masculine voice of JCCV4 answered.

"Good to meet you. Major Bids and Lieutenant Emly Bids here, at your service."

"Thank you, Major, Lieutenant," Casi greeted. "It's good to have you with us. I'm Lieutenant Casi Geaardt."

"If you don't mind me saying," Major Bids said, "I have never heard of, much less ever seen patrol fighters being conveyed by Q-Ships into a fight."

Casi smiled. "The colonel feels it is important for cadets and patrol fighter pilots to get the most experience they can during their training."

"A very good intention," Major Bids agreed. "I doubt the opportunity is available often in a cadet's training."

There was a short crackle of static and then a feminine voice said, "My apologies for the Major, Lieutenant. He forgets that some commanders have new ideas about training."

"No apology necessary," Casi said and smiled to herself.

"Lieutenant?" Lieutenant Emly's voice asked, "I heard that all of the nav-com's in Able-Squadron are pilots. Is that true?"

"Almost," Casi replied and glanced at Cheral with a smile. "All nav-coms are in pilot training and have passed most of the Academy's Flight Training Syllabus. All nav-com pilots and cadet pilots-in-training have combat time and a number of them have made it onto the honors boards with significant credited kills. And for the record, only the Rings still call us Able-Squadron."

"Nice," Lieutenant Emly said. "If you're not called Able-Squadron, what are you called?"

"The colonel," Casi answered, "has named us Apache Squadron and only Apache Squadron ships wear the red band."

"Thank you, Lieutenant," Emly said. "I know of a couple of Watchers that wear the band and I wondered why."

Casi relaxed and chatted with Cheral and as they neared their rendezvous time, Stran came forward and took the left jump seat.

"Sounds like my reputation for unorthodox methods precedes me," he said as he secured the straps. "Did you girls have a nice chat?"

"Of course," Cheral said with a quick glance at Casi. "Casi's given me all the gritty details of life with a certain colonel we both know, things about him that I never thought possible." She smiled when Stran turned and looked at her, wondering if she was teasing. "Take it easy, Greg. Casi would never divulge family secrets, but it was very nice to share our stories with each other. We're cousins that never knew each other until very recently."

Casi smiled at Cheral just as STSX interrupted.

"ONE THOUSAND CLICKS TO RENDEZVOUS WITH Q-HHRL22. PREPARED TO TRANSMIT IFF POSITION."

"Broadcast cloaking codes. See if there is anyone else around," Casi said as she focused on the scanner display.

"NO RESPONSES. NOTHING LIT."

"Go to the Long Range Scanner, Maximum Range," she continued without looking up from the display.

Suddenly a small cluster of dots appeared to the far left of the display center.

"TARGETS APPROACHING RENDEZVOUS COORDINATES. TARGETS RESPONDED TO CORSECAIN AND KYDDELLAN CODES. APACHE FLIGHT RENDEZVOUS WITH Q-HHRL22 IN SEVEN MINUTES. TARGETS WITHIN INTERCEPT RANGE IN FORTY-SIX POINT SIX MINUTES."

"Send our IFF," Casi said and then, "Apache Leader to Apache Wing," she said to the flight as she placed her left hand on the thrust levers. "Rendezvous in less than seven minutes. Bandits and fighter escorts forty-six minutes out and closing. Decelerate."

"STSX?" Casi asked, "How many escorts?"

"TWENTY-TWO FIGHTERS IN FLIGHT AND ONE LIGHT BATTLECRUISER ESCORT THE TWO FREIGHTERS."

Casi relayed the numbers and told STSX to lead them to the rendezvous. Casi quickly felt the ships on both sides as they slowed. Her apprehension that they might not begin decelerating quickly vanished as each Q-Ship remained in position as the formation responded as a single unit.

⊼

"Prepare for crew transfer," Casi announced to the Wing once they had formed up with HHRL22. She caught Cheral's arm and half turned her chair.

Cheral stopped and clasped Casi's forearm and smiled. Then she pushed herself into the central compartment and down through the floor portal with Stran close behind her.

Casi swung her chair to aft facing and checked on TTYF8 and

KKLC14's position. They and STSX1 were the only ships visually unveiled, but she knew where the other ships were, and she knew they were waiting and watching.

"Are the crews ready?" Casi asked.

"Apache Patrol Two is ready," Cheral affirmed through her helmet mic.

"Apache Patrol Three is ready," Ani said, the difference of the helmet mic also apparent.

"Apache Patrol Four is ready," Wilm said.

"Commence transfer," Casi said.

As movement became noticeable behind the Q-Ships, Casi realized she saw two suited figures leave both ships. *What?*

"THE COLONEL ASKED THE MAJORS TO ASSIST THE CADETS TO ENSURE A MINIMUM OF ERRORS OR CONCERNS."

"Good idea," Casi admitted. "He just forgot to mention it to me."

The transfer took less than five minutes and only another minute for the colonel and the two majors to return to their ships. Casi waited for STSX to cycle the pressure doors and confirm the airlock was resealed. She knew Greg was in the equipment bay, changing out of his pressure suit. She touched the other two ships and confirmed the majors were back inside, but decided to let them confirm it themselves.

"KKLC14, is Major Kooich back inside and secure?" she asked.

"Inside and secure," Leeana answered.

"Inside and secure," Franni replied before Casi asked.

"Thanks," Casi said. "Apache Patrol, power up your ships."

Each cadet responded and counted off each preparation step. Finally, when they were powered and waiting, Casi said, "Disconnect," and STSX and the other two ships released the magnetic stays. "Repulsion pads, off," Casi added and watched as the patrol fighters drifted up on the right side of their mother ships. "Assume formation positions." She watched as HHRL22 shifted and settled beside and behind JCCV4 on their left side.

"Intercept will commence in eight minutes," Casi finally said as she watched the closure distance counter incrementally decrease. She pulled her headband from the utility pouch on her belt and wrapped it around her forehead, tying the knot so the tails hung behind her right shoulder.

᠘

Leeana was watching Casi through STSX's canopy and saw her get her headband out. She quickly pulled hers out of her utility pouch and said, "Apache Wing, headbands on." She absently looked back where she knew the veiled ships were, knowing JCCV4 and HHRL22 nav-coms were not piloting and did not have headbands.

"Headbands on. Apache Wing is ready," Franni announced and Leeana looked across and just under STSX she could see the red in the uncloaked cockpits. She waved at Ani when she saw the headband in Apache Patrol Three's cockpit.

"Last system checks, Apache Flight. Intercept to commence in two minutes. Visual Cloaking on," Casi announced. "Patrol cruiser Brigstoan, Apache Squadron is in position."

Ninety-Four

"One says we have intruders! Nick, the Shields are still up!" she said and turned to the disguised panel Kiile had installed near the kitchen door. *'One, contact Kiile.'* Then she turned to Nick. "Are you armed?"

"Yes," he said as he slipped into the darker, formal portion of the living room. He eased the edge of the sheer drape aside and looked into the darkness.

"I'll alert the house girls," she said as she hit the shields control to roll the edges of the shields down to the ground. She pushed the kitchen door open and found Matti opening the dish washing machine, "Where's Cara and Annie? We have intruders."

Cara stepped out of their commons area and Matti pointed to the pantry.

"Go into an inside room and stay there until I tell you it's okay to come out," she said as she hurried to the pantry. "Annie, come quick."

Once Jill got them into the commons, she slipped back into the dark dining room. Nick was waiting and she quickly crouched down and led him to the coat room. Without rising up, she slipped her coat off the peg and Nick followed her example.

"I sure wish I could've sensed them like Shar would've. No time to get into our Blues now," she said in a whisper. "So don't try to be a hero and get yourself shot. C'mon."

She stopped, crouched by the back door to the long porch. "Damn, that yard light is going to light us up when we go out." She started to pull the door open when the yard light suddenly went out.

"Shit! Don't know if I liked it better lit up, or not," Nick whispered beside her.

'One, where are the intruders?' she asked as she peeked through the crack in the doorway.

'THERE ARE FIVE ALONG THE EAST PROPERTY BOUNDARY. FOUR ARE HALFWAY BETWEEN THE SOUTH BOUNDARY AND

THE MAIN HOUSE. TWO ARE BEHIND THE BUNKHOUSE. TWO ARE BEHIND THE FEED BARN. THEY CUT POWER TO THE YARD LIGHT. FIVE ARE WEST OF THE ANIMAL BARN. TWO ARE OUTSIDE THE SHIELDS AT THE FRONT DRIVE. THEY CANNOT GET IN.'

Jill quickly stood up between the door and the first coat room window and keyed the intercom. "Hank, intruders behind the bunkhouse and the feed barn. Five coming from the east. Eighteen inside the shields." Then she dropped back down and grabbed Nick's arm and pulled the door open.

Crouched in the darkness, Nick slowly pulled the door closed. Jill was on the west side of the door and motioned for him to go toward the apartments and that she would go the other way. He nodded and moved toward the corner of the building.

'Two. Where are you located' Jill asked the darkness.

'TWO IS BEHIND THE FIVE MEN WEST OF THE ANIMAL ENCLOSURE,' Two replied.

'One?'

'ONE IS BEHIND THE FOUR MEN SOUTH OF THE MAIN HOUSE,' One replied.

'One and Two. Corral your groups. Contain them and do not let any escape,' she said and the ground to the west of the horse barn erupted in brilliant, luminous energy; spears of light streaked down and formed a cage of super-hot bars encircling the stunned group of men. Dirt and grassy debris flew into the air, carried by clouds of hissing steam. She saw the reflection as One repeated the process and contained the four in front of the house with another circle of light spears and steam. *'One, raise the shields and let the other two come in to help. Then lower them again,'* she said and started a sprint across the yard to the feed barn.

Halfway across the yard, two men come out from between the barn and the bunkhouse; she saw the bunkhouse door open. Someone fired a projectile weapon and Jill dove for the snow covered ground. Her Kaaspr slammed the first man against the barn and she turned to the second as the first's body flopped forward in a smoking pile.

"Hank! To your left!" she shouted as the two from behind the bunkhouse and the five from the east charged through the gap between the buildings. She fired at the multiple muzzle flashes and

Hank's short barreled shot gun boomed. Jill rolled aside as the second man at the feed barn fired his hand weapon and the snow and dirt erupted beside her. The Kaaspr flashed and the man fell back, spread eagle on the ground.

She quickly rolled to see where Nick was and caught her breath when she saw the double flash of two projectile weapons. Almost in unison, the flashes of Nick's Kaaspr silenced the two hurrying between the main house and the apartments.

Jill scurried to the feed barn and knelt against the front wall, searching the darkness.

'One, Two. Status.' She said.

'Two is bringing five men into the yard from the west.'

'One and five Marines are bringing four men from the south. Marine Twelve and four other Marines are bringing three men from the east. Four are dead.'

'Thanks One. Thanks Two,' Jill said as she slowly stood up and faced the group coming around the west side of the stables. Jill stopped in front of the group and shouted, "On the ground! Face down with your hands behind your heads! *'Two, where are their weapons?'*

'They are on the ground west of the animal barn,' Two replied.

'How many of ours are injured?' she asked and turned to the west.

'Two, none dead,' Two answered.

'Thank you, Two,' Jill said and turned as the white winter camouflaged uniforms walked the second group of captives around the end of the main house.

The Marine in charge of the group ordered them on the ground similar to the five Jill already had face down.

'Thanks One,' she said and looked at the Marines. "Thank you for coming so quickly."

"Our pleasure, Miss Thomas," the Marine said just as the yard light suddenly flickered and began to brighten and he pointed to the group coming past the bunkhouse, three men surrounded by Hank, two of the hands, Marine Twelve and four more Marines. "Looked like you were winning without us," he continued with a smile.

She smiled, "We might've had trouble with those last seven if you hadn't shown up. Five is still coming."

The Marine nodded with a broad smile, "You had them all except

113

for three, and that would've only taken you another minute or two."

When Twelve reached the group, he ordered his captives on the ground with the others and the Marines encircled them and began binding their hands behind their backs.

She sensed a movement behind her and turned with a start as Nick limped out of the darkness between the two buildings. She felt pain as she started across the yard toward them.

"Nick?" she shouted and hurried to him. "I told you specifically to not get shot!" She reached him and slipped under his arm and took part of his weight. "Where did you get hit?"

"My side," he said as they staggered toward the Marines. "I've got to learn how to move as quickly as you can." He smiled at her concerned face.

"Twelve, do you have a Medic? Ours is obviously not here," she asked as they reached the circle of Marines. Twelve was already speaking into his earpiece.

"Squad Leader Kiile is enroute and will have our Field Medic here in a couple of minutes," Twelve said as Hank ran up to them with a stool from the bunkhouse. "One of your workers is wounded also."

Hank helped Jill and Twelve get Nick seated.

"One of the hands?" Jill asked Hank when Nick was sitting.

"Yeah," Hank said calmly. "Dusty. Not bad, just in the thigh."

"Thank god it wasn't too bad," Jill said and then stood up and looked to the north. "Five says Wally and Carole are almost here," she said then changed the focus of her thoughts. *'One, raise the shields for the marshal.'*

'SHIELDS ARE RAISED.'

'Thanks One.' Then she turned to Twelve and pointed. "Those two in front of the feed barn are dead and two more are in the dark between the main house and the apartments. Probably ought to add them to our collection."

"We saw the four by the bunkhouse," Twelve said as he signaled his men to get the ones between the house and apartments. "We'll gather all of them for identification."

Then she looked at Nick, "Nick, do you know any of these guys? Like, which one might be in charge?" She knew he had been studying the twelve captives and she realized most of them were young, probably students from the college. As she walked around them, she watched Nick.

"That one," Nick said, pointing to a man in front of her, wearing a nicer looking jacket and slacks instead of jeans. "Let me see his face."

Jill nodded to a Marine and he stepped in and pulled the man's head up and turned it toward Nick. Another Marine turned his hand lamp to shine on his face.

"Well, I'll be," Nick said with a wicked smile. "Mr. Barns. Since when have you started doing Don's dirty work for him?" Nick stared at him but Dave did not answer. "That one, gentlemen, is your squad leader of the evening. He takes his orders from one Mr. Don Nikle—"

Wally's star emblazoned jeep slid to a stop between the apartment garage and the bunkhouse, interrupting Nick as Kiile and the Field Medic came into the light from the west.

⚊

Seeing the ring of Marines and the ranch hands, Wally assumed the situation was under control. He eased himself out of the jeep and went to help Carole out, but she was already on the ground and hurrying toward Jill and Nick.

Jill turned as she approached and looked at Carole funny. She cocked her head and asked, "You're a deputy now?"

Carole stopped, surprised and then remembered the badge. "Oh, no. Wally wanted me to wear the badge in case there was shooting. He didn't want me to get shot by mistake,"

Jill noted Kiile and the Medic, Captain Wrth, were with Nick, so she caught Carole's arm and turned toward the house, "C'mon. I need to tell the girls everything is okay and they can come out of hiding."

Wally heard Carole giggle and whisper something to Jill about him having trouble pinning the badge on her jacket. Jill snickered and looked over her shoulder at Wally with a broad smile. Then they slipped into the house and he saw the dining room light switch on.

Wally sobered his expression and turned to Twelve. "Sorry we were so slow getting here," he said and nodded to Hank. "Ted and Thom will be here in a few minutes."

"Not a problem," Twelve said and extended his hand and shook Wally's. "Good to see you again, marshal. Jill organized everyone when she knew they were under siege and with Nick and Hank and the hands, they almost had them captured before we arrived. She is learning very well."

Wally stared at him, wondering why he had not thought about them needing training.

"How many?" Wally asked before he started counting.

"Twenty total," Twelve said. "Jill stopped four, Nick stopped two and got wounded for his effort and Hank got two when they rushed his shotgun. Two of their remotes captured nine, including their leader. Nick just identified him."

⅄

When Jill and Carole came back out into the yard, Twelve had already taken the dead away and was in the process of removing the captured, a couple at a time. She stopped and saw Dave Barns sitting with his back against the barn and two marines flanking him. Then she realized Nick was not there.

"Kiile's transport is just beyond the light on the west pasture," Twelve said, seeing Jill's searching look. "The Medic took him there to check his wounds and start recovery."

"Thanks," she said, forcing herself to relax and glanced at Carole. "I was worried there for a moment." Then she walked over and stopped, hands on her hips in front of Dave. "Mr. Barns. What were you trying to do tonight?" Kill us? Capture us? Burn the place down? What?"

He stared at her but did not say a word.

'STSX?' Jill said. *'Can you hear me? I need for you to show me how to do a mind scan.'*

'Jill?' Casi's voice asked. *'What's happened? We felt fighting.'*

'We were attacked at the ranch, but everything is under control. I'll explain in a minute,' she said firmly, *'but right now I need to learn how to do a mind scan and have STSX store and analyze the data.'*

'You're not up to that yet,' Casi said.

'I have to do it now,' Jill said and clenched her fists, staring at Dave. He did not look like he liked what he saw in her expression. *'We have to confirm Nick's claim of who's behind this.'*

After a moment, Jill heard Casi say, *'STSX, please run the conditioning program in Jill's mind.'* Then to Jill, Casi said, *'Sit down or kneel and close your eyes and listen only to the phrases STSX will say. Do not try to understand them, just concentrate on him and listen. Are you ready?'*

116

'One sec,' she said and then looked at Carole and the two Marines. "Do not let anyone touch me or bother me until I break contact. I will probably be near faint when I do. Understood?" She looked at the marines until they nodded and then at Carole. "This will take a little while, so be patient. Don't interrupt me." Carole finally nodded and Jill turned back to Dave.

'Okay, Shar,' she said and knelt down with Dave's legs just to the right of her knees. *'I'm as ready as I'll ever be.'*

'STSX, commence please. I'll be listening, Jill,' Casi said softly.

Slowly Jill began feeling and hearing a very soft string of phrases pass into her mind. She could barely hear them and could not understand them, but she remembered and focused her attention on STSX's presence. After what she thought must have been many minutes, she realized the phrases had stopped and Casi was talking to her, calling her. Finally she focused on Casi's voice.

'Okay, Jill,' Casi said. *'Open your eyes and look at the person. Place your hand over his eyes, thumb on one temple and second finger on the other temple. STSX is going to link with you and a flood of information and images and voices and many other sensations are going to well up inside of you. They will try to hang onto you, make you remember them, but you must not listen to them. Focus on STSX and let the information pass, try to ignore it. You will remember what is important later, but do not try to listen during the scan, the transfer.'* Casi paused then continued, *'Jill, this will not be easy for a first time, but REALLY concentrate on STSX's presence.'*

'Okay,' she said. *'Let me get my hand right.'*

Dave squirmed and hollered, fear coloring his voice as Jill placed her hand as Casi told her, squeezing his temples to make him hold still, and then said, *'Okay, Shar. I'm ready.'*

'Push your palm against his eyes and nose and squeeze so he can't shake loose.'

'Done,' Jill said and took a deep breath.

⚓

Carole watched in concerned uncertainty as Jill held the man's face in her grasp. Wally stood beside her with his arm around her, surprised as the man began to shake in Jill's grip. They became more concerned with the growing amount of time taken by Jill's performance, but Carole made sure Wally did not interfere.

Jill began to shudder and rock slowly as time drifted on and the man shook more violently. The Marines turned toward Jill and Carole raised her hand, stopping them. Seconds turned into minutes and minutes stretched as they watched. Then suddenly, Dave fell limp and Jill's hand dropped away. She teetered and started to slump sideways, but Carole and Wally were quickly at her side and held her upright.

Carole looked up at the marines and asked, "Have you seen anyone do this before?"

The both shook their heads.

"I've heard of it being done, but have never seen it. Other than a few very special marines, only Shadows can do that," one of them said as he knelt down beside them. "I was told she was just a cadet. No one ever said she was a Shadow."

Carole noticed the proud smile on the Marine's face and wondered what he meant by a Shadow.

"She'll be all right," he said with a knowing tone. "She cannot have done this many times, might be her first," he said. "I've heard the first few times are very taxing, like she said it would be."

The Marine turned to the second Marine. "To the transport, get a restorative tea and an energy bar. On the double."

The second Marine left at a full run and disappeared into the darkness. Mere minutes had passed when the Marine returned. He knelt beside the first, opened the warm tea container and passed it under her nose, letting the mild fragrance call her back.

Slowly, Jill began to stir and Carole told her to drink, then she told her again, repeating the urging until Jill finally let the fluid slip past her lips. Then, tasting the drink, Jill wanted more and sipped more and more heartily until the tea was gone. When the Marine removed the container, Jill slowly opened her eyes and realized where she was, leaning back against Wally and Carole with two Marines eagerly assisting her.

She tried to straighten up and Wally helped her regain her composure and balance. Then she remembered her task and she asked, 'Shar, did it work?'

'Yes, Jill,' Casi replied. 'I believe it did. STSX is processing the information and says some of it is the same as what we got from Harold and pieces from the judge. STSX says the data is clear and properly focused. You did very well, Jill. Well done. Are you doing okay?'

'I believe so,' she said. '*I think I passed out, though. Carole, Wally and two Marines are tending to me.*'

'*Can you tell me what happened?*' Casi asked. '*We're about to rendezvous with the second Watcher, so I don't have much time.*'

'*Let me know when your skirmish is over. I'll explain then, after I get everything here in order,*' Jill looked at the Marines and said she needed to get up and with the help of the four, she managed to stand and step away from Dave's limp form.

"You can take him now," Jill said. "We have enough information to confront Don Nikle and both police chiefs." She turned to Wally, "Thom will be pleased to know that."

The second Marine handed Jill the energy bar and told her how pleased he was to be of assistance. Then he turned and hurried after the first marine.

Bewildered, she turned toward the house. "I need to sit back down for a minute." Jill settled onto the stool Hank had brought for Nick, and called, '*One, Two?*' Wally stood on one side and Carole on the other as Jill started nibbling on the energy bar. '*Please show Kiile where the captive's weapons were dropped. He'll need to collect them.*'

Suddenly she stopped, "Hank? Where's Hank?"

"Hank's with the Medic. They're looking the ranch hand over," Wally said. "He got hit in the leg, nothing serious. Ted and Thom are here, so we'll take him to the hospital once the Medic says we can."

"No!" Jill said and turned abruptly. "That'll raise too many questions. He has to be treated here. Take me to Kiile."

"Apache Flight," Stran said as Casi led the Wing toward the oncoming freighters and fighters. "Apache Patrols Two, Three and Four concentrate on the fighters. Apache Wing Leader, assign your targets. Apache Leader will attack the battlecruiser."

"Apache Wing," Major Kooich said, "LLRT12 and HHRL22 stay with the two freighters. Keep them from straying. Disable if necessary, but do not damage the cargo. Patrol cruisers *Brigstoan* and *Dorsalt* are waiting one thousand clicks up course. TTYF8 assist Apache Leader, and all other fighters pick targets of your choice. Watch for additional fighters from the cruiser once we strike."

"Apache Leader, patrol cruiser Brigstoan here," the voice filled STSX's cockpit. "The hail has been sent. Launch your attack."

"Attack commencing. Keep your shields up and stay cloaked," Stran said. "Remember, fire and move. Don't give them a lucky hit. Good hunting." Then he turned his thoughts. "STSX, run their diagnostic routines, please. Drop their veils."

Casi shoved the thrust levers forward and focused on the approaching cruiser as its veils switched off, exposing it. "TTYF8, target the belly equipment area. It's similar to the converted freighters but buried deeper. We'll go for the weapons control center on top."

"Will do," Franni confirmed and Casi felt them settle low and a mile off her left.

"STSX," Casi said smoothly as she rolled STSX so the left pylon would aim at the top of the cruiser when they passed. "Double volleys from all turrets. Target the area on the centerline, one-third of the length forward of the engines."

Casi focused on the cruiser, envisioned the target area and added a little braking. She wanted a quick pass, but not so quick that she jeopardized the accuracy of the shot. Then she had a thought and pitched STSX's nose up, flipping him one eighty and then she looked back over her left shoulder as the cruiser rapidly grew in size. She kept the left pylon aimed and when the cruiser streaked past and the turrets unleashed their twenty-four shots, a blinding fury of light exploding against the dull golden hull, she slammed the thrust levers full forward.

"Sorry love," she said, straining to speak against the forces that slammed her back in the cushioned chair.

"Go get 'em," Stran said from the back. "I was ready for it."

In a matter of seconds, STSX had reacquired the cruiser and closed for a second barrage along its backbone. She felt TTYF8, trying to get back in the fight. Franni had passed head on and turned after the pass. It cost her many seconds before she was ready for a second strike, but Casi smiled, Franni's first volley had been effective and the cruiser had developed a slow roll to the right.

"Stay with it, Franni," Casi said as she fired a second double volley of twenty-four, followed by a third. "Fighters are coming out of the right side hangar bay."

Casi jinked STSX, repositioned and fired into the hangar bay on an angle from the front, sweeping across the fuel cell storage inside.

The bay burst in fire and smoke, and three fighters spun away and then burst in fiery clouds of their own.

TTYF8 hit the bay from behind and below and a huge panel on the opposite side tore away behind the tapered nose and the cockpit area.

STSX was picking off fighters at random as Casi focused another volley just forward of the engines. A second volley in the same area as she jinked cut the aft section through and the engines twisted, but hung onto the main body of the ship. The cruiser began to spin and tumble from the misaligned thrust of the skewed engines.

"Pull back!" Casi shouted. "Get some distance for your next shots."

She felt Franni increase their radius of attack and moved STSX ahead of the cruiser. They both fired another volley and the engines separated completely and the main body split down its back, peeling open like an over cooked shellfish.

TTYF8 circled behind the cruiser when the engines exploded in a huge, blinding flash and expanding cloud of flames, smoke and debris. Casi caught her breath, "Franni! Report!"

A long moment passed as Casi maneuvered STSX around the ruptured and gutted forward section, now silent with no glow of fires or traces of smoke, no emissions of power.

"Franni! Report!" Casi shouted again.

"We're... okay," the feeble response finally came. "TTYF8 got a little fried and took a hit from some of the debris, but he says he's okay."

Casi smiled, then started to chuckle. "Good to hear you. I did that once. Hell of a 'Bang.'"

"Yes, ma'am. It sure was," Franni agreed.

Casi turned and looked at the space around them, not seeing any indications of bursting targets or the freighters. "What's the Wing's status, STSX?" she asked before she thought to ask Greg.

He was laughing softly when STSX answered.

"ALL ESCORT VESSELS HAVE BEEN DESTROYED. THIRTY-THREE FIGHTERS DESTROYED IN FLIGHT. SEVENTEEN COUNTED DESTROYED WHEN THE LAUNCH BAY EXPLODED PLUS THREE THAT TRIED TO ESCAPE. Q-LLRT12 AND Q-HHRL22 HAVE STOPPED THE FREIGHTERS AND ARE

RENDEZVOUSING WITH PATROL CRUISERS BRIGSTOAN
AND DORSALT. APACHE PATROL TWO, THREE AND FOUR
ARE SAFE AND UNDAMAGED AND HAVE ADDED KILLS TO
THEIR TALLY. KCMM9 SUFFERED INTERMITTENT SHIELD
FAILURE AND DEBRIS DAMAGE TO THEIR RIGHT PYLON.
NO CRITICAL SYSTEMS DAMAGED. JCCV4 LOST SIXTY
PERCENT OF ITS SHIELDS AND ONE TURRET FAILED. ALL
OTHER SHIPS REPORT NO DAMAGE."

"Wow," Casi said as she turned her chair to aft facing and stared
at Greg in disbelief. "Total engagement time?"

"SEVENTEEN TERRAN MINUTES."

Casi's mouth dropped open as she watched Greg's broad smile.
Then chuckling, she turned her chair to forward facing and said,
"STSX, let's regroup alongside of the patrol cruisers. Tell the Apache
Wing to join up, visual cloaking off. We'll collect the Apache patrol
fighters when the cruisers are finished." Then she said over her
shoulder, "Better put our report together, love. I think the director
will want to know how this one turned out."

C.3482.389

Prince Kiese stared at the communications console in disbelief.
He slowly turned in his chair and swept the walls of his large, ornate
private office, suddenly not seeing the beauty he tried to bring into
the other-wise dreary confines of his daily business.

"Tell me again, Chairman Sorgat," he said in a low tone sounding
suspiciously like a soft growl.

"Yes, yes," the chairman said softly, holding his demeanor steady
and his voice calm. "I have just been informed by my Director of
Merchandise that yesterday's shipment from Copus Two's secreted
base disappeared. Intelligence received a very short transmission
from one of the freighters saying they were under attack by two Peace
Force heavy fighters. The message mentioned the fighters wore a red
slash and then the message terminated." The chairman took a deep
breath. "We suspect the Peace Force intercepted and boarded the two
freighters. There has not been a response from any queries sent to
the freighters, or from the battlecruiser or any of its fifty-five fighters
assigned as escort."

"That is what I thought you said," the prince said as he slowly rose up from his chair and threw a large paper weight across the room, knocking a finely sculptured statue of a warrior spearing a fallen slave off an ornate credenza.

"Prince Kiese," the chairman said in an entreating tone. "Please! Do not upset yourself. I will increase the escorts for our next shipments. I will—"

"Chairman!" the prince shouted. "You lost fifty-six escort vessels! And you said you lost them to two of the Force's heavy fighters?"

"My Intelligence staff feels there were more than two," Chairman Sorgat said firmly. "I must admit, I do not know how many, but I intend to find out the Force's strength."

"And what about my shipments?" Prince Kiese demanded. "You have lost the last seven of my orders! I want those orders filled!"

"Yes," the chairman said, "I understand. I will do everything I can to fill those orders quickly."

The prince slammed his fist down on the console, terminating the conversation. Then he keyed for his battle commander.

An aide answered, "The Supreme Battle Commander is not in, sir."

"Where is he?" the prince demanded.

The aide withdrew noticeably from the screen on his end. "Handling the unrest in the remote sectors of the Pico mines as you ordered, sir. The adjunct commanders are engaged in the water war in Aridont and the civil revolt in Pordenl."

The prince nodded sharply and paced a moment. "Have my battle commander contact me within a par!"

"Yes, sir. I will send him your order," the Aide said and the prince disconnected.

Thursday, January 5

"Morning, Matti," Shara said as she set her carrysack down and hung her coat in the coat room. "How is everyone this morning? Jill said you had some trouble last night."

"Morning Mrs. Shara," Matti said with a half-smile. "We're okay, 'cept Dusty got shot in the leg and Mr. Nick got shot in the side. Mr. Kiile said they both will be fine, so that is a good thing." Matti wrung her hands, then continued when Greg came in and set his carrysack beside Shara's. "We were all scared, but Miss Jill knew what to have us do and she knew what she needed to do. Honestly, Mrs. Shara, in all the years I've known that girl, I never saw her so level headed. I never thought I'd hear myself say it, but I'm glad she was here." Matti took a deep breath. "Morning Mr. Greg. Will you be wanting breakfast?"

"Certainly, Matti," he smiled at her. "We've missed Annie's cooking and your pleasant smile." He glanced at Shara and added, "I think we'll get cleaned up first, and we are a little early yet. Give us a half an hour or a little longer. Major Kooich and Leeana just got back as well and it'll take them a bit to get cleaned up."

"Will Miss Cheral be joining us?" she asked glancing at her watch.

"I think she'll be eating with the other cadets this morning," he said as he turned Shara toward the hallway.

When he had closed the bedroom door, Shara looked at him and said, "You know, I don't think I've ever heard Matti say hardly anything about Jill, especially anything complimentary. Most people felt Jill was a little too pompous and opinionated to get to know her very well."

Greg smiled as he slipped out of his Blues and started the shower. "Well, I like Jack and Amy, but they did almost ruin her."

"I like them too, Jack anyway," Shara said and followed him into the bath. "Amy's harder to like, too much of her dad, James, in her, always with the airs, worried about what everyone thinks about them. Jim's dad Bill was the only one of the Woods' boys with any practical, common sense. He appreciates people."

Greg caught her and turned her too him, "Well, Bren. With her training and now with your help, it sounds like she may have found herself. And with you leading her through a mind scan, she has certainly accomplished more than any of us ever thought possible."

Shara stretched up and kissed him. "Maybe, but enough about her for now, love. I've waited an entire mission to have a minute or two alone with you."

⁂

"Franni asked me," Leeana said as she finished one of Annie's sweet rolls and sipped her coffee, "where you came up with the attack maneuver you used. She said there was no way she could keep up with you."

"Which one was that?" Shara asked, surprised by the comment and glanced at Major Kooich, Greg and then Jill.

Shara had settled into breakfast and was enjoying the conversation after a rocky start. Her nausea had flared up right after she sat down to eat, but she was able to force it down with only one hurried trip back to their bathroom.

"I wasn't watching, of course," Leeana continued, "but she said when you went in head-to-head on your first pass, you seemed to turn around and glue yourself to the cruiser. She said she made her pass and by the time she got turned around, you were already pounding it a second and a third time."

Shara smiled and sipped the refreshing juice Matti had poured her from a separate carafe. "I just sort of, made it up as I went. I didn't want them to have time to recover or regroup, so I turned around and started catching up before it got to me."

Major Kooich watched her steadily as he finished his plate of fruit.

"Before?" Leeana asked.

"Yes. That way when the cruiser passed me the first time, I got off a clean, focused volley and was already accelerating for my second volley. Franni got its controls on her first pass and I got the weapons on mine."

"Then you just opened it up to see what was inside?" Major Kooich asked with a huge smile.

"Well, not really to see what was inside," Shara said, "but I knew there would be more fighters and I figured a few shots through the roof might slow them down some. When Franni and I got to the hangar bay portal, we pretty well shut them down."

Major Kooich chuckled softly, his eyes dancing as he glanced up at Greg. "I'd say that's a pretty accurate assessment. It was over, completely disabled in what, six, maybe seven volleys?"

Greg smiled at Shara. "Pretty much. STSX said they caught more than a third of the fighters before they could launch, significantly reducing the threat to the other ships."

Major Kooich nodded. "I'll have the counts for the debriefing. Do you have a time, Colonel?"

"Let's assemble at 1300 hrs at Obscure," Greg said, "Casual dress."

Major Kooich nodded and refilled his cup and Greg turned to Jill.

"Give us a briefing on the attack here, Jill," he said and refilled his own cup.

Jill smiled, a concerned smile with uneasy thoughts hiding behind her eyes. She commenced and explained the sequence of events from Nick's noticing a flash of light in the field south of the house through the collection and capture of the assailants, twelve alive and eight dead. She explained that she felt the mind scan was the only way she could confirm Nick's claim that Dave Barns was acting on Don Nikle's orders, and thanked Shara and STSX for the help and guidance.

"Unfortunately," Jill concluded, "the scan also confirmed that Don wanted you and me," she looked at Shara, "alive or not, to stop us from interfering in the Family's business."

"Alive or not?" Shara repeated softly. "Seems to always be the case, doesn't it?"

"Yeah," Jill answered. "He seems to have figured out that in our absence from society we haven't just been hiding. He knows we were here when Bernice came and Harold ran, leaving her behind. We expected that. He also thinks we had something to do with Harry and Harold's disappearance, but doesn't actually know. He also doesn't know you have any connections with the loss of the freighters, the Clotter brother's disappearance or any of the people they sent to see what happened at Obscure during or after the attack."

Shara and Greg thought about Jill's news.

"If I remember right," Greg said, "Nick had said there were only the two Elders left, Don Nikle and Dave Barns and you said you caught Dave last night with the attackers." Jill nodded. "That means that only Don Nikle is left."

"The only Elder, maybe," Jill admitted, "but you remember what we found out last week, Chief Russell and Chief Parks and their deputies? None of them were very cordial or pleased to see Deputy Baines."

"Yeah," Greg admitted. "There is still a lot of distrust and anger in the southern valley."

"There's still some around here," Jill added with a little disgust in her tone. "All of the guys Dave brought last night were from the college."

"Well," Greg said as he finished his coffee and stood up. "I think I'll talk to Wally and see how his background checks are coming. He was trying to link the missing people to current residents. Maybe he can expand his investigation to see which families have tendencies toward the Family and the Elders." He looked at Shara. "But, for now, I think I am ready for a nap before we meet for our debriefing."

She looked up and smiled. "I think I am as well."

Ninety-Five

"Abe?" Don Nikle's voice asked when Abe answered the phone console.

"Yes," Abe answered. "It is a little early for you to be calling. What do you need?"

"Did you see Dave yesterday?" Don asked tersely.

"Yes," Abe said. "About three or so. He was recruiting some guys to help him with something last night, but I was tied up."

"You were not with him then?" Don pressed.

"No. I just said that," Abe said. "Why?"

"Do you know if he was able to recruit the men he needed?"

"I think he did," Abe said as he made his way to the kitchen and poured a cup of coffee. "I think he said he had about twenty total."

"That was the number we discussed," Don admitted. "Did he explain his need?"

"Only generally," Abe said. "He just said you had him on some kind of an errand that needed a lot of manpower."

After a minute, Don continued, "He was supposed to meet with me at midnight with the fruits of his errand, but he has not returned. It is not like Dave to not come to a meeting when I call one."

"Okay," Abe said, "so he is overdue. What do you want of me?"

"Will you go to the college and talk to the fellows that were with him last night and see what has happened?"

"Sure. I can check," Abe said, and looked out his front window to see how the morning was shaping up. "I will call Ben and get him to help."

"Good, good," Don said, suddenly in a slightly better mood. "Call me as soon as you know why he is delayed."

"I will," Abe said and Don disconnected.

Abe sipped his coffee and toggled Ben's code.

▲ ▲ ▲ ▲ ▲

Greg, Shara and Leeana, wearing their Blues, sat behind the long table in Obscure's Flight readiness room as the room began to fill with the squadron crews. Major Kooich stood behind a slender podium and watched everyone file in and stop in front of the seats of their choice. When his count confirmed the number, he announced "At ease," and told them to sit.

"As some of you may know, we have an extra ship and crew with us for a few days," Major Kooich started. "I'd like to introduce Major Bids and Lieutenant Emly Bids of Q-JCCV4."

The crews nodded and extended welcomes as they turned to greet the standing couple.

"Q-JCCV4 had some shield damage and a turret malfunction to repair," Major Kooich explained, "and we are closer than any other facility with spares. Good to have you with us."

"Thank you, Major," Major Bids said and they sat back down.

"I want to thank all of you for a mission well done," Major Kooich continued. "There are a few constructive criticisms that the colonel and I would like to discuss with one or two of you, but we will hold individual face-to-face sessions immediately following the general briefing.

"First matter of business is the damage and repairs. Lieutenant Tam?"

"Yes, sir," Lori said and quickly stood up.

"Your report says you had a shield failure. Explain," Major Kooich said and waited.

"Sir," Lori began, speaking clearly. "KCMM gave me a warning indication just as I engaged one of the fighters at close range. The right and top shields lost power and when the fighter exploded, our right pylon was pierced numerous times by its debris. After investigating, Maintenance said KCMM had a failed harness between the power unit and the two associated antennae."

"What is the repair estimate?" Major Kooich asked as he looked at his notepad.

"Harness will be fixed today," Lori answered, "and skin repairs possibly as early as midmorning tomorrow."

"Very good," Major Kooich said with a smile. "Thank you, Lieutenant. Any other damage or repairs that need to be reported?" He slowly glanced at the assemblage of twenty-four. "Colonel, do you have a word?"

Major Kooich sat down beside Leeana as Greg stood up.

"Yesterday," Greg began, "we intercepted two more of the Traders Union's freighters carrying slaves stolen from their homes and on their way to delivery in Prince Kiese's numerous markets. These two freighters were the eighth and ninth consecutive freighters intercepted by the Peace Force in our new and aggressive role to stop the slavers. I asked Major Kooich to assign one of our Squadron to help intercept the freighters, visually uncloaked, in the hopes that if a message or a fragment got sent back to the Traders, the squadron marking might be again mentioned."

A soft murmur drifted through the room.

"Apache Squadron has been involved in a few interceptions, but the director has marked a couple of Watchers to help spread the word. I want the Traders and eventually the prince himself to know who we are and that we mean business.

"My apologies to LTVC21 for missing the fight, but I thank you for the help you gave guarding our home front. My congratulations to each and every one of you, and double congratulations to the lieutenants that flew yesterday's combat. I thank you."

Greg was pleased with the smiles, nods and the happy murmurs that filled the room.

"Our next foray is most likely in two or three days, either Saturday or Sunday is my opinion," he finished and sat down.

Major Kooich stood up. "Now the news you've all been waiting for. For Apache Squadron, yesterday's kills will be tallied for the pilots by name rather than for the ships. That said,

"Cadet Captain Haak in Apache Patrol Two added eight for a personal total of sixteen.

"Cadet Tigs in Apache Patrol Three added four for a personal total of ten.

"Cadet Moss in Apache Patrol Four added his first four.

"Lieutenant Colbee Donnr in MKCC5 added her first four.

"Lieutenant Lori Tam in KCMM9 added her first four.

"Lieutenant Leeana Kooich in KKLC14 added her first six.

"I would also like to mention that JCCV4 is credited with three."

The room turned to Major and Lieutenant Bids and added their thanks.

"In addition," Major Kooich continued, "Lieutenant Franni Kaal in TTYF8 and Lieutenant Casi Geaardt destroyed one battlecruiser and twenty-two fighters before they had the opportunity to provide the rest of you with additional targets."

A soft chuckle drifted across the attendees.

"Lieutenant Casi Geaardt also added four fighter kills while attacking the cruiser.

"For Lieutenant Franni Kaal, her first eleven and one half kills are added to the board," Major Kooich said with a smile.

"And for Lieutenant Casi Geaardt, eleven and one half kills plus the four are added to her tally, bringing her personal total to eighty-three and one half."

For a long moment the room hung in awed silence. Then someone started to clap, and then another and another put their hands together until the entire room was standing and clapping at Casi's accomplishments.

▲

Franni and Cheral descended upon Shara as soon as Major Kooich dismissed the squad, happily congratulating each other and Shara.

"How am I ever going to catch up?' Cheral asked as she stopped in front of Shara and clasped her forearm.

"Just stay focused," Shara laughed. "You're doing pretty good yourself."

Franni looked uncomfortable, but Shara put it to now being in the esteemed ranks of fighter pilots and clasped her arm with a smile. "You were great Franni. A good wingman," Shara said.

"But you should get the credits," Franni said. "It... was your shot that blew the hangar bay."

"We were partners, Franni," Shara said, still smiling. "We both took our shots before the bay came apart. I'm perfectly happy with sharing the credits."

Cheral laughed. "Don't worry Franni. You earned what was given and maybe more."

Slowly Franni began to smile.

"At this moment, we're all just fighter pilots," Cheral said, "Casi just happens to be a very good fighter pilot, and of course, a few other things besides."

Shara looked up and nodded to Cheral as she pointed across the room. Cheral turned as Paul walked up and gave her a long hug.

"Commander Haak, sir," Franni said and started a salute.

"At ease, girl," Paul said softly with a wide smile as he turned back to Cheral. "Just had to tell my granddaughter what I thought about her going off to war without tellin' me."

"It's sort of a family affair," Shara said to Franni as Cheral and Paul talked. "Cheral was my husband's nav-com for three years and when we set up for the battle to capture this facility, the colonel, major then, realized Paul and Cheral were related. Neither knew the other was here until then."

"My word," Franni said as Cheral turned to her, "it truly is a small universe."

"Franni," Cheral said, "I want you to explain to Paul what you feel about the training now that you've put some of it into practice, like we talked over lunch."

"I'll be back in a minute," Shara said to Cheral and turned to the door to the hallway.

She stopped briefly and caught the door jamb as she glanced up the corridor. Then she turned and hurried to the women's necessary.

Cheral was listening to Franni's discussion with Paul, but casually watched Shara as she went quickly to the door, gripped the jamb securely before hurrying through and up the corridor. She wondered what Greg thought about Shara's behavior.

▲ ▲ ▲ ▲ ▲

Ben glanced into Abe's den, looked at the dark computer monitors and slowly shook his head. "It was a good idea," he said as he came back into the living room.

"What?" Abe said absently as he pulled two beer containers from the refrigerator and handed one to Ben.

"Oh, the monitors," Ben said as he took the beer and pointed to the den.

"Yeah," Abe said and pulled a chair from the table and sat down. "I just can't figure out how the marshal knew when you put the transmitters out." He took a long pull on the beer. "I guess this will not delay the inevitable for long. I better call Don."

Abe turned his chair and keyed the sequence. Don's voice answered.

"It's Abe and Ben," Abe said.

"Good," Don said. "What did you find out?"

"Nothing. At least nothing good," Abe replied. "We have not been able to find anyone that went with Dave yesterday. We talked to a number of the guys that spoke to Dave when he started asking for help, but they were tied up one way or another and couldn't get away to help. They all said they could have helped if they had had a little heads up."

"We even searched for Dave's car," Ben added, "but we haven't found it either."

Don did not say anything for a long moment. "Did anyone say where Dave was going to take the guys that went with him?"

"No," Abe said. "They all said he said it was to be a surprise, but nothing more."

Again, Don did not say anything for a long moment. "Did anything unusual happen around town last night?"

"Nothing of any note," Ben said. "The deputies were patrolling off and on all night, but no sirens or flashing lights."

"Okay," Don said sharply. "I'll get back with you," he said and broke the connection.

Abe stared at the console. "Man, he is not happy."

"How can you tell?" Ben asked.

"I just can," Abe said. "Something happened last night and he is not telling us. Apparently Dave was supposed to do something, pretty big I take it since he needed twenty or so guys to help. And I don't think he got it done." Abe looked at Ben and took another pull on his beer. "And Don does not know what to do next."

"He will figure something out," Ben said.

"Yeah, that is what I am afraid of," Abe said and finished his beer in one long gulp.

⏶ ⏶ ⏶ ⏶ ⏶

"I'm very proud of you, Franni," Major Mooren said as they talked over a mid-afternoon snack in the Mess, "and to fly with Lieutenant Casi. That was a nice honor."

"Yes, it really was," Franni admitted. "To see her in action was incredible. Did you see how quick she is? You'd think STSX1 was just a part of her the way she handles him."

"Handles who?" Major Bids asked as he and Lieutenant Emly stopped beside them, trays in hand. "Mind if we join you?" he asked and gestured to Major Bradg and Lieutenant Mri.

"No," Major Mooren said as Franni nodded. "Please." And he motioned to the table around them. "Good to have a few minutes to visit."

Major Bids and Emly took places on one side of Major Mooren and Franni and Major Bradg and Mri settled on the other side.

"Mind if I ask," Major Bids asked, "who you were talking about? The lieutenant's comment caught my attention. I apologize if we're intruding."

"That's fine," Franni said with a wave of her hand. "I was just stating how incredible it was to fly Lieutenant Casi's wing in combat, to see firsthand what she does and how she does it. She's incredibly quick and thinks far ahead of me in those situations."

"I know we're new," Lieutenant Emly said, "but is she for real? Lieutenant Casi, I mean. Eighty-three kills?"

Major Mooren winked at Franni and smiled. Then he said, "And a half. Lieutenant Casi is very much for real. I will give you a little history as it was explained to us." He glanced from one to the other, drawing them all in with his gaze.

"Lieutenant Casi grew up here in this valley and apparently knew the major for a little while during his undercover activities. The colonel, major then, working undercover in this area with his nav-com, now Captain Haak, had been searching for the slavers launch facility for three years and that search brought him to the valley. When they met, Casi did not know who the major really was, and when she and the major's sister were taken by the slavers, he went after them. When he found Casi, she had been poisoned and between him and STSX1, they saved her.

"Marine Seventeen explained that she and the major led a six man team, divided into a two man and a four man squad, and attacked and captured this facility." He pointed to the floor. "The major's sister was on a ship that was to launch that night. Casi led the four man squad to find captives and with a small group of captives in tow, she led the group through this facility, across the launch bay and up what used to be stairs and balconies across the south side of the bay and out into the field south of the portal. All against heavy ground opposition."

"How many were here when they attacked?" Lieutenant Mri asked.

"Over three hundred," Franni said softly. "Only about ten percent survived when they got through."

The four just stared at the major and Franni.

"That nice clearing outside that we park in," Major Mooren said, continuing, "was a dense forest. The frigate that took the major's sister crashed there, with both the major and his sister on board. Casi went into the burning inferno and guided the major and his sister out, with seconds to spare. That clearing is what's left. There was almost no wreckage to haul away."

He waited a moment for them to absorb some of his words, then he started anew.

"The Marines here think of Casi as one of their own. They sincerely respect her abilities in hand-to-hand combat, her abilities to know things and her spirit and courage. Seventeen mentioned that while they were rescuing captives down south by the town of Grants, Casi took out an armed sentry barehanded and in a matter of seconds neutralized him. He said he was glad they didn't keep count of hand-to-hand kills since she could easily make his men look like they weren't trying. She is also deadly with the Kaaspr, Brekshiirs and throwing darts."

"I had no idea," Major Bradg said softly. "She seems so personable, normal..."

"She is," Franni said with a smile. "She has a firm, yet pleasant demeanor, even when she's on your case, but don't ever disregard the undertones. From firsthand experience, I will tell you she is forgiving, caring and your finest ally unless you do something stupid, or against orders. That's when you better watch out."

"But she's—" Major Bids said.

"Only a lieutenant?" Franni asked sharply. "Is that what you were going to say? Well, she may officially only be a lieutenant, but she has a bite, knows what needs to be done, expects it to be done, and the colonel backs her up. And she backs the colonel up. They are both our commanders, a unified team." She paused a moment, then added, "But if you think she's hiding behind the colonel's influence, remember, she personally answers directly to the Peace Force director. She can't hide from him. And 'he' brought her into the Peace Force as a lieutenant, the first time ever that anyone has started with rank."

Again she waited.

"Also remember," Major Mooren said, "that she was caught alone with nowhere to go, facing two full battlecruisers, each with a full complement of fighters and came out damaged and shaken, but the sole survivor. Unfortunately, she only got credit for the fifty-nine fighters she got in flight. They didn't give her credit for the other fifty some she kept from launching when she destroyed the cruisers with them inside. And she didn't get credit for the legion of troopers they were delivering to attack this base."

"I guess my comment sounded a little arrogant," Lieutenant Emly said softly. "She definitely 'is' for real."

"Yes, ma'am," Major Mooren agreed.

"Well," Franni said, "enough expounding on the attributes of our commanders, so here's a little personal info for everyone. I'm from Casimir on Betolle in the Daneets system. Where are you from?"

Greg toasted the small group again as they finished dinner at the ranch and again he complemented Annie for her fine cooking.

"Matti?" Greg asked when she came to begin clearing some of the plates from the table. "How is our wounded ranch hand doing?"

"Oh my, Mr. Greg," she said in a bit of a fluster, "Dusty is doing better than I ever expected." She turned to Kiile. "Thank you, Mr. Kiile. For treating him and for letting him stay here at the ranch to mend."

"You're very welcome, Matti," Kiile said, "but it was Jill that convinced the marshal that he needed to stay here."

Matti nodded and muttered another "thank you" as she picked up the plates and swept into the kitchen.

Greg looked at Shara. "I get the feeling there's more than a casual concern there."

Shara smiled and nodded. "She's had a thing for Dusty for quite a while and this is the first time an opportunity has shown itself."

"An opportunity?" Greg asked, noticing the interest of the others around the table.

"So she can legitimately dote over him," Shara said with a soft chuckle, "since, in her words, the Head House Woman is responsible for the well being of everyone on the ranch."

"Is it reciprocated?" Leeana asked.

"I think so," Shara admitted. "He's come to fix things around the main house more often, especially since late August or early September, volunteering more instead of waiting to be asked."

Greg smiled.

"How's Nick?" Leeana asked as she turned to Jill.

"Kiile says he'll be up and around tomorrow," she answered with a smile. "I'm not going to dote on him any more though."

"Why not?" Leeana asked in surprise.

"I specifically told him not to get shot," Jill stated and folded her arms across her chest. "And he did anyway. It wasn't like the last time when he charged the sheriff and all of those troopers."

Leeana smiled and held back the laugh she felt coming.

"Anyone for coffee in the living room?" Shara asked as she got up with her cup and a carafe.

Greg followed and took his place in the overstuffed chair beside the fireplace. Major Kooich and Leeana claimed the loveseat, Kiile and Cheral settled on the long couch and Jill took a chair near the foyer.

"Does anyone want anything besides coffee?" Shara asked as she set her cup on the table beside Greg's chair. When no one did, she took her place on Greg's lap.

The conversation commenced, starting with a more detailed evaluation of the Wing's effectiveness and performance during the intercept, moving through Major Kooich's crew selections and then into a general recap of the attack on the ranch and Jill's acknowledgement that the attack was meant to capture her and Shara.

"Where would they have taken you?" Major Kooich asked, thinking out loud. "I mean, where would this Don Nikle think he could take you and be able to keep you without anyone finding you?"

"I'm not sure that was his concern," Jill said softly, looking at the major. "He didn't need us alive."

The major inhaled sharply, realizing he had glossed over a key point.

"Sorry, Jill," he said. "I didn't mean to sound insensitive. But this Don Nikle must have someplace that he feels is secure enough that he can go there and hide if necessary."

"Deputy Baine indicated Don hung around Clay a lot," Jill said, "but when we went with him to Hawthorne, it seemed like the chief of police there knew a lot about the Elders and the Family. It wasn't what he said, but how he said things."

"Can we do a little searching around down there and see if anything jumps out at us?" Leeana asked.

"We can include over flights when we come and go from Obscure," Greg admitted. "Not sure what we are looking for, though."

"Wait a minute," Jill said, her eyes widening brightly. "Major Kooich, didn't you do some mapping to find where the tunnel goes from Obscure?"

"Yes," the major answered, "we did. What are you thinking?"

"Kiile?" she turned and asked. "Have you cleared the collapsed section of the tunnel at Obscure?"

"Partially," he answered, leaning forward as if to hear better.

"I'm wondering if Don and his affiliation as an Elder," Jill said, absently rubbing her chin, "would have given him any opportunity to use the tunnels. It would let him move from Clay to Hawthorne to Grants undetected."

"And a back door into Obscure if we clear our end," Kiile said with a slight scowl on his face.

"Kiile," Greg said, thinking about Jill's points, "Let's see if there is any activity at Bernice's old mansion in Clay. Then let's see if we can get one of the train cars, or whatever they are called, to use from Obscure." He paused a moment, then added, "If Don is using the tunnels, I'm betting he has a place somewhere along its route, possibly near or past Hawthorne."

"Kiile," Major Kooich said, "I will have to look again, but I remember the mapping indicated a number of maintenance hatches along the tunnels, which could be used to set up security between Clay and Obscure."

'STSX,' Shara said, focusing her mind, '*do you have a copy of Major Kooich's map?*'

'YES.'

'*Very good,*' she continued, '*Where does the tunnel go after passing Hawthorne?*'

'EAST FOR THIRTY MILES.'

'*Is there anything obvious at the terminus?*'

'A NUMBER OF BUILDINGS LOCATED IN NUMEROUS CLEARINGS IN THE FOREST, POSSIBLY A RANCH OR FARMSTEAD.'

'*Thank you, STSX,*' she said and turned to the room. "STSX says your mapping shows a ranch or farmstead thirty miles east of Hawthorne, at the end of the tunnel network."

"I think an over flight is absolutely necessary," Major Kooich said with a smile.

"Absolutely," Greg agreed.

When Major Kooich started to rise, Leeana caught his arm. "First thing in the morning," she said. "If I may be so bold as to impose on your hospitality, Colonel, I think we should break out something better than coffee for the occasion of Jill's speculations and curiosity."

"Certainly," Greg said as Shara got up and hurried to the kitchen.

◢

It was getting late when Cheral got up and reminded everyone that they had escort missions to tend to in the morning. Kiile rose with her and thanked Greg and Shara for a pleasant evening and followed her through the dining room. Greg escorted them to the back door and Shara turned down the hallway to their bedroom. Major Kooich and Leeana noted the morning would come sooner than they wanted it to and headed for their apartment.

When Cheral and Kiile stepped out onto the back porch, Cheral stopped and leaned close to Greg.

"Have you been watching Shara?" she asked softly in a guarded tone.

"In what way?" he asked.

"She seems to be having periods of dizziness and nausea," Cheral explained. "She excused herself three times during yesterday's mission, twice going and once coming back. Then again today, just after the debriefing."

"Yes," Greg said. "I've noticed. They seemed to have started nearly two weeks ago, but STSX says she's fine."

Cheral just looked at him, then shrugged. "I just wanted to mention it. I don't know if anyone else has noticed."

"Thanks," he said and squeezed her shoulder. "I'll keep watch."

⏶

After everyone had gone and Jill was back from visiting with Nick, she turned in herself. Greg and Shara settled into bed and Shara snuggled as close to Greg as she could, stretching out against his length and stroked his back, she absently ran her finger along the remains of the ragged scar just above his waist. She remembered the story of Corsecain and squeezed him tighter.

"You know yesterday took a lot out of you," Greg said softly as he returned her caresses.

"How so?" she asked and pressed her forehead against his chest.

"You fell asleep so fast this morning that I didn't get a chance to tell you how impressed I was with your flying."

"Well I'm not asleep now," she said and tilted her head back to kiss him.

"I see that," he said and tickled her lightly. "And I'm not very interested in yesterday's mission anymore."

"Me either," she said and kissed him again.

Friday, January 6

Wally followed Carol into her place, through the garage like he usually did and she closed the door behind them. He checked with his remote as he hung their coats on the pegs and WL-One assured him there were no voice transmitters placed anywhere on the house and no one was watching the house.

He smiled and hung his utility belt on a peg, slipped his pistol in the back of his slacks and stopped at the living room end of the short hallway beside the stairs.

"Is there anything I can get you?" he asked her slightly ajar bedroom door.

"One of the lagers, if you don't mind," she answered.

He went into the kitchen for the beer and was relaxing on the living room couch when she came out and joined him. As she settled beside him, she took a long sip from the bottle.

"Difficult day?" he asked, knowing last night had upset her more than she admitted.

"Just long," she sighed and reached across him to set the lager on the end table. "Things from last night just kept running around in my head. All day, it was one startling memory after another."

"I know how that is," he admitted.

"Did we really see Jill do what she said she did?" Carole looked at him, trying to understand. "A mind scan? How can she do that?"

Wally put his arm around her and pulled her close.

"Carole," he began, trying to figure out how to say what he wanted to say. "Remember when we were out at the facility they called Obscure, when I told you how some people have the ability to mentally read my POI tag?"

"Yeah," she admitted.

"That's what Jill did," he said softly. "Whatever Jill did, it was definitely done mentally."

Carole pulled away a little and looked at him. "How can that be?"

"I know it is hard to understand," Wally said, holding her eyes as he spoke. "The Marine said she was a Shadow and you saw his possessive expression, the pride in his realizing she had that capability."

"The capability to read something mentally?" she asked. "Next you'll tell me she can communicate and talk to others mentally."

"Yes, I think she can," Wally said. "I saw it done many years ago, and last night she was linked to someone, maybe getting instructions or setting up the scan. Didn't you notice the long periods of blank stares and her deep thinking when she closed her eyes?"

"Yeah," she admitted, "I saw that."

"When I came under the Force's custody many years ago," Wally continued, "I was told that mental communications was a trait, almost a prerequisite for a Shadow."

"And you think Jill has this ability?"

"I do after last night," Wally said with a knowing smile. "I certainly do."

"That means," Carole said, still studying his expression, "you think Greg and Shar have that ability also."

"Yes, I would have to say I do," Wally admitted and smiled at her.

"But, Shar's from here," Carole argued softly. "She's not from..."

"From where?" Wally asked. "Jill and Shar are both from here and Greg is from lower New York State, the same area that I'm from. They're normal people with extraordinary gifts and training. It's a bloodline thing, I think."

"And we sure don't know anything about their bloodlines," Carole remarked softly, thinking. "Why did they attack the ranch?

"Jill said they were trying to capture Shar and her," Wally said. "She said they wanted them removed so they would not interfere anymore."

"Interfere?" Carole asked. "Was she talking about when they captured the facility they call Obscure, or when they went after the man that shot you?"

"Maybe more than just those," Wally said. "Remember when we were taken to the ranch from Obscure, Greg and Major Kooich talked about their hidden, parallel existence, trying to restore the security of the valley? I think this Don Nikle and the chiefs of police are deeply involved and they see them, specifically those two, as threats."

"Maybe Five ought to be watching them," Carole said and squeezed him, "instead of watching you."

"From the way Jill and Nick responded," Wally said, "I think they are being adequately watched. "Someone tipped Jill off to the attack."

"Yeah," Carole admitted. "Like you said, 'extraordinary gifts and training.'"

Wally pulled her back to him. "With all of the daily stress and suspense and all of this impressive, high caliber talent floating around our little corner of the world, I just hope you can be happy with a simple, no-account, common, law-enforcement marshal."

"Very," she said and looked into his face. "And I don't think you are no-account or common, and you certainly are not simple." She kissed him fully.

When she relaxed in his arms, with her legs curled beside him, she was thinking. "You know, having that capability would answer a lot of questions when you think about how they handle the remotes."

"How so?" Wally asked.

"When Jill came to Hap's to get me," Carole said, remembering, "when you were shot. She didn't say a word to the remote we were on, but I could hear Nick talking to his remote, even though I couldn't figure out where he was to what he was doing."

Wally nodded, smiling and said, "Enough speculation. I had a few other things I wanted to talk to you about before the night gets away from us."

"Fair enough," she said and snuggled closer. "I guess I'll just listen to what you have to say."

Ninety-Six

Thom threw on his jacket and smiled at Wally as he left their office and started across the parking lot. He crossed Main and entered Connie's Deli to pick up the to-go order he had called in. He planned to grab the order and eat during his rounds, but when he entered and stopped to remove his cap and gloves, he saw Eddie at a table along the wall near the back of the large dining area. He made his way around and through the congestion of small tables and patrons to the pickup counter and the young woman at the cashier's station looked up.

"Order for Deputy Baine," he said softly when she was ready for him.

"Your usual sandwich, homemade chips and a medium dark roast coffee," she said and rang up his total.

He paid, collected the sack and stepped aside so the next in line could pick up their order. When he had put his card away, he walked over to Eddie's table and stopped.

"May I speak to you a minute?" he asked.

She looked up from the paper she was reading and smiled. "Sure."

Thom sat down in the chair opposite her and set his sack on the table. "I was wondering how your mother is doing," he said softly, not wishing his voice to be heard by others.

"About the same," Eddie said. She folded the paper and tucked it under the edge of her plate. "The doctors don't give her much longer."

"I'm sorry, Eddie," Thom said, looking at her. "I would have spared you and asked at the care facility, but I'm not family and unless there is a criminal need, they won't, and shouldn't, give out information on their patients."

She nodded. "Thanks for asking," she said with a weak smile. "Not many people do."

"I know I'm not much of a comfort for you," he said and glanced at the table, "but I am a good listener if you ever need or want to talk

145

about things, or even just want to get away for a while."

"Thanks," she said and watched him, "but I—"

"I know," he said. "Just saying."

Again, she nodded and looked away.

"I also wanted you to know that I received a short message this morning," he continued. He kept his stance the same and did not lean in to converse, being careful to not make her feel he was intruding. "I sent that list of sixteen names I told you about, to some undercover connections that we have. And the message was a reply saying that the list had been received."

"Received?" Eddie asked, "I don't understand."

"An undercover agent inside the mining company that I told you about," Thom said, glancing around to see if anyone was close enough to hear him, "has replied that he has received the list. It means he has the list in hand and will try to find out more about the names, where they went or where they are, what their status is, anything he can find out."

"Really?" she asked, disbelief still coloring her eyes. "Someone is actually checking?"

"Yes," he said, "but don't get your hopes up. He might not be able to find out anything, or he might be discovered searching."

"Discovered?" she asked, her tone falling in concern. "What will happen if he's discovered?"

"We won't hear anything more," Thom said, looking down at his folded hands in his lap. "He'll be terminated for spying."

She involuntarily covered her mouth. "Terminated," she repeated in a whisper. "I didn't realize your asking would put someone in that kind of danger."

"I know," he said with a tight smile. "But that's why the agents are placed where they are, to find out what certain organizations want to keep secret."

She studied her plate for a long moment. "Thank you, Thom. I know this sounds like you could be making this up, but I believe you. And thank you for your friend and my sincere hope that he doesn't get discovered, for any reason."

"You're welcome, Eddie," he said and smiled warmly. "I wanted you to know when I found out." He picked up his cap and gloves and then collected his sack and checked to see if the coffee was still warm.

"Thom?" Eddie asked as he turned to leave. "Are you going out on your rounds?"

"Yes," he replied.

"Could I... ride along?" she asked. "Just to get away for a little while?"

"Certainly," he said after he mastered his surprise, "but you'll have to stay in the car if I have to take care of anything."

"Deal," she said and got up, put her coat on and put the folded paper in her shoulder bag. She dumped her plate and napkin in the trash and said, "Ready when you are."

⅄ ⅄ ⅄ ⅄ ⅄

Marine Twenty-two raised his hand and the eight remotes slowed to a silent stop. Twenty-two stepped down off the stirrup and began probing the ground. A second Marine stepped down off his remote and began checking the ground a few feet farther southeast of Twenty-two. The whistle of the probe identifying something just below the surface stopped the search and the Marine looked at Twenty-two.

"We have something, sir," he said and dropped to the ground as he unfolded a small utility shovel. A few quick strokes and he smiled at a square, metal hatch buried under a foot of snow and a few inches of dirt.

Twenty-two turned to Thirty-one, still poised beneath his remote. "The next service hatch is supposed to be nearly six miles farther down tunnel, but I think we should consider making a new entrance about a hundred yards down, maybe less. Take a look at the ground structure and see if it looks like there is a suitable site for a new entrance."

"Yes sir," Thirty-one said, and motioned to three others waiting on their remotes to follow him as he slowly drifted away, following the indications on his handheld ground penetrating sensor.

"Let's see what we have found," Twenty-two said and turned back to the kneeling Marine clearing the last of the dirt off the hatch. The third and fourth Marine dismounted and joined the two of them.

"Hinged, but no obvious lock," the second Marine said as he unfolded the handle and stood to straddle the hatch.

"Wait!" Twenty-two said and flipped his digital notepad open. "USL15 said something about a detector circuit they found when they went searching down by Hawthorne. Aah, there's his note."

Twenty-two read the short item and then knelt at the hinge side of the hatch. He brushed the dirt away and uncovered a small covered sensor.

"Carefully remove the cover," he said to a Marine standing beside him, "and short the contacts where the wires go into the structure. It appears to be a magnetic switch that opens when the hatch is lifted and rotated open. A broken wire will give the same indication as opening the hatch and someone will come to investigate."

"Do you think anyone is watching for an indication?" the fourth Marine asked.

"Probably not continuously," Twenty-two said, "but if an indication is illuminated someone will see it sometime and will know this access point has been violated or at least investigated. And I don't want to be the one that lets them know,"

"Yes sir," the Marine said.

"Another thing to keep in mind," Twenty-two said, "is that all of the interlopers have come above ground, which means those that sent them know this tunnel is blocked, or they do not know about the tunnel."

"Okay, open it," the Marine bent over the sensor said as he straightened up.

Twenty-two stepped in and helped the Marine bending over the handle. Together, they slowly lifted the hatch and swung it open. The fourth Marine pointed his hand lamp into the dark opening and noting the descending series of rungs cast into the side wall of the shaft, stepped in and started down. The third Marine followed quickly.

Twenty-two went third and the last Marine crouched beside the open hatch and kept watch of the area around them. He set his remote to orbit around his position with visual, infrared and mass sensing on.

▲

At the bottom of the tall shaft, the first two Marines stepped forward, side-by-side in the wider chamber and Twenty-two stepped up behind them as they slowly moved toward the blackness of the tunnel passing just ahead of them.

"Only enough room for three or four men and that work trolley," the Marine on the right said and he shone his lamp around the small chamber.

"Looks like it'll do nicely," Twenty-two said softly. "We can install a gate to keep a car from continuing toward Obscure and set a shift of two here to meet anyone coming." He looked into the dark tube as it disappeared to the southeast, and continued. "If the second group is happy with the ground and rock composition, we can fabricate another entry, like this one, just a hundred yards down tunnel to stop any attempts at a retreat."

"Maybe we could find out how long a car is," the Marine on his left said, "and expand this access point to trap a car here, before it can start back."

"I think I like doing both," Twenty-two said as he turned and looked at the work trolley. Something was nagging at his mind and he knelt down to study the manner of its construction. "Nineteen?" he asked absently, "could we secure a remote to one of these, or something like it, to travel in the tunnel?"

The Marine turned and followed Twenty-two's gaze. "Yes sir," he said, smiling. "I think we could, and we'd have independent power and armament."

"Can we get the trolley out through the hatch?" Twenty-two asked, glancing back to the vertical shaft.

The Marine made a few quick measurements, then said, "No sir. But we can run it up the tunnel to Obscure, as soon as they have the collapsed section cleared and the tube resurfaced."

"Very good," Twenty-two said. "Gentlemen, I think we have a plan."

Twenty-two led the way back to the surface and quietly surveyed the surroundings as he stood beside the Marine on guard. "Any signs of surveillance or activity?"

"None sir," the Marine said without rising.

"USL15," Twenty-two said softly as he touched his ear. "Release a surveillance remote to stand guard over the entrance we have uncovered. The squad is returning with a plan."

"Understood, Twenty-two," Kiile's voice answered. "Remote M-Twenty-six is on its way."

149

▲ ▲ ▲ ▲ ▲

Greg, Shara and Jill had just finished an afternoon with the horses, cleaning their stalls, water and feed buckets, checking their hooves and shoes and a full brushing of each. Greg knew these tasks were usually done by Hank and the hands, but with the break in the weather Hank had taken Tommy and Bobby out to check fences and the lower pastures for fallen trees or other debris that should be repaired or removed. And Shar enjoyed her time with the horses and took her time getting into the rhythm and details of the chores. Jill, on the other hand, was quite willing to let Shara do as much of them as she wanted.

When they had finished replenishing the feed and water for the eight horses, Shara had finally called an end to the day and led the group back to the main house. She checked the time as they entered and hung their coats on the pegs in the coat room, and asked Jill if she wanted coffee or tea, or something stronger.

"Do you have any rum around?' she asked as she slipped her boots off. "I haven't had a Cuba Libre in a long time."

"We do," Shara replied and stepped to the kitchen. "Greg? What would you like?"

"Tea, I think," he said and headed for the living room.

He sat down in his customary overstuffed chair and half turned to watch the fire. Jill sat down across from him on the loveseat and curled her legs up under herself.

Shara was half way to the living room when Matti darted through the dining room and opened the back door.

"Come in, come in," she said and led Kiile and Nick into the house.

"Afternoon, Matti," Kiile said, smiling at the girl as he followed her through the dining room and stopped in front of Shara.

"Can I get you two anything to drink?" Matti asked, then looked at Nick. "Are you able to have anything substantial?"

"Medical says I am fine," Nick said with a smile as Jill got up and stepped up beside him, hooking her arm through his. "I'd love a scotch with a splash, Matti. I haven't gotten to celebrate defending the home front yet."

Kiile settled for a beer and Matti hurried off to the kitchen as they found their way into the living room. Greg sat back down and Shara joined him with a sincere hug. Nick took the end of the loveseat and Jill curled up next to him and Kiile took the near end of the long couch.

"I'm still mad at you," Jill said with a gentle poke at Nick's shoulder.

"For heaven's sakes, what for?" Nick asked in complete surprise.

"For getting yourself shot," she admitted, "again, and after I expressly told you not to."

"Oh?" he questioned as he slipped his arm around behind her, looking at Greg with a completely puzzled expression. "And I don't get credit for keeping those two coming around the house from joining the party?"

He squeezed her and she hugged him in return. "Yes, you get credit for those two."

"Since Medical didn't need to keep him," Kiile said, "I figured he ought to be back here. You fed him up to fightin' weight quick enough last time, so I figured the sooner you got started, the sooner he'd get his strength back."

He glanced up as Matti arrived with a tray of drinks and Cara with another tray with two cups and a carafe of tea. Once they finished serving, Matti stopped beside the couch, holding the tray in front of her and asked if there was anything else they needed.

"Thanks, Matti, Cara," Shara said. "I think we're all right for now."

Kiile watched absently as the two went back to the kitchen before he started again. "A small squad of my marines went down along the tunnel heading off toward Clay this afternoon."

Shara hesitated as she poured a cup of tea for Greg and noticed Jill's intense interest.

"About four miles from Obscure, they opened a maintenance hatch and checked out a small work area beside the tunnel. Twenty-two says it is large enough to set up a security point and install a gate to keep anyone from coming into the facility unannounced."

"Really?" Jill said softly. "So it was a good idea."

"Yes, ma'am," Kiile agreed. "They looked the area over and devised a plan to enlarge the work room in length. They want to make it long enough to trap and hold a tunnel car coming to the gate, and house more than a one-man security detail."

Greg nodded with a pleased smile.

"Secondly," Kiile continued, "they presented a plan to add a new entry point 50 yards down tunnel where they found a crossing that branched off to the south and to the north. Those tunnels weren't on Major Kooich's map."

"Wow," Jill said in an almost inaudible whisper.

"I approved their concept and they have set up cloaking and a shield generator," Kiile said with a smile as he sipped his beer. "They've already started excavating."

"Do you expect to see traffic coming up the tunnel?" Nick asked.

"Yes," Kiile said. "Hopefully, just ours and not theirs. Twenty-two and one of his men figured out how they can modify a work trolley they found and secure a remote to it. That'll give them fast, reliable and armed transportation up and down the tunnel complex."

"Very nice," Greg said as he sipped his cup. "And, if you can secure possession of the properties served in Clay, Hawthorne and Grants, maybe we can effect some changes in how the southern folks get along with the northern folks."

"Yes, Colonel," Kiile said softly. "My thoughts, exactly."

"Are there any other tunnels that we don't know about?" Jill asked, then smiled as she realized what she had asked. "Sorry. You know what I mean."

"Maybe," Kiile chuckled, "but as soon as the security check-point is in place and the armed sled is working, we'll search for those that we don't know about." He turned to Greg, "but the tunnel that runs north from the crossing probably comes to somewhere in Riggin. Our penetrating scans don't go deep enough to see under those hills. I need one of the ships to map north of the junction to see where it goes."

"So," Shara asked, "you think they may have a connection to Harry or Brian's place?"

"Maybe," Kiile said, again. "At least, a connection to somewhere in the upper valley, here in town or up towards the old mill. Hard to tell at the moment, but I think we will make more than one sled for searching and security. Or we figure out how to power up that spare tunnel car we found at Obscure."

"Both are probably good ideas," Greg said and raised his cup in a toast.

Kiile raised his beer in response.

Saturday, January 7

Greg woke with Shara's stirring and tossing. She got up and he felt her nausea as she knelt and vomited in the bathroom. She was only gone for a couple of moments, but once back in bed she could not relax. He tried to comfort her, putting his arm around her, but it did not seem to help.

After another half an hour, he felt her sudden spasm and she threw the covers back and darted into the bathroom again. He waited patiently, but she did not return. He felt the turmoil in her mind, but she kept the content tightly contained. After another few minutes, he got up and put his robe on, picked up her robe from where it had fallen beside the bed and took it to her.

She was shaking in the cold, hunched over the stool, still spitting out phlegm and reluctant bits of the evening's meal. He gently dropped her robe over her bare shoulders and tucked it around her as he knelt beside her. He held her tight. After a few minutes, her trembling subsided and he got up and filled a cup at the sink. She sipped some and rinsed her mouth.

When she looked up, he could see in the dim light that tears were streaking her cheeks and her expression was full of sorrow. He pulled her to him and held her until her soft sobs abated.

"Bren, love," he whispered to her, "please tell me what's wrong. What can I do to help?"

"No," she whispered softly, pressing her face tightly against his shoulder. "I can't."

He forced himself to patience, and not rise to the anger he knew was lurking in his mind, tenuously held at bay. Her silence and separation was slowly gnawing away at his ability, and desire, to remain calm and compassionate. He had never felt like he was feeling now. When he had thought he had lost her six years ago, he simply felt despair and defeat, both very foreign feelings for him. But that was nothing compared to the anguish he felt at being cut off from her thoughts, her spirit, her continual touch, purposely pushed aside. Now their connection seemed lost, her support simply physical, and he felt helpless.

"Bren," he said a little firmer than he intended. "You have to tell me what's wrong, what's going on."

"No!" she said sharply and hurried out of the bedroom.

He got up slowly and felt her in the living room and then he followed. She was setting in their chair when he found her. He went to the fire, stirred the embers and added two small logs to the pile. Then he turned and scooped her up from the chair and sat down with her on his lap so she could see the fire.

He said nothing and watched the fire with her, holding her close and as tight as he dared. Time slipped by as invisible as a shadow in the night, unacknowledged other than the knowing that it was passing. The embers had ignited the logs and the dancing flames made the room twitch and flicker. Finally he whispered to her.

"I hope you know I love you more than anything. I care a great deal about you and I want you to be happy and confident. I want you to trust me and know that I am always here for you."

He waited and watched the fire for many minutes before she whispered back, "I know. I love you more than anything too."

He kissed her forehead as she stared at the fire and the minutes fled, snowflakes disappearing in the night on a strong north wind.

"You know," he said softly, "someone told me once that I could tell her anything, and I wouldn't lose her. Just so you know, I feel the same way, Bren."

He felt her shake and heard her soft sobs. "I know," she whispered between breaths. "But I just can't."

"I'm here when you feel like you can," he said, "but I think you know that as long as this condition continues, you're going to have to fly in the back."

She jerked her head up and glared at him. "I can fly," she said in a hoarse voice as she coughed at the congestion in her throat.

"I know you can," he said firmly, "but if you have a dizzy or nauseous spell in combat, you will put us all in danger, even our wingmen. You can't just unbuckle and float to the necessary during an engagement, Bren."

Slowly her eyes filled with tears again and she threw her arm around his shoulder and buried her face against his neck. "You're right," she whispered, "but please don't ground me. Please don't. We're a team and I have to do my part. Please don't ground me."

Sunday, January 8

TTYF8 and Apache Patrol Four were already joined when Stran settled STSX in a low hover. They stopped and watched as KKLC14 and Apache Patrol Three joined up.

"Apache Patrol Two," Stran said, "STSX1 is ready to receive you."

"Apache Patrol Two is ready, Colonel," Cheral said as she slowly guided the patrol fighter under STSX.

'Eight is coming to bring you aboard,' Casi said to Cheral as the magnetic stays engaged.

After a few minutes, Cheral exited the belly hatch and mounted Eight. She reclosed the hatch and drifted up to STSX's aft portal and again stowed her helmet in the equipment bay. At the top of the ladder she turned forward.

"Mind if I ride in the jumpseat again?" she asked.

"Not at all," Stran said and unfolded it for her.

"Morning Cousin," she added as she turned and strapped herself in.

"Morning," Casi greeted with a wave and then turned back to the consoles. "Launch status, please."

She heard the ships call in one by one and realized the whole squadron was going except MKCC5. She knew Major Kooich had to leave someone to watch over the space station and the valley, and Colbee had done well on the last mission, so it wasn't unexpected when they were asked to stay behind. JCCV4 was not actually part of the squadron and was still under repairs, but she knew Major Bids and Emly wished they were going.

'Jill?' Casi called. *'MKCC5 is the Q-Ship that will be here while we're gone. Call Major Romaan or Lieutenant Colbee if you need their help.'*

'Thanks,' Jill answered. *'I'll remember. I hope this time it will be nice and quiet around here.'*

'Me too,' Casi said. *'We'll see you late tonight.'*

"Colonel," Leeana's voice said, "Apache Fighter Wing, Apache Wing Leader and Apache Patrol Three are ready."

"Apache Leader and Apache Patrol Two are ready," Casi said to the Wing. Then to Stran, "The Wing is ready."

"Apache Wing," Stran said, "Proceed to the outbound fix. Cloaking on, sensor blocked and shields full, please."

Casi did not turn around when she felt Stran add thrust and pull STSX's nose up. It was just after three a.m. and she knew without looking that it was deep night and very few lights were on to see. They quickly broke into the clear, starry morning sky and though she could not see the formation from where she sat, she could feel their positions and noted the small amount of jockeying they each did as they climbed out of the atmosphere. She felt the space station to the east on its northward swing over the eastern portion of the country as Stran leveled STSX and they closed on the outbound fix coordinates.

"Outbound fix achieved," Leeana said. "The Wing is ready for the jump."

"Rendezvous Bravo-Bravo-Charley coordinates loaded and ready," Casi said.

"Apache Wing," Stran said. "Coordinates Bravo-Bravo-Charley. On my Mark all ships match speed with STSX1."

"Will do," Leeana answered.

"Mark."

Casi leaned back and stretched her arms high over her head, feeling the reassurance in STSX's strong acceleration.

'STSX, call me if the scanner sees anyone looking for us. I'll be below for a few minutes,' Casi said as she unbuckled and drifted to the opening in the floor. She drifted down without Cheral turning to see her, but she knew Stran knew where she was. She tried to keep her stay in the necessary short, but this morning was almost as bad as last night, except the cramps were more severe.

Finally, she forced herself to straighten, cleaned up and drifted into the galley and fixed herself a container of tea.

"Do either of you want some tea?" she asked as hers warmed. "Or one of Annie's sweet rolls?"

"Sure," Cheral said. "Stran says yes also."

Suddenly she felt irritated. Cheral knew she knew what Greg said or thought, but she forced herself to calm. Cheral was just being her normal pleasant self and she wondered if her 'condition' was affecting her tolerance and temperament.

'STSX,' she said with her mind tightly focused, '*is this irrational irritation normal?*'

'*YES. MEDICAL SAYS IT WILL COME AND GO AND OCCASIONALLY GET WORSE.*'

'*Thanks,*' she said, trying to hide her sarcasm.

'*YOU MUST TELL THE COLONEL.*'

'*No! You know I can't.*'

'*I DO NOT KNOW THAT.*'

'*You know he'll hate me for letting it happen. He'll ground me and I won't be able to help.*'

'*I DO NOT KNOW THAT, EITHER. GROUNDING WILL COME ANYWAY. IT WILL BE BETTER IF HE IS NOT ANGRY AT YOU FOR KEEPING IT A SECRET.*'

'*He'll hate me when I tell him what I've done.*'

'*HE WILL BE HAPPY FOR BOTH OF YOU. YOU ARE CHOOSING TO IGNORE HOW HE REALLY FEELS ABOUT YOU. YOU MUST STOP BLAMING YOURSELF FOR DOING SOMETHING THAT IS NATURAL.*'

'*I can't, STSX. I can't. I've betrayed him. How can I expect him to be happy with me, to forgive me?*'

The warmer chimed.

'*YOUR TEA IS READY. THINK ABOUT HOW BAD IT WILL BE IF HE HAS TO FIND OUT FROM SOMEONE ELSE. HE TRUSTS YOU WITH HIS VERY LIFE. YOU HAVE NOT BETRAYED HIM. NOT YET.*'

STSX's words stung her like a bee. She took her canister from the receptacle and placed another into the depression. As it warmed, she stared at the cabinet. Greg would feel very betrayed if he found out from someone else, and she knew that would happen. *Too many people already suspect, Coleen, Matti. Who else?* she asked herself. *People at Obscure may have noticed already, Cheral or any of the nav-coms. Shit!*

She was putting the third canister into the warmer slot and turned in start when Stran stopped in the portal. He stood there and watched her as she fidgeted, turning from the warmer to him and back again.

"Give me one of the canisters," he said softly, "then go back and sit down. I'll join you in a minute."

157

He took the canister up to Cheral and Shara had barely buckled into the aft doublewide chair when he returned. Casi pointed to the other chair and he sat down and buckled himself in. He waited, watching her as she opened her container and sipped the tea through the straw, but he did not say anything. A long, uncomfortable moment passed.

"I owe you a very big apology," she started, stumbling over the words as she tried to put her thoughts together. "I have compromised my ability to support you like you expect me to." She sighed and sipped the tea again. "There will come a time, not too far away, I will have to ground myself and I will no longer be able to go with you on your missions."

"What are you saying?" he asked, stunned. "STSX says you're in good health, that you're not ill. How—?"

She held her hand up. "I've caused a situation, a lapse in judgment on my part that will affect us both for the rest of our lives. It was an accident, but I'm to blame for letting it happen." Her eyes began to fill again and her lips trembled. "And I know you'll hate me for it, but STSX has been after me to tell you, so you won't find out from someone else, so you won't—"

"From someone else? Someone else knows?" he asked, holding onto his temper with everything he had.

"No," she said, staring at him, realizing the hurt she was causing him. "But some may suspect, and soon they'll know."

"Know what?" he asked in a much softer tone. He unbuckled and moved to the chair with her, buckling her lap belt around both of them. "Sorry, but I'm not going to sit across the room and discuss this. What will they know?"

"Greg," she turned to face him, tears filling her eyes. "Oh, Greg. I'm so sorry to have done this to you."

"Done what, love?"

She buried her face against his shoulder. "Greg, I'm... pregnant."

He squeezed her shoulders and stared at the sleeping couch across the aisle, a smile slowly spread across his face.

"Are you sure, Bren?" he asked in a whisper.

"Yes," she said between sobs. "I shouldn't have let it happen, but when you came home and asked me to marry you, I forgot about everything else. I forgot to take Medical's contraceptive potion and...

and..."

He thought a moment, then said, "So you're almost eight weeks. That explains a lot."

She looked up at his cryptic comment and stared at his wide smile.

"Didn't you hear what I said?" she asked as she watched him intently.

"Yes, I most certainly did," he said and squeezed her again. "I hope you're not kidding me."

"Kidding? How can you think I'd kid about something so—"

He smothered her words with a full and firm kiss and he held her until she began to respond. *'I think you're amazing! I think this is amazing!'*

"Are you crazy?" she asked as she pulled herself back to look at him. "I won't be able to do any of the things we do now, any of the things you expect of me, any of the—"

He kissed her again. *'Stop,'* he said. *'Why can't you fly? Why can't you do the things we've trained to do? The nausea will pass, probably be completely gone in another couple of weeks. The only limitation after that might be the fit of your flight suit, but I can get that fixed, and you'll probably have to stop the hand-to-hand combat for a while.'*

She stared at him, disbelieving her eyes and ears.

"I... thought you'd hate me for letting it happen, for changing our lives forever," she said and glanced away. "You had no say in it and I've trapped you into a future that you didn't choose. I... knew you'd hate me—"

"Bren, love," he said softly and squeezed her again, "I was so worried that something was really wrong, an illness or something, and you wouldn't let me take care of you, you wouldn't talk to me. When you closed your mind to me, you about killed me. I'm lost without your touch, your spirit, without 'you.' Don't you know that yet?"

Slowly, she nodded.

"And to build a life and a family with you," he continued, "is the greatest thing we can do together. Yes things will be different, especially after our child is born, but we'll figure it out."

"But what about our missions?" she asked, a little bewildered. "I won't be able to go with you and raise a child at the same time. We won't be a team anymore. I won't be there to help—"

"Missions change, Bren," he said. "And we'll always be a team. We'll do what we're trained to do as long as we can. When it's time, we'll figure out our next step. The director is already criticizing his campaign commander for flying dangerous combat missions. We'll figure it out, Bren, together. Maybe we'll do less combat and more training and more managing. We'll figure it out."

He wiped her eyes dry and then opened his container and drank his tepid tea.

"Whatever we do, we'll do it together, Bren. Don't ever forget," he said, "I'm in love with 'you' and I'm always here for 'you,' and now I'm here for 'us.'"

She turned and wrapped her arms around him and held him very tight.

Ninety-Seven
C.3482.392

The slightly hunched, middle aged clerk, known locally as Technician Kilp, shuffled down the dimly lit corridor and carefully carried his hot canister of tea back to his data entry terminal. He turned at the correct opening in the shoulder high wall, stopped at the third and last terminal folded out from the wall cabinet and set his canister in the thermal receptacle to the left of his input board.

With a soft sigh, he settled into the cushioned chair and waited for it to readjust to his seated form. He sipped his tea and then reentered his access codes to log back into the system. After a moment, the large, high definition screen blinked back to life and the lists of arrival data for the various mining colonies and support facilities filled the right half; the list of requests filled the left half. He slowly selected the requests for the first facility, matched it with an entry from the arrival list. He carefully worked down the facility's list, matching the supplies to the requests in an orderly progression, basing his choices on the many specifications listed for each. When he finished the first facility, he continued with the next, providing a verification of the need for the articles requested and identifying any unfilled requests. Those he simply shifted to a backorder file and continued with the next line on the list.

After a par or more of tagging and verifying, he glanced at the time icon in corner of his screen. It indicated he had ten centipars left to his shift and he closed his activity screen, selecting the main database menu screen. It blinked into focus and he keyed a request for data on sixteen specific names he had received and waited for the database search to complete.

One at a time, each name came up on the screen and he read the specifics, identification processing code, date of arrival, destination, transfer status if any, work record, current placement and so on. When he finished reading the display and had committed the details to memory, he keyed for the next.

After reading and memorizing the last file, he entered a note to

161

'Database Maintenance' that the 'Thirty Turn Verification' search was successful and complete. Then checking the time icon, he saw that he had a couple of millipars to the end of his shift. When the time display reached the appropriate number, he logged off and terminated his session on the terminal.

As he did every day, he then gathered his drinking canister, thermal receptacle, his entry stylus and the time chip verifying his time on station and log in. In his usual appearance of absently moving by habit, he dropped his personal items in a small carrysack as he got up and pushed his cushioned chair under the input panel's shelf, turned and slowly shuffled out into the long corridor toward the facility exit.

If anyone watched him, they would see that he followed his usual routine as he stopped at the small eatery on the busy artery just beyond the extent of the facility building and ate a quiet dinner. From there he would walk the short distance to the company provided lodging where he would retire, watch one of the many company provided entertainment video channels or quietly read a digital selection from the company sponsored library.

No one ever really watched him, much less paid him any attention at all, but today might be different he told himself as he sat and ate his quiet dinner. He focused his mind and gently reached out. Between bites of the new dish he had spotted on the seldom changed menu, he slowly recalled each of the names that he had entered into his terminal and repeated the data from his nearly photographic memory. When he finished repeating the data on the last name searched, he sat quietly and ordered a delicate sweet he had recently discovered and savored it with a mild, nutty liqueur. He thought the comingling flavors were the perfect end to a long awaited for, perfect day.

Finished with his meal, he shuffled along the street toward the small three room dwelling the company had assigned him and listened to the bustling evening. Angrilat was a vast, sprawling city of industry and commercial businesses of every sort and it never actually slept. Shifts overlapped in all areas of business and the bustle of to and from traffic never diminished, day or night. But Technician Kilp was listening for something else.

As he entered the outer door to the building he dwelled in, he smiled. He sensed the two company security people waiting in one of the corridors he would pass and as he stopped to call the lift, one of them stepped forward.

"Technician Kilp?" the man with a security emblem on his sleeve asked.

"Sir?" he asked and looked up at the man.

"The Superintendent of Data Filing would like to speak with you," the man said.

"Now? I have finished my shift," Kilp said innocently.

"He asked to see you before the evening becomes too late," the man continued.

"All right," Kilp said and turned and began shuffling back toward the entrance.

"Come this way," the man said and pointed to a side door. "We have a conveyance waiting."

⅄

The two security men stopped at the superintendent's door as Kilp entered and waited inside the small anteroom. After a moment, the superintendent opened an inner door and asked them in. He gestured to a chair near his small desk and the security men stopped on either side of the door.

Kilp sat down as the superintendent settled into his own chair.

"Technician Kilp," the superintendent said. "I understand you did a database search today and sent a notification to the Database Maintenance people that it was successful."

"Yes," Kilp said without emotion.

"And why did you do a database search?" the super asked more directly.

"Revised Policies and Practices Manual," Kilp said, "requires a validation search be done every thirty standard turns to ensure the database integrity is maintained."

"It does?" the super asked in surprise, then continued when Kilp nodded, "And who authorized you to do the search?"

"Day Shift Leader Bitz," Kilp said, again without emotion. "When I asked him if we ever did a search like that, he said he never heard of one being done. I told him the revised manual required it be done by someone on his staff at the end of the normal work day every thirty standard turns."

The super looked at him and gestured for him to continue.

"Day Shift Leader Bitz suggested, that since I knew about it and

163

what was supposed to be done," Kilp explained, "that I should run the search and notify Database Maintenance when it was accomplished. He did warn me though, to wait unit I had time available and to not interrupt my logging and verification demands."

"Sensible of him," the super admitted. "When did you speak to him about this?"

"Four turns ago," Kilp said, making a show of thinking back to remember. "Today was the first time I had a few centipars available."

"And what did you search for?" the Super asked.

"A random date, three thousand, one hundred to two hundred turns past," Kilp said knowing the system did not record whether the search was by name or by date. "I figured a significant number of turns back would give a good test."

"I see. And what did you find?"

"The files of a few names came up and all of the data fields seemed to be filled in, nothing obvious was missing," Kilp said with a shrug. "It looked like the data was valid and not corrupted, so I notified Database Maintenance the search and validation was successful."

"I see," the Super said and turned his chair to one side and looked out of the window at the illuminated windows of the next building. Then he slowly turned his chair back to face him. "Tell me, how did you know the manual required the search?"

"Why sir?" Kilp said in mild surprise. "Your office notified every employee ten... or was it fifteen turns ago? ...that the Manual had been revised and you said you expected every employee to review the revisions and to be cognizant..., yes that was your word, cognizant of the changes. You allotted two pars each shift for up to four shifts for reviewing the Manual."

"And you read the Manual?"

"Why, yes sir," Kilp said confidently. "And you were right. There were a number of significant changes, including a number in the validity and security of the database section. Ah, Section 2466... or 69 or something like that, I do not remember exactly, changed the validation from every sixty standard turns to every thirty standard turns. Others were in the proper manner of logging on and logging off, and terminal security when one is on breaks, and there were some in—"

"I see," the super said with a sigh.

Kilp waited as the super sat quietly, thinking.

"Thank you, Technician Kilp," the superintendent said and rose from this chair. "I appreciate your diligence and your seriousness in the matters of you work. That will be all."

"Yes sir," Kilp said, got up and turned to the door. He stopped between the security men and turned back to the super, "Sir? If I may ask. Can these nice men take me back to my dwelling? It is late and a long walk back."

The super stared at him, surprised at such a request, then slowly smiled. "Yes, yes. One of them will take you back."

"Thank you sir," Kilp said and shuffled out of the office and into the corridor.

Sunday, January 8

"RENDEZVOUS WITH WATCHER, Q-RBSL10, IN EIGHT MINUTES. READY TO TRANSMIT IFF POSITION," STSX announced.

"Go to the long range scanner and see who might be around," Casi said as she studied a monitor on the nav-com console in front of her.

"TARGETS ARE INBOUND AND WILL BE WITHIN INTERCEPT RANGE IN NINETY-SIX TERRAN MINUTES. TARGETS CONSIST OF ONE CLASS XII FREIGHTER, TWO BATTLECRUISERS AND THIRTY ESCORT FIGHTERS IN PRESENT FORMATION."

"Send our IFF," Casi said and then turned to the Wing, "Apache Leader to Apache Wing. Begin deceleration for Rendezvous." Immediately, she felt STSX begin to reduce speed.

⅄

"Prepare for Apache patrol crew transfer," Casi announced to the Wing after they formed up with RBSL10. She turned as Stran swiveled the pilot's chair to aft facing and unbuckled.

"Bren," he said and motioned for her to come to him. "Watch over the Wing while I get Cheral aboard Apache Patrol Two."

Casi unbuckled and pushed herself forward into the central compartment. Stran caught her and kissed her before he dropped through the floor portal. Casi settled into the chair and checked

KKLC14 on her right and TTYF8 on her left, waiting while Stran suited up.

"Are the crews ready for transfer?" Casi asked.

"Apache Patrol Two is ready," Cheral confirmed.

"Apache Patrol Three is ready," Ani said.

"Apache Patrol Four is ready," Wilm said.

"Commence transfer," Casi said, and watched for the activity behind the two other Q-Ships.

Once again, the transfers took less than five minutes, including the time for the colonel and the two majors to get back aboard their ships. Casi waited for STSX to cycle the aft portal airlock and was about to inquire of the others when Leeana announced, "KKLC14, inside and secure."

"TTYF8, inside and secure," Franni announced.

"Inside and secure," Stran said as he drifted up through the floor portal.

"Thanks," Casi replied, "Apache Patrol, power up your ships."

When all three acknowledged they were up and waiting, Casi gave the order to disconnect and to power the repulsion pads off.

"Assume attack formation positions," Casi said as Stran settled into the right side jumpseat. Startled when he did not ask her to change places, she hesitated, then recomposed herself. "Intercept will commence in twenty-five terran minutes."

A strange expression crossed Stran's face and Casi questioned him.

"Get a *feel* of the battlecruisers, Bren," he said and closed his eyes.

"Strange," she admitted as she focused her mind on the sense of the two ships "A more intense sensation than other cruisers we've encountered."

"Remember it," Stran said seriously. "These are not converted freighters. They are designed and purpose built battlecruisers and... they are from the prince's Royal Naval fleet." Then Stran said, "STSX, put up the known information on the cruisers. Show Casi where the weapons control centers are and where the flight control centers are."

"Major Kooich," Stran continued, "Our two battlecruisers are Prince Kiese's own Kyddellan battlecruisers. STSX is passing the details across. Plan your strikes for quick penetration at the specified control centers."

"Thanks Colonel," the major replied. "We'll concentrate on them first. I'll distribute the ship details to the rest of the Wing."

"Casi?" Stran asked as he looked at her. "Are you up to this one?"

She grinned at Stran and pulled her headband out of its pouch. "Apache Wing, headbands on." Then to Stran she said, "Thank you, love."

He smiled and squeezed her arm before she turned the chair back to forward facing.

"Headbands on, Apache Wing is ready," Franni announced as she looked at the red flashes in the cockpits across the Wing.

🔺 🔺 🔺 🔺 🔺

Kiile heard the sentry's alert and had just reached the clearing south of the launch portal as Jill and Nick drifted to a stop and dismounted. Jill straightened her Blues as they both removed their head masks and put them in a pouch on their utility belts. She quickly patted her hair to catch the flighty, static possessed strays as Kiile walked up to them.

"Good morning," he greeted and shook Nick's hand, and then Jill's. "What brings you two out so early, and to this dull and dreary outpost?"

"Shar got us up early before they left," Jill explained, "and after a while we had to decide if we were going to go back to bed or come and see how the tunnel effort is coming."

"Aah," Kiile said, understanding Jill's motives. "And just what do you expect to see?"

"I'm just curious," she admitted. "But I really can't wait to see if you can find out who else is using the tunnels."

"I'm anxious to find that out also," Kiile said with a smile. "Have you eaten yet?"

"Yes," Jill said, "but we'll take coffee with you. Annie sent some of her sweet breads for you and for Twelve and Seventeen for helping the other night."

"No need to thank us for the helping," Kiile said as he turned and led the way inside through the portal hatchway. "But please thank

Annie for the sweet breads."

▲

Kiile led them to a table near the serving counter in the Mess and proceeded to get coffee for each of them while Jill and Nick seated themselves. She placed the tin with Annie's sweet bread on the table as Kiile set the mugs in front of them and sat down.

"Tell me, Jill," Kiile asked as he opened the tin and savored the aroma of the glazed breads and took one out. "You seem to have a deeper interest in the tunnels than you've been letting on."

"I do," she admitted. "When Rose and I went down with Deputy Baines to Clay and Hawthorne, it was pretty obvious the Family feelings are still alive and well in that part of the valley. My thinking is that the marshal and the deputies are not going to be able to keep watch on what's happening down there, or to be able to get the information they need to close the missing person's files if they are seen driving into town and asking questions."

"So you think," Kiile surmised, "they could use the tunnels to get into town and see what's going on?"

"Yes," she said. "I don't know what information they are looking for, but it would help them get access to the towns without their patrol cars giving them away."

"Well," Kiile said as he finished the first roll and took a sip of coffee. "I think I should talk with Wally and see if he also sees the tunnels as an asset. Yes, they might be of some help to him like you say."

"Thanks, Kiile," Jill said and glanced at Nick.

"When you finish your coffee," Kiile said and opened the tin again to check the count of sweet breads, "I'll take you down to see the new security outpost they're building."

"That'll be nice," Nick said as he looked around the room. "Sure is quiet with everyone away. Are Doug and Rose still coming out for instruction?"

"Tomorrow," Kiile said. "Three days a week. The session was shortened since you were out of commission after the attack, so the plan is to resume tomorrow."

"Good," Nick said with a tight smile, "after my performance during the attack, I think there must be something more I need to learn to keep my hide in one piece."

"Certainly, yes," Kiile said softly. "I think I need to have you four spend some time with Seventeen for some night training. There are some things he can certainly show you."

"Thanks Kiile," Nick said. "Name the time and place and we'll be ready."

⌃ ⌃ ⌃ ⌃ ⌃

"Apache Flight," Stran said as Casi started the flight forward. "Apache Patrols concentrate on the fighters. Stay cloaked and sensor blocked. Apache Wing Leader, assign your targets. Apache Leader will take the near side cruiser."

Major Kooich assigned RBSL10 and KCMM9 to stop the freighter, reminding them that the patrol cruisers *Brigstoan* and *Climatus* were waiting down course. TTYF8 was again teamed with STSX and LTVC21 was teamed with KKLC14 to take on the two cruisers, leaving LLRT12 and KVWC33 to hunt escorts along with the Apache patrol fighters.

"Remember, fire and move," Major Kooich said. "Make your shots count."

"STSX," Stran said as Casi led the formation on a converging course with the targets, "Has the Cruiser Brigstoan hailed the freighter?"

A quick moment passed and the Brigstoan commander's voice replied, "Apache Leader, begin your attack."

"Okay, STSX, run their diagnostic routines. Drop their veils." Then to the Wing, "Apache Squadron, commence."

Casi shoved the thrust levers forward and concentrated on the nearside cruiser. She felt the confusion in the ships when their veils 'failed' and noticed RBSL10 and KCMM9 as they changed their course slightly to intercept their freighter.

"TTYF8," Casi said as she confirmed their relative positions, "There are three weapons control centers. You take the one on the top side and we'll go for the two on the under belly. Controls will come second. Watch for fighters as they are launched."

"We're with you," Franni said. "I've got the top side center locked in."

Casi rolled STSX, again using the pylon to 'aim' at the underside of the cruiser as she came from behind. She noticed that TTYF8 was copying her methods as Franni lined up for her run. Casi smiled and then focused on the quickly approaching target. "Double volleys from all turrets, both targets."

When STSX released the first and second volley, Casi jinked up and to one side, fired a third and fourth volley and jinked again. She felt Franni's shots hit their mark and then fired another double series of her own to ensure the weapons control centers were destroyed.

"Go for the flight controls," Casi said, louder than she needed to, "between the forward and aft hangar bays."

As she rolled for a shot, she saw the flash of TTYF8's cannons and the explosion on the far side of the cruiser. "Fire through the launch bay," Casi said as she maneuvered. STSX's volley erupted inside the hangar bay and Casi jinked for another shot through the now gaping hole in the upper hull. As she moved from one alignment to another, STSX hit escort fighters that were within range.

Suddenly Casi felt new ships. "KKLC14, jink now! We have cloaked fighters!" Casi felt their presence and had STSX plot them for the other ships.

"I see it," Leeana said as she turned KKLC14. A quick volley and one of the sensations disappeared. "Thanks."

Another sensation disappeared and Lieutenant Debira whooped. In short order the remaining four sensations disappeared and Casi refocused on the slowly rolling cruiser.

"Keep some room, Franni," Casi said as they jinked around the cruiser, slowly cutting huge sections away from its mass. They filled the hangar bays repeatedly with cannon fire, catching nearly twenty fighters as they tried to launch and join their defense. When the cruiser finally began to break into pieces, Casi slowly let herself begin to relax, feeling the strain in her shoulders and abdomen. She focused on the major chunks as they separated from the ship and broke them into small, unrecognizable pieces of debris. She synchronized her attacks with Franni and worked the opposite side of the ship until the engine cluster erupted in one huge, defiant explosion. The fiery smoke cloud spread and quickly dissipated, leaving a silent void where the ship had been.

Casi felt for KKLC14 and saw the final explosion of the other cruiser. She turned and searched for other indications of continued engagements but saw none. "Wing status?" she asked.

"ALL ESCORT VESSELS HAVE BEEN DESTROYED. FIFTY-SEVEN ESCORT FIGHTERS DESTROYED IN FLIGHT, NINETEEN ESCORT FIGHTERS DESTROYED WHILE ATTEMPTING TO LAUNCH FROM THE FIRST BATTLE CRUISER AND TWENTY-TWO DESTROYED ATTEMPTING TO LAUNCH FROM THE SECOND BATTLE CRUISER. RBSL10 SUFFERED DAMAGE BY CANNON FIRE FROM THE FREIGHTER BEFORE KCMM9 DISABLED THEIR WEAPONS. FIVE ESCORT FIGHTERS WITH THE FREIGHTER WERE DESTROYED. PEACE FORCE PATROL CRUISERS *BRIGSTOAN* AND *CLIMATUS* HAVE TAKEN CONTROL OF THE FREIGHTER. APACHE PATROL TWO, THREE AND FOUR ARE SAFE AND UNDAMAGED AND HAVE ADDED KILLS TO THEIR TALLY. ALL OTHER SHIPS REPORT NO DAMAGE."

"Well, I'm glad everyone is okay," Casi said as she turned to look at Stran, "I really feel like we worked for this one. Those cruisers were a lot tougher than the converted freighters."

"More layers to get through," Stran said and smiled back at her. "Form up with the patrol cruisers and get Apache Patrol joined up. STSX, put those details into a message for the director."

🔺 🔺 🔺 🔺 🔺

Don Nikle saw Chief Parks' patrol car in the lot next to Charley's Bar and Grill as he approached on the narrow sidewalk along the highway just south of Hawthorne's town center. He rapped on the passenger's side glass to catch the chief's attention and slid in when the chief motioned for him to open the door.

"Afternoon Don," the chief said as Don closed the door. "What is going on? Your message was a bit cryptic."

"Afternoon. Go somewhere where we are not so easily seen."

Chief Parks drove south about a mile and took the street back to the west to the small park nestled in a quiet neighborhood.

"We may have a problem," Don said as the chief pulled into the parking lot and stopped under a large pine with bows reaching down, nearly to the top of the car.

"What sort of a problem?" the chief asked and turned in his seat to look at Don more easily.

"I am all that is left of the Council of Elders and only four of you on the Family Council are left," Don said as he put his thoughts together. "I am assuming that because all of the Elders, except for me, have disappeared is the reason why the four of you have not provided names for replacements."

"Now Don," the chief said defensively, "You know we have been trying to get people to agree to be considered."

"So I have been told."

"Everyone we have talked to have serious reservations," the chief explained. "Almost to the man, they all have said they see joining the Elders is a sure ticket to disappearing themselves."

Don thought about the chief's answer a long moment. "I think you and the Council know that I think Clea Smallwood's daughter and Jack Thomas' daughter have something to do with the judge's disappearance."

Chief Parks nodded. "Or the three or four others that were there at that time."

"And I am speculating," Don continued, "that they may have had something to do with Harry and Harold's disappearance. The best I can tell from what Chief Russell says, Harry Woods and Harold left Clay together the day they disappeared, so I am thinking they were together when they did disappear."

"It is possible," the chief said, "I suppose. But the new marshal was asking a lot of questions about that time, and he somehow took care of Pat's brother and the five other students that jumped him on Thanksgiving. And I understand, Pat shot the marshal twice and came up missing himself. I do not think that was the Smallwood and Thomas girl's doings."

"Yes, I suspect you are right," Don admitted, "but Wednesday night Dave Barns went to Riggin and the Smallwood Ranch to collect and bring the Smallwood woman and the Thomas woman to me for questioning. But he and twenty students seem to have disappeared instead."

"Where was the marshal when all of this happened?" the Chief asked.

"Abe and Ben said the two deputies were called out of town that evening," Don said, rubbing his chin as he thought, "A little after dark. They did not see the marshal."

"I think we need to get rid of the marshal and his deputies," the chief said. "I said so when he came down here snooping around."

"And like you were reminded then," Don said, catching the chief with a stern stare, "if they all are killed or simply disappear, the state will send a swarm of marshals and deputies in here to find out who is responsible. No, we do not want that, so we must think of some way to stop their investigations without removing them."

"Without removing them?" the chief asked in disbelief, "How?"

"I think I have a plan," Don said and turned to look at the chief with a wicked smile. "We simply need to nurture distrust of the new marshal and his new deputies. We just need to change the perceptions of the people and let them do the rest for us."

"I don't understand?" the chief asked.

"I'll explain later," Don said, "but right now, I need to get a little more information and start a few rumors."

Chief Parks smiled, "Okay. Tell me what I need to do."

Don's smile widened, "I'll have something for you soon."

⁂ ⁂ ⁂ ⁂ ⁂

From her pilot's chair, Casi monitored the recovery of the Apache patrol fighters and the transfer of the pilots back to their Q-Ships. When Stran drifted back up to the cockpit, he smiled at her as she unbuckled and pushed herself up.

"Cheral will be up in a few minutes, Bren," Stran said as he caught her and pulled her close. "You were absolutely wonderful," he said and then kissed her long and tenderly.

"Thanks," she said. "But I'm suddenly very tired. Would you mind flying the first part of the trip home?"

"Certainly, love," he said and kissed her again. "Why don't you go down and get something from the galley. You haven't eaten in four or five hours."

"That sounds good," she admitted, "then maybe a short nap." She smiled at him as he gently pushed her toward the floor portal.

"Come up when you wake up," he said and pushed himself to the pilot's chair. He waited for STSX to readjust the settings and then buckled himself in. "Apache Wing, status please," he said and listened to the responses as each ship called in ready for the return trip.

"Patrol Cruiser Brigstoan, Apache Squadron is departing. Our pleasure to be of service," he said.

"Many thanks," the Brigstoan commander responded. "It was very good to work with Apache Squadron again. Looking forward to working with you in the future. Safe trip home."

"Thank you. Apache Leader out." Then Stran switched to their ship-to-ship channel, "Apache Wing Leader, let's be off. Inbound fix."

"Inbound fix," Leeana replied. "Apache Wing has formed up. On your Mark, Apache Leader."

And with that, Stran pushed STSX's thrust levers forward and said "Mark."

▲

Casi drifted down and into the galley as Cheral came out of the necessary and saw her.

"Very good hunting," Cheral said as she stopped and watched Casi rummage through the various canisters of soups, broths and food pastes.

"You certainly did very well yourself," Casi said and smiled at Cheral. "And Franni has grown so much in capability. My word, I don't think I had to warn her about anything today."

"That's good," Cheral smiled, remembering pieces of the engagement. "But tell me, when did you see the cloaked fighters? I heard you, looked and suddenly they were on the scanner."

"That's when I saw them," Casi admitted. "I was so wrapped up in my part of the engagement that I almost missed them. I had just moved to a new firing position and there they were. One was almost on top of Leeana and I yelled. I thought they were going to collide."

"I'm sure glad you saw them."

"I think maybe Greg was right."

"Right? About what?"

"That I should do some of the fighting from the back seat," she said and stared at a canister in her hand. "I would've seen the cloaked fighters sooner, if I hadn't been flying and so focused."

"Well, that's always the dilemma," Cheral said. "You can never be in all of the right places at the same time. No one can."

"I know."

"But I will say, Cousin, you do manage to be in more of the right places more often than anyone I know. Thank you for that."

"Thanks," Casi said and Cheral turned and drifted up through the ceiling portal. Then Casi turned her attention to the labels on the canisters and began reading the contents. After a few frustrating minutes, she said *'STSX, what's in these? I don't recognize any of the names or the ingredients listed? How should I know what I will like or should be eating?'*

'MEDICAL SAYS YOU SHOULD TRY THE COMBASSA BEANS AND THE YARROL FRUITS, ONE CANISTER OF EACH. ADD A SWEETENER IF YOU FEEL THE NEED. THESE ARE HIGH IN THE NUTRIENTS AND MINERALS YOU NEED AT THIS TIME. DRINK ONE CANISTER OF THE SPICED TEA INSTEAD OF THE RATION TEA AND THEN SLEEP. RATION TEA WILL REFRESH YOU WHEN YOU WAKE.'

'Thanks,' she said and searched the canisters until she found the two foods Medical had recommended and then she found the Spiced Tea. She warmed all three and took them and a squeeze tube of sweetener to the forward facing doublewide chair and settled to eat. The bean paste was a delightful sensation to her dry mouth and she suddenly realized she was hungrier than she thought she was. The Yarrol fruit did need the sweetener, but the resulting delicate flavor enticed her to eat it all, and as she stowed the empty canisters in the trash bin, she realized the tension that had been knotting her stomach was all but gone.

She felt her stomach, slowly thinking about the new life that was growing within her. She had been so worried about what she thought Greg would say that she had not slowed down to think about the reality, a life slowly forming and growing from a blend of their two beings. She focused her mind inward, knowing it was entirely too soon in her term to sense it, but the thought made her smile. She knew it was happening, and one day soon she would *feel* it, she would *know* it, long before she gave it actual birth.

She unbuckled and drifted to their personal bunk and Medical's right hand couch, retrieved a pillow and the retention netting and secured herself. She stretched out and sipped the tea through the canister's straw and was fast asleep before she finished it.

Ninety-Eight

Monday, January 9

It was just after midnight when Greg carried a still sleeping Shara through the back door into the coat room, through the dining room, past a concerned Matti, Cara and Annie in their nightgowns and robes and down the hallway to their bedroom. After a few minutes, he returned and met Major Kooich and Matti and the girls in the dining room.

"She's fine, Matti," Greg said with a huge smile, nodding to each of them. "She was great today and just wore herself out. She ate about six hours ago and slept all the way back. Medical made sure she got a strong dose of restoratives."

Matti wrung her hands slowly and smiled. "Thank you Mr. Greg," she said and nodded to the major. "I'm glad she's all right. Breakfast at the regular time?"

"Yes, Matti," Greg said, "Thank you, and thank you for your unwavering support and for caring."

Matti smiled and slowly turned, ushering Cara and Annie back through the kitchen to their rooms.

"I know the cruisers were tougher," Major Kooich said, "but I didn't think it was that much harder. Are you sure she's alright?"

"Yes," Greg smiled. "She's fine, and I'll bet she'll wake hungrier than she has been in weeks. No nausea since the episode just after we left here. Medical thinks those should be declining."

Major Kooich looked at him with a curious stare. "Declining?"

"Yes, her appetite ought to start picking back up now."

"So she's getting over something?" Major Kooich was confused.

"No. Nothing like that, but I want Shara to explain when she's ready. Now Major, my extreme gratitude for your continued friendship and support, but I think I'm getting a little tired myself. We'll debrief midmorning. Good night and get a good night's rest yourself."

▲

Casi woke early, frisky and playful and tickled and kissed Greg awake, demanding to satisfy a hunger that had nothing to do with food. She felt alive and energetic, her anxiety and worry had disappeared. After a passionately lingering shower, they dressed for the morning and Shara led him to the dining room, looking to take the edge off her now urgent need for nourishment.

Matti greeted them with a carafe of coffee and a 'special' carafe of tea for Shara and a plate of Annie's glazed sweet breads.

"Glad to see you're feeling good this morning," Matti said as she set cups in front of them. "Mr. Greg said you would wake hungry. Breakfast will be just a few more minutes. Do you want to wait for the others?"

"Yes, Matti," Shara said as she grabbed a roll, "With a bit of Annie's breads, I can wait a little bit." Then she sat down and poured a cup of coffee for Greg and a cup of 'Matti's tea' for herself.

She and Greg chatted comfortably and had finished their second cup when Major Kooich and Leeana came through the back door with Nick close behind.

"My, but don't you look all aglow this morning," Leeana said to Shara as Hench pulled a chair out from the table for her.

"Morning," Nick said as he followed them in and closed the door.

They returned their greeting as Jill came out of the hallway and quickly searched for a cup to go with Greg's carafe.

"Morning to you too," Nick said as he caught Jill and gave her a quick kiss. She started to pull away in her pursuit of coffee, but stopped and responded to Nick's greeting, kissing him in return.

"Am I going to have this much trouble getting your attention every morning?" Nick asked as he turned her and pointed to the carafe.

"Maybe," Jill said absently as she grabbed the carafe and filled her cup.

Greg smiled at the major and Leeana through his chuckle as they sat down. Then he looked at Nick. "I think you'll have to spend a few minutes each morning getting Jill awake before she gets up."

He was still chuckling as Nick guided Jill into a chair and took the one beside her, nodding in agreement.

Matti stepped in and placed another plate of sweet breads on the

table and checked the carafe of coffee. "I'll bring another right out."
When she returned with another carafe, Cara followed her with a tray
of breakfast plates.

"I'm glad to see you're back among the living," Leeana said to
Shara and Jill stopped and looked at her. "I don't think I've ever seen
you as tired as you were last night."

"Sorry," Shara said meekly and took another sip of her juice. "I
don't remember getting home at all."

"What happened?" Jill asked, suddenly concerned. "Was it a bad
engagement?"

"No, I was just overtired, Jill," Shara said. "I fell asleep when we
started back and don't remember anything," and she smiled at Greg,
"until this morning."

"Medical helped," Greg admitted. "If he had arms and legs, I
would suspect he laced your tea or something."

Shara chuckled. "But he doesn't."

"No, he doesn't," Greg said with a knowing smile. "But he
prescribed a different tea and a different food selection, and I think he
knew they would relax you and let you sleep."

"Prescribed?" Jill asked. "Honestly, you're not making any sense at
all."

Shara ate heartily without answering and Jill finally conceded and
began eating. Leeana smiled at Greg with a questioning expression
and then looked at Shara. When Shara looked up and saw Leeana
watching her, she glanced around and noticed they were all watching
her.

"What?" she asked and washed a bite down with a gulp of tea.

"Nothing," Greg said with a broad smile. "Nothing at all, except I
don't think I've ever seen you this hungry."

She glanced at her empty plate and then at everyone else's,
realizing they were just starting to eat. "Sorry, I guess I was a bit
hungrier than usual."

Matti stepped in to check on the carafes just as Shara spoke
and stopped beside her with a startled expression. She also glanced
around the table and then looked at Greg with a slow, half smile.
"Mrs. Shara, would you like more?"

Leeana burst into laughter and nodded at Shara. "I certainly think
she does."

"Yes, ma'am. `Bout time," Matti said and quickly returned to the kitchen.

Leeana looked at Shara's blank, almost stunned look. "Well? Are you going to tell us?"

"Tell you what?"

"Don't," Leeana said. "I think some of us have it figured out. Weeks of no appetite and spells of nausea and dizziness, and I suspect a few cramps to go with them. Matti's been giving you different things to eat and drink, and now you're suddenly tiring easily and sleeping for twelve hours straight and waking with a ravenous appetite. Do I need to say more?"

Matti came in and set another plate in front of Shara and hearing the conversation she stepped back to wait.

Shara glanced around at each of their expectant faces and then at Greg's broad smile. *'They know, love. They just want you to admit it and let them share in the joy.'*

She glanced down at her plate, realizing she already had another bite stabbed on her fork, "Okay, okay." She focused her thoughts, *'Hey Cousin, Coleen, listen up.'* Then she looked up and smiled, took a deep breath and said, "Greg and I are going to have a little one. I'm..." she smiled at Greg, "pregnant."

▲ ▲ ▲ ▲ ▲

Major Kooich stood up beside the dais as Greg sat down. "I agree with the colonel that yesterday's engagement should definitely send a message to the prince himself. You all performed up to and beyond your potential and I must congratulate the new pilots. The director will most certainly be pleased with your accomplishments. As a side note, the Patrol Cruisers reported four hundred and thirty-seven captives released."

He smiled at the room. "And now, the tallies," he said and consulted his notepad.

"As in the past missions, the tallies are by pilot's name," he reiterated.

"Apache Patrol Two, Cadet Captain Haak is credited with fourteen additional kills for a personal total of thirty.

"Cadet Tigs in Apache Patrol Three is credited with twelve

additional kills for a personal total of twenty-two.

"Cadet Moss in Apache Patrol Four is credited with an additional six for a total of ten. Many thanks to our cadets."

He smiled at each of them and then continued, "Lieutenant Tam in KCMM9 while flying with RBSL10 in stopping the freighter and its cargo of captives is credited with five additional kills for a personal total of nine. I would also like to mention that RBSL10, though not officially part of Apache Squadron, is credited with one kill and did suffer minor damage from the freighter before KCMM9 could silence the freighter's cannons. Well done.

"Lieutenant Mri Bradg in LLRT12 is credited with her first ten.

"Lieutenant Meecia Miiles in KVWC33 is credited with her first eight.

"Lieutenant Debira Glean in LTVC21, paired with Lieutenant Leeana Kooich in KKLC14, is credited with her first five and another one half for her portion of the Kyddellan battlecruiser for a total of five and one half.

"Lieutenant Leeana Kooich is credited with seven and another one half for her portion of the same battlecruiser, bringing her total to thirteen and one half.

"Lieutenant Franni Kaal in TTYF8, paired with Lieutenant Casi Geaardt in STSX1, is credited with one half for her portion of a Kyddellan battlecruiser and an additional fourteen fighters for a personal total of twenty-six.

"Lieutenant Casi Geaardt in STSX1 is credited with the other half of the battlecruiser and an additional eighteen fighters for a personal total of one hundred and two."

Someone started clapping as soon as the major had finished reading the tallies and the room quickly stood and joined in, audibly congratulating each other and especially their co-commander and her incredible score.

Major Kooich held up his hand and slowly the room came back to order.

"My congratulations to each and every one of you," he said with a proud look at each of them. "And thanks to MKCC5 for defending the home front while we were away. You will be scheduled for the next mission. Refreshments are available in the Mess. Dismissed!"

▲ ▲ ▲ ▲ ▲

It was after seven when Eddie finally left the Hospital and drove down to Hap's, hoping Monday evenings would not be too noisy. She stopped at the convenience store across the street and bought a case of her favorite brews, deposited them on the floorboard of the back seat and then crossed the street and parked in Hap's back lot.

She was relieved that the ambiance was softer than normal and the music was mellow and not raucous. She settled into a booth to one side of the bar, piled her heavy coat against the wall beside her and scanned the digital menu.

"Hey, Eddie," Carole said as she stopped at the end of the booth. "Good to see you. What can I get you?"

She sighed without looking up, "Get me a double Black and White and a four cheese Queso appetizer with chips. Some hot peppers on the side. I'll decide if I want more after a bit."

"Sure," Carole said, recording her order in the hand held.

Mel fixed the drinks and Carole collected it when the Chili con Queso came up.

"Mel," Carole said as she passed the end of the bar, "I'm going to take a short break." Then she set the appetizer and drinks in front of Eddie and slid onto the empty bench. "You sound pretty down. Something you'd like to talk about?"

"No," she said sharply, then looked up at Carole and slowly softened her glare, "and yes." She sipped her drink and inhaled slowly. "It's mom. She was almost unresponsive tonight. Even the nurses are having a hard time keeping her attention when she's awake. If you can call her being awake when she has her eyes open."

"I'm sorry Eddie," Carole said and caught her hand. "I wish there was something I, we could do."

"Just being here helps," Eddie said and forced a smile. "I've spent so many years closing myself off from everything, everyone, I'd forgotten there are some that really care. I thank you for that." She nibbled on the Queso and peppers, thinking about her situation. "You know, I think I owe Thom for waking me up and making me see that I do have friends." She smiled.

"Wally mentioned you went with Thom on his rounds Friday,"

Carole said with a smile. "How did that go?"

"Wally knew?"

"Of course," Carole replied frankly. "Thom had to tell him he wasn't going to be alone. It's policy to know who and how many are in a patrol car at any given time."

Eddie nodded and forced herself to accept Carole's explanation.

"Don't worry, Wally hasn't gone talking about it," Carole said, "other than mentioning it to me. Like I said, we talk about what goes on but we don't spread it around. I don't spread around what friends tell me either."

Slowly Eddie relaxed and realized Carole was just making conversation, just between the two of them.

"I decided to do some checking on Thom," Eddie said as she pulled the folded sheet of paper out of her handbag, "after he ordered a bouquet for the Widow Banks."

"Checking, huh?"

"Did you know Thom's dad was a policeman in New York?" Eddie asked as she unfolded the sheet, "in the Queens actually. He walked a beat for most of his life, but he died just before Thom was born."

"That's probably why he went into police work," Carole surmised.

"He said it was," Eddie said, "when I asked him about it. He became an officer when he was eighteen."

"Is that why you went with him?"

"Yeah. When he saw me at lunch on Friday, he offered to listen," Eddie admitted, "if I ever wanted to just talk, or get away for a while and after the news he's given me, I wanted to talk some in private."

"News?" Carole asked, curious and Eddie realized she might not know. She remembered Thom had said he wouldn't tell anyone and if anyone did hear, it would not be from him.

"Since you and Wally talk about his work, I'm surprised you don't know," Eddie said and dipped her chip and added a pepper slice.

"We do talk about his work," Carole defended, "but he doesn't tell me everything."

Eddie leaned close and motioned for Carole to do the same. "Thom told me that he and Wally started a search and has proof my dad was taken from us. He didn't run off like we've thought all these years."

"Oh, Eddie," Carole said and squeezed her hand again. "I'd like to say that's great news, but I know he's still missing and that doesn't help your situation."

"But it does," she explained, "at least a little. So many questions I had growing up have vanished, knowing that we didn't do anything wrong, that we didn't cause him to not want us anymore. You can't imagine how guilty those questions can make a fourteen year old girl feel."

"No, I can't," Carole said, "but I can see the news has helped you."

"I just wish I could tell mom," Eddie said with a sigh and took another sip of her drink. "But you asked about riding with Thom and I'll say it was enjoyable. He is very courteous and respectful, keeping his distance almost to an irritating degree." She smiled wide-eyed and snapped a chip between her teeth to emphasize her 'irritation.'

"He also told me," Eddie said in a very low voice as she glanced around to see if anyone might be listening, "there's an undercover agent searching somewhere that he won't describe, to see if Dad might still be alive."

"No!" Carole said sharply in a loud whisper. "That could be wonderful news."

"Yes, but he cautioned me that it might not be that good," Eddie said, "but I can't stop myself from hoping. Thom says that eight years in some of those places can really change people. And that it's also likely he's not still alive."

"Well," Carole said sitting up straight, "I'll keep my fingers crossed for you."

"Thanks," Eddie said and smiled. "So, we talked for most of his rounds about almost everything. Did you know he likes antique furniture? And has refinished many old pieces himself? Well that certainly surprised me. But you know the nicest thing was when we were coming north from the elementary school, he saw two little girls, maybe ten years old that were standing on a street corner crying. Obviously distressed. Thom got out and crouched down beside them and talked to them for maybe five minutes before he called someone to come and help. I stayed in the car like he told me I'd have to, and I was surprised when Deputy Marks showed up." Eddie took another sip of her drink. "Thom came back to the car and told me they would need to take a few minutes before he could continue and asked me to just sit tight. The little girls were supposed to care for their class' pet kitten over the weekend and had dropped its cage crossing the icy street and of course, the kitten bolted when the cage sprang open. He and Ted and the girls spent the next half an hour searching and finally found the kitten, white of course, huddled in the snow against a tree across the street from where he found the girls."

"I'll bet they will remember that for a long time," Carole said and smiled at Eddie.

"I'm sure they will," Eddie said as she finished the Queso. "I know I will. After he took me back to Mary's I asked him if he'd like to come over sometime." Eddie caught the surprise that flashed across Carole's face, quickly hidden behind a sober expression. "He said he would, but wondered if I would feel better if he took me out somewhere more public first." Eddie smiled and glanced at the empty Queso dish. "He's taking me to the Stone Fence Wednesday night."

"Very nice," Carole said and smiled. Then she picked up the empty dish and asked, "Anything else to go with your Queso?"

"I think so," Eddie said with a smile. "Is the chicken fried steak still a Monday special?"

"Yes it is," Carole said.

"Then that's what I want. Gravy on everything," Eddie said and Carole went to place her order.

⚔ ⚔ ⚔ ⚔ ⚔

"Hello," Abe said as he answered the phone console.

"Abe, it is Don Nikle. I need you and Ben to do something for me."

"Sure," Abe said and set his coffee cup down and picked up his note pad. "Ready."

"I need for the two of you to get me a list of the marshal's and deputies' activities and the associated times they do things."

"You mean like who takes what shift or the route of their patrols rounds?" Abe asked. "Stuff like that?"

"Yes, only more detailed. I want to know when their rounds start, where they go and when they are finished. Where they start from and where they end. I want to know when they are in the office and not patrolling, how long they are usually there and anything else that might help figure out their routines."

"Okay," Abe smiled. "It will take us a few days to double check their routines against the notes we already have and to see if anything has changed. I'll give you a status late Wednesday."

"All right," Don agreed. "I also want to know who they talk to around town. Any regulars, or any one of importance. I need as much detail as you can put together. I need to know their habits and routines and schedules."

"I'll call Wednesday evening," Abe said, "and let you know what we have, if anything."

▲ ▲ ▲ ▲ ▲

Greg settled into their preferred overstuffed chair near the fireplace and stretched his legs onto the hassock as Shara set the carafe of tea on the table and settled on his lap. Major Kooich and Leeana took the loveseat across from them and Jill and Nick settled on the long couch just to his left.

"So, Shar?" Jill asked. "How long were you going to keep us in the dark, letting us fill in the blanks and thinking you had some horrible disease?"

"Jill," Shara rebutted," I wasn't trying to make you think bad thoughts. I..." and she looked at Greg and buried her face against his neck, "thought Greg would hate me for letting it happen. This will definitely have an impact on our future."

"You know," Greg said, "and I don't mean this in a bad way, but your mother was a surprise to Andrew and Katherine and you were a surprise to Henry and your mother, so why would this one being a surprise to us be a problem for you? By the way, I think we need to go up and see your dad tomorrow."

"Really?" she squealed and hugged him very tightly. "God, I'm glad you don't hate me," she said softly.

"Bren, love, I might get mad at you over something sometime, but I won't hate you." Then he turned back to the group. "Leeana, may I be so bold as to ask about this morning? I sensed an undertone when you asked Shara to tell you she's pregnant. Have you had a bad experience?"

Leeana stared at Greg, surprised by his question. She visibly had to compose herself and Greg noticed she glanced at Hench before answering.

"I know you don't mean to be disrespectful," Leeana finally replied, "and yes, I saw in Shara signs I know from experience. I was pregnant with a son and almost made it through the second trimester, but we were sent to join a blockade of Hells Gate and we were hit, severely. Shields didn't hold once they locked onto our position. In the recovery, they didn't realize I was pregnant until after the treatments were administered and the pregnancy failed."

"I'm sorry," Shara said and stretched her hand out to Leeana.

"Thanks," Leeana said after a moment. "I know you didn't know, and I am happy for you and the colonel."

"Leeana!" Shara said sharply, and smiled hugely. "It's Greg, Shara and Greg, unless we are with the subordinates."

"Thanks, Shara. I keep forgetting," Leeana said and smiled in return. "I know we all know loss, and I have always been happy to know the colonel, Greg, and I am very pleased that you two have found each other. You are truly a gem yourself. But after being here with you and Greg in this heavenly place, Hench and I have been given another chance."

"What?" Major Kooich turned and stared at Leeana.

"Yes love, KKLC confirmed it this afternoon," Leeana said with a smile only for him.

"When?" Shara asked, being very forward before Hench could say a word.

"Christmas," Leeana said and smiled at the major, "We had a couple of pretty remarkable nights after Cheral's close call reminded us of our frailties and how fragile and temporary life can be. We aren't waiting any longer for a maybe."

"Oh my god," Jill said in a rush, "I'm going to have nieces and nephews! I'm going to be an aunt and I'm not even married yet!" She turned and glared at Nick.

Shara chuckled and looked at Greg with a huge smile. "I think we're going to have a houseful."

Matti stopped between the dining room and the living room and asked if they needed more coffee or tea, or if they wished something else to drink.

"I don't know, Matti," Shara said softly, "I think there might be something wrong with that tea we've been serving."

"What?" Matti was taken aback. "Something's wrong with it?"

"Yup," Shara said with a wink and smiled at her. "Now, Leeana's pregnant, too. It must be something in the tea."

Matti's mouth dropped open and she looked from one to the other. "You too?"

"Looks like it," Leeana happily admitted.

"Oh my," Matti said and clapped her hands together with a broad smile, "I better tell Cara and Annie to stay away from that tea. It might be catchin.'" Her eyes were dancing as she turned and hurried back to the kitchen.

Tuesday, January 10

"He's in his office," Shara said as she slipped her street clothes over her Blues and swapped her boots. "Amanda is there handling the front counter."

Greg finished changing and stepped to the aft portal. When she was ready, he led her out onto the partially extended ramp. They mounted Seven and made their short descent to the main street in Antelope Springs. On the ground outside the BIA office building, they both scanned the area around them and when they felt it was safe, they dropped their veils and walked around to the front door.

"Morning Amanda," Shara said as they stepped in and Greg closed the door behind them.

"Why good morning, Shara," Amanda said as she glanced up at their arrival, "and Greg, right?"

"Yes, Amanda," Greg said and smiled at her. "I hope you're having a good morning as well."

Shara had pushed Henry's office door open and was hugging him when Greg caught up.

"Good to see you, Greg," Henry said and offered his hand. Then he looked at both of them, "I'm sorry I couldn't make it down for Christmas. I knew you had a houseful and I thought I ought to spend the holiday with your grandma. She's getting pretty old and I just felt I needed to be here. I hope you understand."

"We do understand, Dad," Shara said. "I need to stop and see her on one of these trips up. It's been a long time."

"She'd like that," Henry admitted and settled back into his wood framed chair. "So tell me what's been happening with you two since you dropped by in November."

"I'm sorry it's been so long since we've been up," Shara apologized and settled on the corner of his desk, "but I have to admit the days are all a blur."

Shara started telling Henry about everything that happened in the past two months, beginning with their continued effort to catch the slavers and release those they had captured. She described Greg's promotion to colonel and the responsibilities he now had in directing a campaign to seek out the slavers, wherever they happen to be. Then she explained her surprise when the director had brought her into the Peace Force as an under-lieutenant and about Greg teaching her hand-to-hand combat, to be a crew member and to fly their ship. She told him about the death of Harry Woods and the capture of Harold Danley, the arrival of a new state deputy and his promotion to marshal and his permanent assignment in Riggin with three deputies of his own.

Then she told him about their planning and the attack on the main slaver's complex in Virginia and how she, Jill and Rose found and rescued Greg's mother while Greg, Jim Woods, Nick, Doug and a bunch of Kiile's Marines had secured the rest of the complex. Finally, she explained that the director of the Peace Force had them report to his office in the Rings for a meeting, and a celebration that turned out to be an awards ceremony honoring Greg and her and five other crews.

"The Rings?" Henry asked, curious. "Where are the Rings?"

"A long, long ways away," Shara said and pointed to the ceiling. "Two or three days travel on a very fast space ship."

"It isn't nice to pull your dad's leg so hard," Henry said with a disbelieving smile.

"I can't convince you it's true," Shara said and glanced at Greg, "but I know it is. We've also been on a number of missions millions and millions of miles off planet, the latest was Sunday. The Peace Force rescued over four hundred captives, people stolen to be slaves."

"So, if I should happen to come and visit," Henry said, "and you don't happen to be home, you might really not be at home?" He looked up at the ceiling.

"There's that possibility," Greg said with a smile and a shrug. "We could be hours away or days away, but Shara has one more bit of information to tell you about. The main reason we took a little time to visit."

"Oh?" Henry asked as he leaned forward and looked at Shara. "There's more to this elaborate tale?"

"Yup," Shara said and smiled at Greg. She looked back at Henry. "You're going to be a grandpa."

Henry's eyes sparkled and his grin stretched across his slender face. "You're not pullin' my leg agin', are you?"

"Nope. I'm eight weeks along," she admitted, "and due in mid-August."

Henry got up and hugged Shara again. "That's really great," he said. When he released her and stepped back to look at her, she saw his eyes were filled with happy tears.

"I sort of hid the fact from Greg and didn't tell him until Sunday," she admitted, "but when we talked about it yesterday, he said we had to come and tell you. We never know when we're going to have time anymore, so we have to jump on things when we think of them."

"I'm sure glad you did," Henry said and hugged her again.

C.3482.394

Prince Kiese's gentleman's gentleman was arranging the prince's coats and robes and inquiring if the prince preferred one color choice over a second choice for the morning's court when the chamber courier knocked. He stopped just inside the personal chamber's anteroom and announced that he had a message for the prince from his Naval offices.

The valet crossed the room and received the sealed message, and returned to the prince as the courier left the room and closed the door. The valet handed the envelope to the prince and asked, "Shall I leave you, Sire?"

"That is not necessary, Camerso," he said and slit the seal open.

Prince Kiese read the message and was slowly consumed in rage.

▲

"All communications with Battlecruisers *Gissel* and *Northgate* ceased C.3482.392 at 2247 Galactic Standard Time. It is feared both cruisers have been lost. Adjunct Battle Commander Liket was in command of the battlecruiser *Gissel* and Adjunct

190

Battle Commander Spere was in command of the battlecruiser *Northgate* when communications ceased. No communications have been received from any of the escort fighters."

Two of my best fleet commanders, he thought to himself, squeezing his fingers into tight fists. *Presumed lost! How can this be?* He turned and absently stared at the court robes.

"I take it the message was not a good one, Sire," Camerso said from where he waited a respectful distance from the prince.

"No! It is not!" He said sharply. "I will be back in a few centipars."

The prince hurried to his office adjoining his personal chambers and keyed a sequence into the communications console.

"Chairman Sorgat," he said when the connection was made. "Prince Kiese. What have you heard about the latest shipment?"

"I am reviewing the intelligence reports now," Chairman Sorgat replied drily. "The freighter *Nova Ebon* apparently has been intercepted by the same Peace Force fighter squadron as the others. Communications ceased two turns ago about 2250 Galactic Standard Time. My report indicates they were attacked suddenly with a force large enough to engage the battlecruisers and the escort fighters at the same time. Two Peace Force heavy fighters disabled the *Nova Ebon*, one with a red band like that noted in the messages from the previously captured freighters. We believe the *Nova Ebon* was commandeered by boarding parties from Peace Force patrol cruisers."

"Two battlecruisers with seasoned crews and decorated commanders and fifty fighters each," the prince said with tightly stressed words, "presumed defeated and lost."

"Sad to lose them," the chairman said. "Do you have any ideas to use to stop these surprise attacks, any way to detect when they might strike?"

The prince thought a long moment and then stared at the console. "Yes," he said, "I believe I do. I must consult with my Naval Offices and I will get back to you, but I think we can give the Peace Force a very real surprise of their own when they attack the next shipment."

Shara and Greg's journey continues in
Paladin Shadows Series Book 9,
Operation Retribution Part 3, Luring the Prince into the Open

Riggin Town Map

Elevation 6852 Ft   Population 1845

Operation Retribution

Riggs Valley Map

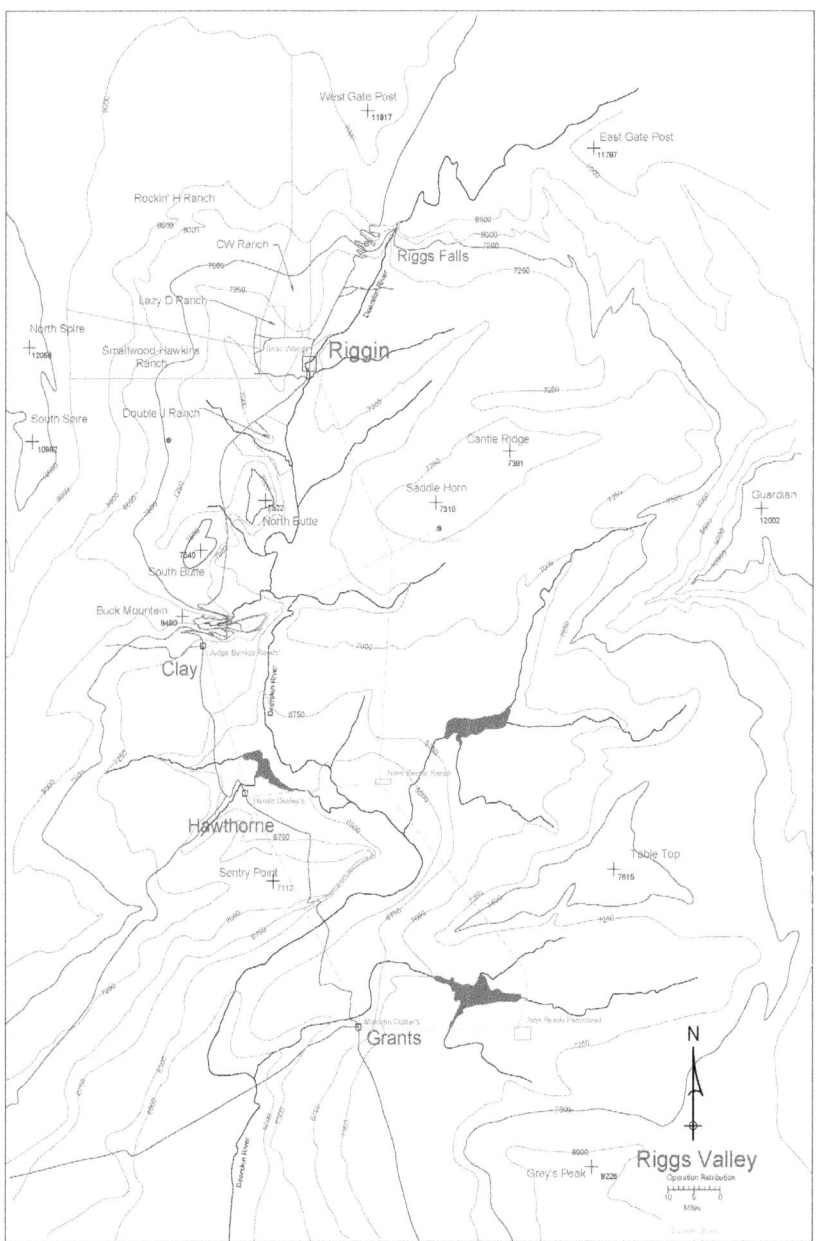

Glossary

Characters:

-A-

Ahaar	Key agent for the Trader's Union.
Arkir, Captain	Captain of the freighter, Dai Horizon.

-B-

Bernice Reeds; Judge	See Reeds, Bernice; Judge
Bren	Short version of Greg's nickname, 'BrenCara,' for Shara. Old Country meaning: "Special Raven Haired Friend."

-C-

Cadet Pilots	Cadet students training in the art of space combat.
	Apache Patrol Two: Captain Cheral Haak
	Apache Patrol Three: Cadet Ani Tigs
	Apache Patrol Four: Cadet Wilm Moss
	Apache Patrol Five: Cadet Loni Grenn (Reported Jan 11)
	Apache Patrol Six: Cadet Gill Kast (Reported Jan 11)
Camerso	Gentleman's Gentleman to Prince Kiese.
Cara	Second house girl at the Smallwood-Hawkins Ranch.
Cassel, Brendan	Coleen Malone's second husband, mate. (IAL01-SS3)
Cassel, Coleen	Husband/mate to Brendan Cassel, second marriage. Previous marriage: Coleen Reese. Maiden name: Coleen

	Malone.
Chairman Sorgat	Principal Officer in the Trader's Union
Clark, Della	Daughter of Widow Clark and sister of Steve. College student in Riggin.
Coleen Malone	See Malone, Coleen
Coleen Reese	See Reese, Coleen
Colette Marsin	See Marsin, Colette
Collier, Eddie	Floral Arranger at Mary's Flower Boutique. 23 yrs old. Daughter of Daniel Collier. No siblings.
Collier, Daniel	Eddie's missing father.

-D-

Danley, Harold	Banker in Clay, one of Bernice's Elders.
Danny	Shara's black stallion.
Davis, Carole	Waitress at Hap's Place. Shelly's younger sister by one year. 23 yrs of age.
Davis, Marty	Married to Rusty Davis. Father of Shelly, Carole and Todd Davis.
Davis, Rusty	Married to Marty Davis. Mother of Shelly, Carole and Todd Davis.
Davis, Shelly	Raised in Riggin, wife of Lt. Jim Woods. Mother of Carrie Anne Woods. 24 yrs of age.
Davis, Todd	Older brother of Shelly and Carole Davis. Moved away from the valley before Shelly graduated from high school.
Deputies, Special	Thom Baine. See Baine, Thom.
	Dan Lupis. See Lupis, Dan.

Ted Marks. See Marks, Ted.

Dílis   Shara's black-faced roan. Greg's favorite and named by him. (Pronounced Jee + lus)

Director Korveel   Merchandise Director for the Trader's Union.

Director, Peace Force   Identification AGL36Q

-E-

Elders, The Family   Brian Woods   (deceased)

Harry Woods   (deceased)

Harold Danley   (captured)

Malcolm Clotter   (captured)

Charley Clotter   (captured)

Dave Barns

Don Nikle

-G-

Geaardt, Stran   A Shadow. An undercover agent. A Major in the Galactic Peace Force. GPF ID: HQZL09-ES. Pronounced "Gee (as in Geese), + art."

Geaardt, Casi (Casey)   A Shadow. An undercover agent. Stran Geaardt's partner, wife. HQZL09-ES2 GPF ID. Pronounced 'Casey.'

Geaardt, Moira   Registered name of Coleen Malone

Greg Malone   See Malone, Greg

Grenn, Loni   Cadet Pilot of Apache Patrol Five, Class 1 Patrol Fighter.

-H-

Haak, Cheral   Captain in the Galactic Peace Force. Cadet in the Peace Force Flight Academy. Cadet Pilot of

	Apache Two, Class 2 Patrol Fighter. Granddaughter of Paal Haak. Previous Upper-Lieutenant Nav-Com on Q-STSX1.
Haak, Paal	Commander, Galactic Peace Force Academy, Retired. Grandfather to Cheral Haak
Hank	Forman at the Smallwood Ranch.
Hawkins, Andrew	Deceased brother of Paul and Nancy Hawkins. Married Katherine Reeds. Father of Clea Hawkins. Shara's Grandfather.
Hawkins, Nancy	Sister of Paul and Andrew Hawkins. Second wife of Dave Ashley, no children.
Hawkins, Paul	Brother of Andrew and Nancy Hawkins.
Hawkins, Clea	Unplanned daughter of Andrew Hawkins and Katherine Reeds. Married to Henry Smallwood. Mother of Shara, and surrogate to two daughters.

-J-

Jordan, Robert (Bob)	Owner of the Jordan Double-J Ranch. Nick's father.
Jordan, Darcy	Nick's Mother. Darcy Reeds married to Ben Jordan. Deceased.
Jordan, Nicholas	Aka, Nick. Friend and class mate of Jill Thomas.

-K-

Kast, Gill	Cadet Pilot of Apache Patrol Six, Class 1 Patrol Fighter.
Kiese, Prince	Warlord Prince of Knobaal.
Kiile	A Marine Squad Leader in the

services of the GPF. (Pronounced as Kī īle.) GPF Marine ID: USL15-EFM (Upper Squad Leader, Earth Force Marine)

Kooich, Hench; Major   A Shadow. Major in the GPF, commander of Q-KKLC14. GPF ID: RWKR17-SC.

Kooich, Leeana   Major Kooich's partner (wife). Lieutenant in the GPF, Nav-Com officer on Q-KKLC14. GPF ID: RWKR17-SC2.

Korveel, Director   Trader's Union Merchandise Director, under Senior Chairman Sorgat.

Kraast, Director   Trader's Union Intelligence Director, under Senior Chairman Sorgat.

-L-

Lima, Wally   State assigned Deputy to Riggin. Assigned to Riggin after Sheriff Black and his six deputies disappear. 26 yrs of age.

Lupis, Dan; Deputy   Special State Deputy assigned to Riggin under Wally Lima. Wife Mandy. Daughter Blaire (age 7).

-M-

Malone, Coleen   Married to Tom Reese (1), and to Brendan Cassel (2). GPF Planet-side ID: IAL01-SS. Registered Moira Geaardt.

Malone, Greg   Great Nephew to Gary Woods. Son of Coleen Reese (Malone). Stran Geaardt's registered birth name. Born March 17, same year as Shara Smallwood. GPF Terran ID: IAL02-SS

Malone, Shara (Shar)   Greg Malone's wife. Maiden name:

	Shara Smallwood. GPF Planet-side ID: IAL02 SS2.
Marks, Ted; Deputy	pecial Stat Deputy assigned to Riggin under Wally Lima.
Mary	Owner of Mary's Flower Boutique.
Matti	House girl at the Smallwood-Hawkins ranch.
McIntire, Doug	Significant friend of Rosalee (Rose) Mitchell's. (IAL38-SS)
Mitchell, Rosalee (Rose)	Friend of Shara Smallwood and Jill Thomas. Doug McIntire's significant friend. (IAL37-SS)
Moss, Wilm; Cadet	Cadet Pilot of Apache Patrol Four, Class 1 Patrol Fighter.

-P-

Parks, Chief	Police Chief in Hawthorne

-Q-

Q-STSX1	Colonel Stran Geaardt & Nav-Com Lieutenant Casi Geaardt. Campaign Commander for Trader's Union Offensive; Terran and non-terran forces.
Q-KKLC14	Major Hench Kooich & Nav-Com Lieutenant Leeana Kooich. Campaign Commander's lieutenant and Wing Commander under Colonel Geaardt.
Q-KVWC33	Major Daaws Miiles & Nav-Com Lieutenant Meecia Miiles
Q-LTVC21	Major Neel Glean & Lieutenant Debira Glean
Q-MKCC5	Major Aiilx Romaan & Lieutenant Colbee Donnr

Q-TTYF8	Major Mooren & Nav-Com, Lieutenant Franni Kaal
Q-LLRT12	Major Deni Bradg & Nav-Com Lieutenant Mri Bradg
Q-KCMM9	Major Pti Fila & Nav-Com Lieutenant Lori Tam
Q-JCCV4	Major Ronl Bids and Nav-Com Lieutenant Emly Bids. Joined Apache Squadron after supporting the attack of 4 January and getting repairs done at Obscure.
Q-QRTT7	Major Amel Clef and Nav-Com Lieutenant Pela Clef. Apache Squadron B-Group Wing Leaders.

-R-

Ranch Hands	At the Smallwood Ranch: Jimmy, Tom (Tommy), Billy and Dusty.
Reeds	Terran family name of the controlling Family in southern Riggs Valley.
Reeds, Bernice; Judge	Great Aunt of Shara Smallwood. Head operative in the Family affiliation with the Traders and Slavers. Riggs Valley Circuit Judge.
Reeds, Thad & Betti	A stranded couple that Wally helped on his way through Grants on his way back to Riggin (Dec 20). Son Sam, age thirteen, and daughter Glory, age nine.
Reese, Coleen	Married to Tom Reese (1), mother of Hew and (by an Affair) of Greg Malone. Maiden name: Coleen Malone.
Reese, Tom	Husband of Coleen (Malone). Distant relation of Gary Woods. GPF Planet-

side ID: IAL01-SS2.

Riviera, Ensign	QuickSilver Tracnav Surveillance Specialist.
Russell, Chief	Chief of Police in Clay.

-S-

Shara Malone	See Malone, Shara
Smallwood, Shara (Shar)	Unplanned daughter of Henry and Clea (Hawkins) Smallwood. Youngest of three. 28 yrs old. Born June 20 (solstice), same year as Greg Malone.
Smallwood, Henry	Full blooded Apache, American Indian. Married Clea Hawkins, father of Shara Smallwood.
STSX	Q-STSX1 is a late generation, Shadow Class Corvette, nicknamed as a type as Q-Ships, operated under the command of Stran Geaardt. The latest in the long evolution of the GPF's Shadow ships. The name is synonymous with the ship's central computer system ID.

-T-

Thomas, Jack	Married Amy Woods, daughter of Gary Woods. Father of Jill. Financial Officer at the Woods Lumber Mill. (Father of Greg Malone by pre-marital affair with Coleen Reese.)
Thomas, Jill	Daughter of Jack Thomas and Amy Thomas (Woods). Six years younger than Shara Smallwood and Greg Malone.
Tigs, Ani; Cadet	Cadet Pilot of Apache Patrol Three, Class 2 Patrol Fighter.
Tina	Pert, brunette waitress at Hap's Place.

Townsley, Thomas, Colonel	Watch Commander, space station S.S. QuickSilver.

-W-

Wardly, Anne, Lt.	Staff Assistant and Aide to Admiral Baker, space station S.S. QuickSilver.
Woods, Harry	Son of Horace Woods. Longtime head of the Woods Lumber and Mill (Retired). Father of Gary, James and Brian.
Woods, Gary	Son of Harry Woods. Father of Bill Woods.
Woods, James	Son of Harry Woods. Father of Amy Woods.
Woods, Brian	Son of Harry Woods. Unmarried. Current head of the Woods Lumber and Mill.
Woods, Bill	Son of Gary Woods; no siblings. Father of Jim Woods, Lieutenant (USAF).
Woods, Jim, Lt.	Son of Bill Woods; no siblings. Married to Shelly Davis, father of Carrie Anne Woods.
Woods, Amy	Daughter of James Woods. Married to Jack Thomas, mother of Jill Thomas.

Places and Things:

-A-

Angrilat	A Principal commercial complex in the Kyddellan System
Antheria	Major Commercial Planet in the Tunst System. Known as a Heavy World with a gravity index of 2.02 times Galactic Standard.
Aridont	City on Listera, cite of water rioting.

-B-

Baile	Planetary system of the planet Rygon.
Betolle	Planet in the Daneets System. Home planet of Lieutenant Franni Kaal and her hometown of Casimir.
Brekshiir	A wrist mounted laser weapon, consisting of one or multiple optics and fired by a unique sequence of mental commands. Specifically designed for the GPF Shadows.
	Brekshiir 170 Single Optic wrist Unit, 50 pulses with a range of 300 yds in air.
	Brekshiir 490 Wrist Clusters is the most common in the GPF, consisting of 4 laser units, 50 pulses each with a range of 300 yds in air. Individually fired or in combination.
	Brekshiir 710 Wrist Clusters, upgrade of the 490. 70 pulses with a range of 300 yds in air.
Brigstoan, Patrol Cruiser	GPF Patrol Cruiser designed for interception and boarding of suspect transports. Operated with a standard pilot crew, fifty aerial marines, a separate pilot crew and a Medical staff.

-C-

C.Date	A date referenced to the galactic calendar. A galactic year is comprised of one thousand galactic turns.
	Example: C.3482.329 is the 329th day of the galactic year 3284. It is

also the 310th day of the current story year, November 6th.

Caldite Throwing Dart — A coveted and highly guarded GPF tool, used to inject a sedative or toxin upon impact.

Casimir — City on the planet Betolle, home town of Franni Kaal.

Cellystoan — Planetary system in which the Warlord Prince's home planet, Knobaal, orbits.

Centipar — One hundredth of a par. Similar to a terran minute.

Clay — Town in central Riggs Valley, 93 highway miles south of Riggin.

Colbr — Planetary System with three agricultural planets: Copus One, Two and Three.

Corsecain — Planet in the Gashii system. Prominent for numerous bloody battles in the Moulit Wars.

-D-

Dangcee — Mining colony on the fourth planet of the Greel system.

Double J Ranch — A 43,138 Acre (67.4 sq. miles) horse ranch owned by Nick's father, Bob Jordan, situated between the North Butte and Riggin.

-G-

Galactic Peace Force — Galactic policing organization headquartered in the Gridelin Rings.

Galactic year — Equivalent to 1000 terran days, or 2.7397 standard terran years. See C.Date.

Grants — Town at the south end of Riggs

Valley, 186 highway miles south of Riggin.

Greel System — Planetary system in which the Pico Mining Company has established numerous mining colonies.

Greymn — Major Industrial complex on Omerai Two, renowned for its weapons manufacture. Model 40 is hand weapon most widely used by the Trader's Guild.

Greymn Model 40: 40 destructive pulses with a range of 400 yds in air.

-H-

Hawthorne — Town in central Riggs Valley, 128 highway miles south of Riggin.

-I-

IFF — Identification, Friend or Foe. An identification system to determine if an entity, craft or forces are friendly, and to determine their bearing and range from the interrogator. The system is capable of transmitting a hail to another system on command.

-K-

Kaaspr — The standard issue brand of hand laser weapon for the Galactic Peace Force. Model 106 is the current standard laser hand weapon used in the GPF. Replaced the previous standard, Model 88.

Kaaspr Model 106: 50 destructive pulses with a maximum range of 350 yds in air.

Knobaal — Home planet and seat of the Royal Throne of the Warlord Prince Kiese.

Located in the Cellystoan planetary system.

Kyddel
System in which Angrilat's home planet resides.

-L-

Lazy D Ranch
Martin Davis' 15,455 acre ranch (24.15 sq miles).

-M-

Millipar
One one-thousandth of a par. Similar to in concept but equivalent to 3.456 terran seconds.

-O-

Omerai Two
Industrialized planet in the Kyddel system, noted for its arms manufacturing.

-P-

Par
A fundamental galactic unit of time. Twenty-five pars in a Galactic Standard Turn (Day). Similar to a terran hour.

-Q-

QuickSilver
Planet Earth's multinational, manned orbital space station. (S.S. QuickSilver.)

Q-Ships
Nickname for the Galactic Peace Force's two man Recondite Corvettes. Specifically used by Shadows in their various roles of information gathering, defense and protection.

-R-

Riggin
A small college town in the northern point of Riggs Valley, western United States, planet Earth.

Rockin' H Ranch
A 1,263,950 Acre (1975 sq. mile)

	horse and cattle ranch belonging to Paul Hawkins and Nancy Hawkins (deceased), situated NW of Riggin.
Rygon	Home planet of the very old Geaardt family name, located in the Baile System.

-**S**-

Shadow	Undercover agent of the Galactic Peace Force with specialized training and abilities in clandestine operations and information collecting, generally thought to be able to hide in plain sight.
Smallwood-Hawkins Ranch	Horse ranch belonging to Shara Malone (Smallwood). 209,275 Acres (approx. 327 sq. miles) split off of Paul Hawkins' larger ranch to its north. Situated West of Riggin.

Books by Aidan Red

Paladin Shadow Series
Terran Assignment Triptych
Book 1: Things are not as they seem.
Book 2: When luck is not enough.
Book 3: Fate has a different idea.
Terran Recruits Triptych
Book 4: In the wake of chaos.
Book 5: Terran Talents join forces.
Book 6: New rules of engagement.
Operation Retribution Triptych
Book 7: The training phase.
Book 8: Taking the fight off-world.
Book 9: Luring the Prince into the open.
Garda Nua Triptych
Book 10: The proliferation of Talent.
Book 11: When a planet is stolen.
Book 12: Right does not ask permission.
Assignment: Casha-Six
Book 13: No Warning
Book 14: The Best Laid Plans
Book 14: A Change of Heart

Eight's Warning
Book 1: The Past Hunts.
Book 2: The Past Attacks.
Book 3: The Price of Escape.

More Books by Aidan Red

Keeper and His Tiger
Book 1: An Unexpected Complication.
Book 2: Deadly Undercurrents.
Book 3: The Trap.

Fearin' the Banshee

About the Author

Aidan Red's passion for aviation and aircraft design, engineering, and a deep interest in space and space travel go back many years. An avid reader from an early age, Aidan, with great trepidation, ventured into the world of writing during college. With real world experience in business aviation, Aidan's creative side led him to create an alternate world where the beautiful Riggs Valley was born and Shara's life became chronicled in his epic science fiction series, Paladin Shadows.

Paladin Shadows consists of the five triptychs (three-part works), *Terran Assignment, Terran Recruits, Operation Retribution, Garda Nua* and *Assignment: Casha-Six*. In between the Paladin triptychs, Aidan has penned two, three book series, *Keeper and his Tiger,* and *West's Ghost Ranch* and a novel, *Fearin' the Banshee.*

Unpublished books in his various series are scheduled for release on a regular basis in the coming months.

Visit *www.RedsInkandQuill.com* or *www.AidanRedBooks. com* for more information on Aidan Red's books and where to purchase them.

www.ingramcontent.com/pod-product-compliance
Lightning Source LLC
Chambersburg PA
CBHW070823180626
46818CB00001B/374